She wanted to kiss him. Let him make the terror go away.

He brushed his fingers along her cheek. Murmured her name. He wanted it, too. All she had to do was tilt her head, close her eyes, relinquish control.

But bitter words about her being imperfect echoed in her head. She couldn't lose control again. Control was all she had. The only way to protect herself. The only way she'd survive.

She couldn't risk getting hurt once more.

And this man had the power to do it, because he made her feel again. Made her want things that she'd learned long ago were impossible.

RITA HERRON

FORCE OF THE FALCON

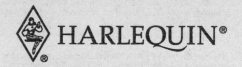

TORONTO • NEW YORK • LONDON
AMSTERDAM • PARIS • SYDNEY • HAMBURG
STOCKHOLM • ATHENS • TOKYO • MILAN • MADRID
PRAGUE • WARSAW • BUDAPEST • AUCKLAND

For my grandmother, who taught me to love stories…

ISBN-13: 978-0-373-88731-6
ISBN-10:   0-373-88731-0

FORCE OF THE FALCON

Copyright © 2006 by Rita B. Herron

www.eHarlequin.com

Printed in U.S.A.

ABOUT THE AUTHOR

Award-winning author Rita Herron wrote her first book when she was twelve, but didn't think real people grew up to be writers. Now she writes so she doesn't have to get a *real* job. A former kindergarten teacher and workshop leader, she traded her storytelling for romance, and writes romantic comedies and romantic suspense. She lives in Georgia with her own romance hero and three kids. She loves to hear from readers, so please write her at P.O. Box 9?¹??⁵, ..., GA 30092-1225, or visit her Web site at www.ritaherron.com.

Books by Rita Herron

HARLEQUIN INTRIGUE
710—THE CRADLE MISSION*
741—A WARRIOR'S MISSION
755—UNDERCOVER AVENGER*
790—MIDNIGHT DISCLOSURES*
810—THE MAN FROM FALCON RIDGE
861—MYSTERIOUS CIRCUMSTANCES*
892—VOWS OF VENGEANCE*
918—RETURN TO FALCON RIDGE
939—LOOK-ALIKE
957—FORCE OF THE FALCON

*Nighthawk Island

CAST OF CHARACTERS

Brack Falcon—His only love was his falcons—until he met Sonya Silverstein and her little girl. Now he must protect them or die trying....

Sonya Silverstein—When a twisted psycho tries to kill her, she must put her life in the hands of Brack Falcon. But can she trust him with her heart?

Katie Silverstein—She may be physically handicapped, but will her sixth sense help her survive a killer?

Stan Silverstein—Sonya's ex blames her for their daughter's physical handicap. But what is he hiding?

Sheriff Cohen—He railroaded Brack's father into jail twenty years ago for a crime he didn't commit. Is he going to do the same thing to Brack?

The Talon Terror—This villain kills women and animals with his birdlike talons. Is he animal, man or both?

Jameson Viago—The artist who draws the cartoon character The Talon Terror. Is he imitating the character in real life to boost his comic-book sales?

Emerson Godfrey—An expert from the government who is researching diseased animals. Is he going to destroy Brack's beloved falcons?

Darrien Tripp—A reporter for an occult magazine called The Tween Zone. Has he really seen supernatural creatures?

Dr. Aaron Waverman—He wants Sonya for himself. How far will he go to win her?

Dr. Phil Priestly—The local veterinarian tends to birds of prey and has been attacked himself. Has his work with animals turned him into one?

Jerry Elmsworth—Katie doesn't like Jerry, the veterinarian's assistant. Is she right when she senses that he is untrustworthy?

Chapter One

"Mommy, save me!" The chilling cry whispered through the eaves of the old farmhouse and echoed off the walls, terrifying and insistent.

Sonya Silverstein jerked awake and sat up, a shiver rippling through her as if the icy fingers of a ghost had touched her neck.

Had Katie cried out for help?

She clutched the sheets and listened for her daughter's voice, for the sound of her small crutches clacking on the wooden floor, but an eerie silence seeped through the cold, dark room instead, and fear gripped her.

Something was wrong. Sonya felt it deep in her bones.

Her heart pounding, she slid from the bed, pushed open the bedroom door and searched the murky gray den for her little girl.

The dying embers of the fire they'd had going earlier glowed. A wild animal howled in the distance. A tree limb scraped the ice-crusted glass, and the shutter flapped against the weathered boards encasing the window.

Wind, vicious and blustery, tore through the dark room, hurling dead leaves across the plank flooring through the open door. Her breath caught.

She had locked the door when she'd gone to bed.

Had an intruder broken in while she'd been sleeping?

Panic seized her. Dear God, Katie had to be there. She had to be all right. Katie was everything to her. She was all that mattered.

She'd moved here to Tin City to raise Katie, to give her a safe life. To take solace in the small mountain town and heal from the pain her ex-husband had caused them.

But the house she'd rented was practically in the wilderness. What if Katie had gone outside hunting for the kitty? Or what if a madman had broken in and kidnapped her?

The door to her little girl's room was cracked open, and she pushed it, praying she'd find Katie snuggled in bed with Mr. Buttons, her favorite teddy, and their kitten, Snowball. But Mr. Buttons lay on the floor, and she didn't see the baby cat. The covers were tousled, and the bed was empty.

"Katie!" She searched beneath the bed, then yanked open the closet. But Katie wasn't inside. Frantic, she screamed her name again and checked the bathroom. Katie's Hello Kitty cup. Her damp toothbrush. Her fluffy bedroom slippers.

But no Katie!

Sonya whirled around, scanning the room for Katie's small crutches.

They were gone.

Terror streaked through Sonya as she ran back into the den and grabbed her coat, her hat and a flashlight, then jammed on her snow boots and darted outside.

The bitterly cold Col..... wind clawed at her face as she searched the porch, then the snowpacked ground below, for her daughter or her footprints.

Snow whirled in a blinding haze, covering any tracks that might have lingered. A sob welled in Sonya's throat as she scanned the thick, snow-capped woods surrounding the farmhouse. The rigid cliffs and peaks climbed toward the heavens like stone boulders. While she'd thought they'd offer a perfect place for her to hide, a sanctuary, now they looked ominous, threatening.

Katie was out there somewhere all alone. No telling what dangers lay waiting in the dense patches of firs and aspens. Katie was so small. She'd never survive the elements or be able to fight off an attacker.

"Katie!" A scream tore from deep in her throat, but got lost in the howling wind.

"Save me, Mommy!"

The whisper of her daughter's plea reverberated through the chilling tension. Whether Katie had cried out for real or not, Sonya didn't know. But she heard her daughter's silent plea for help anyway.

She ran into the woods, blindly searching. She had to find her. She couldn't lose Kate. Not now.

Not ever.

FRESH BLOOD dotted the powdery white snow, the scent of death floating in the whistling wind of the forest surrounding Falcon Ridge. Brack Falcon knotted his hands around the flashlight as rage rippled through him. A loud screeching sound had awakened him and brought him outside. And now, out here, he'd heard it again and found fresh blood. He hadn't yet found the source of the blood this time, but he instinctively recognized the pattern.

Another one of the precious creatures of the forest had been attacked. He had discovered several dead birds of prey already this week. Most had been viciously slaughtered and mauled, their talons ripped off, their blood drained as if some creature had virtually sucked the life from them.

What kind of animal would do such a thing? Or could it be a man?

Stories of the ghosts and legends that thrived in Tin City haunted him. The dead that lingered. Miners trapped below the town, screeching in terror, haunting the very place where they'd died—the underground tunnels and caves that had been built as escape routes back in the 1800s.

And now a revival of the tales of wild animals that attacked without provocation. Stories of hybrid and mutant creatures, half human, half animal. With the bizarre attacks on the falcons this week, the fables had risen from the depths of the past, creating panic and hysteria.

All the more reason for the citizens to once again look at the Falcon men with suspicion.

Brack followed the blood-dotted snow, trekking farther into the bowels of the towering aspens and fir trees. The bitterness he'd lived with since he was six years old and his father had been falsely accused of murder ate at his insides. Granted, he and his two brothers, Rex and Deke, had finally helped exonerate his father, and his parents were now reunited, but twenty years of hating the people in the town who'd shunned the boys and their mother had stolen a part of Brack's soul.

A part that was lost forever.

And now his brothers were back at Falcon Ridge, and had decided to settle in Tin City and relocate their private detective agency to Colorado, back at the old homestead. They'd built offices in the basement and had installed high-tech security and state of the art computer systems. Deke and his new wife, Elsie, had bought one of the historical houses in town and were renovating it, while Rex and his wife, Hailey, had built a beautiful Victorian on her parents' property.

Brack had moved in to Falcon Ridge. Alone.

But the cries, anger and pain from his childhood still echoed in the stone structure as if twenty years had never passed, as if he were that little boy again watching his father being dragged away to jail.

He'd listened to his mother's sobs at night, had seen the anger and helplessness in his brothers, and he'd virtually shut down. Had learned to suppress any emotion.

Never get close to anyone and you'll never hurt like that again.

And he hadn't.

Instead, he'd pulled away from people and befriended the birds. And over the years, he'd honed his natural instincts with the falcons, instincts he'd inherited from his father and his grandfather before that, until he had such a deep connection with the animals of the forest that they communicated in their own silent language.

The crackle of twigs being severed in the wind jarred him from his reverie. A branch snapped off, and layers of snow and ice pelted him. Above, he heard the flapping of a falcon's wingspan stirring the frigid air, then the faint, heartwrenching cry of a bird in pain.

He picked up his pace, knowing it was too late to save the creature, but hating for it to die alone.

Seconds later, fury welled inside him as he studied the mauled remains. Its body had been ripped apart as if killed by one of its own kind. Blood streaked the muddy white ground. Feathers were scattered across crimson patches of ice, and the eagle's head lay against a stone.

Dammit. The head had been severed.

Rage shot through him, primal and raw, all-consuming.

When he found what or who was doing this, he'd kill it.

Then another cry of terror floated from the distance. It was so faint he had to strain to hear it.

This cry was human.

A chill shot through him, and he took off running.

AN ODD SCREECH rippled through the air, sending a chill through Sonya. What kind of animal made a sound like that? Nothing she'd ever heard before.

The wind was so strong she had to fight to keep from being knocked against the trees. The snow was almost ankle-deep on her—what would it be like for Katie?

Each footstep she took intensified her fears. Katie must be freezing. Terrified. What if she'd fallen and gotten hurt? What if she slipped off one of the ridges? What if a man had her, and he hadn't brought her into the forest?

No, Katie had to be out here. Sonya hadn't heard

a car engine. She grabbed a vine and pulled herself along, shining the flashlight across the snowpacked ground, pushing through bramble and broken limbs. The white haze of swirling snow blurred her vision, and she swiped at her eyes, willing them to focus.

Up above, she saw a faint flash. The color red.

Katie's red pajamas?

Her pulse raced. "Katie!" She began to run, slogging through the thick weight of the downfall. Cold bit at her cheeks and nose, and her limbs felt heavy. Wet sludge squished beneath her boots, and twigs and dead leaves crackled.

She spotted the red again, just a quick flash, then the outline of a small form. An animal? A deer, maybe?

No, her daughter hobbling on her crutches, her frail body swaying as she struggled against the elements.

Sonya screamed Katie's name again and launched into a jog. A limb shattered, then crashed to the ground. Ice and snow rained down on her. Sonya jumped over the limb and pushed forward. Another splintered and slammed into her arm. She threw it aside and tore through some fallen branches, desperate to get to her little girl.

Suddenly Katie went down. Her small body disappeared, lost in the blizzard. Panic ripped through Sonya. Where was Katie? The heavy snow could bury her alive within minutes.

Swiping at tears, she sprinted faster, searching,

praying, turning to scan the area where she'd seen Katie a moment earlier. Finally she spotted one crutch sticking up from the ground. Her heart throbbed as she closed the distance.

Katie was lying in the thick snow and ice, trying to battle her way up against the ferocious wind, but it pulled her down as if it were quicksand.

Oh God, her poor baby.

Sonya's paramedic training kicked in. She had to hurry and get Katie warm before hypothermia set in.

Her breath puffed out in clouds of white as she jogged to her. Katie looked up, her eyes full of terror. "Mommy!"

"Shh, Mommy's got you." Sonya leaned forward to scoop Katie into her arms, but a loud, horrifying animal-like cry splintered the air. Katie screamed, and Sonya's lungs tightened as something slammed into her back. She pitched forward, clawed at the air, anything to break her fall, but ice and snow pelted her face and stung her hands as she collapsed.

"Mommy!"

Something sharp clawed at her back through her coat. Sonya sent Katie a panicked look, but waved to her daughter. "Run, Katie! Run! Find shelter!"

Katie's cheeks ballooned with exertion as she grabbed the crutch from the ground and dragged herself up to stand.

The animal tore at Sonya again, viciously assaulting her, shredding her jacket and ripping through her flannel gown.

Sonya grabbed a broken limb and swung it backward, trying to fend off her attacker long enough for Katie to escape.

"Mommy!" Katie cried.

"Get out of here, Katie! Run now!"

Katie's chin wobbled and tears streaked her cheeks, but she began to hobble through the woods, pushing her crutches through the snow.

Pain shot through Sonya as the animal's talons bit into her skin. She tried to roll over and fight, clawing at the ice and snow, but the screech echoed off the mountain, and her head swam as the animal ripped into her flesh.

The stench of death assaulted her. Then she tasted blood, and terror seized her. She was going to die tonight at the hands of this creature.

Then who would take care of Katie?

AN ANIMAL'S vicious attack cry split the air, and Brack froze, listening, focusing on his senses to lead him. The sound was vile, primitive, inhuman. Had it come from the same creature who had mauled the eagle?

Was it attacking again?

He shined the flashlight on the ground and headed in the direction of the noise, the snow swirling in a thick fog in front of him.

The sickening screech erupted again, and he pivoted, zeroing in on the rustle of the trees and movement to his right. He still smelled the blood of the eagle, but the scent of fear and death teased his nostrils, too.

A human's fear.

Anger sizzled through his veins. His beloved birds weren't assaulting humans, were they? No, there had to be another explanation.

He glanced up and oddly, through the haze, saw a falcon circling above. Following the falcon was not a question, but his only option. He trusted the bird implicitly. Wind whistled through the bowing branches as he pushed his way through a thicket of pines and hiked toward the caves buried in the mountain. The falcon moved ahead another seventy-five feet, then stopped and flapped his wings, diving downward as if to warn Brack of impending danger.

Brack darted through the fir trees, branches tearing at his jacket sleeve, his heart racing. Seconds later, he spotted blood dotting the milky-white snow. A woman lay on the snow-carpeted ground facedown, the back of her coat and gown ripped to shreds, blood streaking her pale skin. Her hands were outstretched as if she were reaching for something, the delicate skin red and bloody from defense wounds.

His heart lurched to a stop. She was lying so still… Was he too late? Was she already dead?

Chapter Two

Brack scanned the woods for the woman's attacker, but the swish of trees and slight tremor of the earth below his feet told him that he had frightened off the creature. He slowly knelt to check the woman's pulse, pushed her long, curly hair aside, then pressed two fingers to her neck. Her skin still felt warm, and a slight pulse throbbed in her throat. Thank God.

But he had to get her help. She was bleeding and would die if he didn't hurry.

He reached inside his pocket to call 911, but his cell phone showed no service. Damn. Knowing he had to get her out of the elements, he gently eased her to her side, carefully bracing her against his arm to support her. Her face was covered in snow, her complexion ashen, her cheeks dotted with ice crystals and chafed red from the cold. He brushed away the flakes and gently rubbed his thumb over her cheek. She slowly opened her eyes and whimpered, then tried to pull away.

"Shh, I'm not going to hurt you." He lowered his voice to a soothing pitch, the same tone he'd perfected with the falcons.

Her eyes widened in terror, and she moaned and pushed at him. "No, get away!"

"My name is Brack Falcon," he murmured. "I live at Falcon Ridge. I'm going to carry you out of here. You're bleeding."

"No…"

Why the hell was she fighting him? Women had been afraid of him before, due to his large size and his affinity for wild animals. But she needed him. "Listen, Miss, you need a doctor."

She gripped his arm with bloody hands. "No, g-got to find K-Katie first."

His breath puffed out in a white cloud. "What?"

"My little girl," she moaned. "She's out here…I have to find her."

A child. That explained why she was trudging into the blizzard at night.

"I can't leave you. Whatever attacked you might come back." *Or you might bleed to death*, he added silently. And she was much too young and beautiful to die.

"He might get Katie!" she cried. "Please, she's only four…she's so little, and she's all alone, and she can't walk very well…"

Brack's gut clenched. A four-year-old lost in the woods with something attacking humans close by.

He didn't want the picture in his head, but the image flashed there anyway, sending fear through him.

Their gazes locked, and something shifted inside him. Some emotion he didn't want to identify. He had connected with the woman on some instinctual level.

"Please find her," the woman pleaded.

Brack searched his brain for another option. She felt so small and vulnerable in his arms, and she was hurting. Yet she was more concerned for her daughter than her own safety. If he carried her back to Falcon Ridge, by the time he returned, the creature might have hurt the little girl. Or she'd be so lost he might not find her in this weather.

He had to go after the kid.

His chest tightened as he jerked off his coat and wrapped it gently around the woman, then lifted her and moved her beneath an overhang. The jutting cliff would protect her from the new falling snow and somewhat from the bitter wind. But he had to hurry.

She clutched his hand again and squeezed it. "Please go now. You have to save her."

She stared at him. In her eyes, he saw terror, and the realization that she might not make it, but that she didn't care. She'd sacrifice her life to save her daughter's. In fact, she'd probably been attacked doing just that.

Emotions swelled in his throat, but he pushed them aside. He didn't have time for them.

He had to find Katie and bring her back to her mother. Then he had to make sure they both survived.

SONYA FELT her little girl's fear as if it were a physical part of herself and tried to stay alert.

But her head swam, and the world danced in a haze in front of her eyes. She was bleeding, felt so weak, her body was throbbing…

Her head lolled backward…she could hardly keep her eyes open.

No, don't go to sleep. Don't pass out.

She had to hang on. She had to be awake if that man found Katie. What had he said his name was?

She forced her eyes open, but she was completely disoriented. She could no longer see two feet in front of her. Panic gripped her, and she tried to move, to get up, but nausea rose in her throat, and she swayed and collapsed back against the ridge. Pain throbbed relentlessly through her back and arms. But she refused to give in to it. She had to stay calm.

The man would be back. He'd promised. He knew where he'd left her.

Brack Falcon. He said he lived nearby. She'd heard rumors in town about the men at Falcon Ridge. They were strange. Dangerous. They lived in the wild like animals.

But he had spoken so softly to her and had promised to find Katie.

Wind ripped through her coat and tossed debris through the air, the throbbing in her body intensifying as the minutes dragged on. Panic gnawed at her again.

Katie. Dear God, had the creature gotten her? Had Katie stumbled and fallen in the snow? What if she stepped off a ridge or embankment and was hurt? What if Brack Falcon couldn't find her?

She curled up inside his coat, a sob wrenching from deep in her soul as her little girl's face flashed in her mind. Katie, with the big brown eyes. Katie who liked Cheerios and peanut butter cookies. And strawberry shampoo and bubble baths and picking wildflowers in the yard.

Katie with the guileless smile and the determination to overcome her handicap. Katie, who never complained about being left out or struggling to walk, all the things other kids took for granted.

Katie, with no father.

Or rather, one who hadn't wanted her.

The agony of Stan's betrayal and parting words felt like a heavy weight slamming into her every time she thought about it. He had wanted a baby but with Stan, everything had to be perfect.

Katie wasn't. At least not in Stan's eyes. And neither was Sonya because she carried a genetic disorder that had caused Katie's physical problems.

She'd been heartbroken at his cruel comments, but most of all she hated him for abandoning Katie.

Katie might have a physical handicap, but she was perfect in Sonya's eyes. The most precious child that had ever existed.

She had the heart and soul of an angel.

Pain and fatigue clawed at Sonya, tempting her into unconsciousness. She closed her eyes, a tear leaking out and freezing on her cheek.

Sonya could live without a man in her life. She never wanted that kind of heartache again.

But she'd die if anything happened to her daughter.

WHERE IN the hell was the kid?

Brack stooped to search for footprints, indentations in the icy ground, anything to help him find the child.

Ahead, twigs and debris swirled through the snowy haze, and the sound of a cry floated toward him. It was her. The little girl. He sensed her presence nearby just as he sensed the injured animals in the woods when they needed him.

He was part animal himself, he'd been told enough times. He connected with them on a deep level, much more than humans.

But the woman's pleas had torn through his defenses. He could still see her wide-set green eyes staring up at him in terror.

His pulse kicked up as he scanned the horizon. It was so damn dark. She might be wandering aimlessly in the forest. She might have fallen and hurt herself. She might be hiding from wild animals.

He closed his eyes, forced his mind to siphon through the fear and zero in on his instincts. What would a little girl do if she was lost or scared?

Find a place to hide? Maybe in a cave or one of the old mines if she stumbled upon one.

The soft swish of a falcon's wingspan cutting through the air sliced through the noise of the violent wind, and he glanced up and saw the falcon again. Soaring lower than normal. Heading to the east.

Again, he followed it, and the flashlight beam caught a small scrap of red fabric that had snagged on a broken branch. The little girl's, maybe?

He picked up his pace, then started yelling her name. "Katie! Katie! Where are you, honey?"

His voice floated through the wind and echoed off the mountain. Could she hear him?

Seconds later, he spotted a group of branches piled at the mouth of a cave, and a pair of small crutches was lying near the entrance.

Her mother's pleas taunted him. *Please find her. She can't walk very well....*

He paused, listened. A small cry echoed from within the stone walls. The little girl was inside.

Relief whooshed through him.

He slowly inched forward, knowing she was probably frightened and that he might scare her.

"Katie?" He ducked inside the opening, scanning the gray interior, listening for sounds of her breathing. How far back was she? "Katie?"

He paused, allowing a second for his eyes to adjust to the darkness, and then eased another step forward. "Katie, your mommy sent me to get you."

A small whimper. Almost indiscernible. Still, it chilled his insides.

He glanced to the left, shined the flashlight across the interior.

"Katie, my name is Brack, honey. Your mommy's worried about you."

"Mommy?"

The tiny voice made his heart squeeze. She was huddled into a ball, her arms cradling a small animal close to her chest, her chest heaving with sobs. In between her gulps, the soft meow of a kitten drifted toward him.

"Yes, honey. Your mommy." He squatted down, putting himself more at her eye level, then lowered his voice. "She wants me to bring you back to her."

A hiccup, then she nodded, her chin still resting against her knees. "Is my mommy aw wight?"

God help him, he didn't know. But he had to lie. "She is now, but we need to get her to a doctor."

"It's all my fauwt," she cried. "My fauwt that m-monster gots her."

"Shh, it's all right." He reached his hand toward

her. "Come on, we have to go now, honey, before the storm gets worse."

Her eyes were so luminous with fear that she reminded him of a small bird trapped by a predator. "Can you stand up, honey?"

She sucked in a breath that rattled with fear and then clutched the wall with one hand. But she kept the other one wrapped around the kitten.

"What's your kitty's name?"

"Snowball…" Her voice broke, brittle, like ice cracking in the wind. "That's why I runs outside. To finds him." She wobbled forward, her thin legs buckling, and he caught her. "I needs my crutches."

"We'll get them." He scooped her up into his arms, letting her carry the kitten between them. God, he wished he had a blanket or something to shield her from the cold. She buried her head against his neck, shivering, but she didn't complain as he dashed outside the cave. He stopped only long enough to grab her crutches, then tucked them under his arm and rushed through the woods back to her mother.

He just prayed the woman was still alive when they reached her.

Chapter Three

Brack dashed through the woods, battling the wind, well aware of the tiny child in his arms who had placed her trust in his hands. He couldn't let her down.

But what if they were too late to save her mother? Did Katie have a father at home waiting for her? If so, why had the man let his wife go out into the approaching storm to search for the child alone? Where the hell was he now?

And who would take care of Katie if the woman didn't make it?

His own memories of losing his father erupted from his past to haunt him. Even though his father hadn't died when he'd been carted off to jail, Brack had felt as if he had. Once he had been incarcerated, his father had cut off all communication with his boys. As an adult, Brack realized that his father had done so to protect his sons, but at six, he hadn't understood. Instead, he'd felt as if he'd been abandoned.

He cut through the patches of broken limbs and trees, grateful the falcon had led the way to Katie. Her body jerked with the cold, so he cradled her closer, using his own heat to keep her warm.

"We're almost there, lamb chop," he murmured.

She nodded against his chest, and his lungs tightened at her brave little face. Finally, he made it to the overhang where he'd left her mother. The woman was so still that panic squeezed the air from his lungs. She lay curled on her side, her knees hunched upward, her head buried in her arms. He quickly knelt and checked for a pulse again. Tension coiled in his muscles when he didn't feel one, but he shifted his fingers slightly to the left. Yes, he found it. Her pulse was weak and thready, but she had one.

He eased Katie down beside her mother.

Katie tugged at the coat sleeve. "Mommy!" Katie cried. "Mommy, wake up!"

He tipped the little girl's chin up so she'd look into his eyes. "Honey, I need for you to climb on my back and wrap your arms around my neck. I'll carry you piggyback, then I can lift your mommy, too. Can you do that for me?"

She bobbed her head up and down, then bit down on her lip. "But what about Snowball?"

Hell, he could no more leave the kitten than he could the woman and child.

He tucked the kitten into the pocket of his coat. "There, now he's safe and warm."

Katie smiled at him then, so trusting, that he could have sworn a moonbeam bounced through the dark storm and lit her face like an angel.

He gestured to his back. "Now, hop aboard." He crouched to the ground so she could wrap her arms around his neck. He grabbed her hands to secure them, and she tried to wrap her legs around his waist, but they dangled as if she didn't have the strength. His throat convulsed, but he patted her hands. "Good girl."

She pressed her face against his back away from the wind. He tucked Katie's crutches below one arm pit, then scooped her mother into his arms and strode back toward Falcon Ridge.

SONYA STIRRED from the depths of unconsciousness and cold. She had to live, wake up, find Katie. Make sure her little girl was safe.

But she was so cold. So tired. Her limbs felt like dead weights and pain throbbed through her. Sleep offered a reprieve, and the darkness pulled her into its abyss. She gave in to it, but then she was trapped in a minefield where light had been obliterated by cave-like walls and where strange mythical creatures stalked the night.

Terror splintered through the fog, and she forced her eyes open. She had to escape the tunnel of darkness, find the light. Then she was being jostled, moved. Somewhere in the haze, Katie's small voice soothed her.

Finally, she felt herself being lowered onto something soft. Warm. A blanket being tucked around her. Then another. And a fire nearby. The crackle of wood. The hiss of the flames. So cozy. She sank back into sleep, craving the peace it offered.

"Mommy, mommy, you gots to wakes up!"

Katie's tiny, terrified voice shattered her rest. Sonya forced herself to blink through the fog of pain and cold, but the details of what had happened were fuzzy.

Where was Katie? She couldn't see her, had lost her in the blizzard. No, that creature had attacked her, and she'd warned Katie to run.

A husky, deep voice followed. "The paramedics are on their way." A brush of her hair, and she looked up to see a man's face peering over her. Dark, scruffy hair. Black eyes. A wide-set jaw. He looked dangerous and unkempt, wild like the mystical animal creatures she'd been dreaming about.

Was he the bizarre creature that had attacked her in the woods?

No…he had saved her. And Katie was clinging to his back, her small hands clutching his neck in a choke hold as if she couldn't let go.

The man…he'd found Katie for her… Brack Falcon…

"You're at my place now, at Falcon Ridge," he said in a deep voice. "The paramedics are on their way."

She tried to nod but wasn't sure she had actually moved her head. "Katie?" she croaked.

He brushed his thumb across her cheek. "She's fine. I found her hiding in a cave nearby." He swung her daughter from his back as if he'd been handling her all his life, and Sonya swallowed back tears. He was huge, had powerful muscles and the biggest, widest hands she'd ever seen on a man, but he gently cradled his arms under Katie's weak legs and placed her beside Sonya as if Katie were a delicate china doll that might break if handled too roughly. Then he wrapped a thick blanket around Katie.

Katie's father had never held her like that.

Fresh tears filled her eyes as Katie snuggled into her.

"Mommy, I was s-so scared," Katie whispered. "I…thought you was gonna leabe me." Her voice caught, and she buried her head into Sonya's neck.

Pain shot through Sonya's battered arm as she slid it below Katie's back to hug her. "No, baby, Mommy would never, ever leave you." She brushed Katie's shoulder-length hair from her damp cheek, then rubbed small circles on Katie's back to soothe her. "Do you hear me, sweetie? Mommy will always be here for you."

But fatigue and blood loss had drained all the life from her, and she felt herself slipping back into the darkness again.

"Is there anyone I can call?" Brack asked, drawing her back to reality as if he, too, thought she might be fading off for good. "Your husband? Katie's father?"

Sonya shook her head. "No, no husband.... No one."

Worry flickered in the man's black eyes. He was so serious, somber...maybe she wasn't going to make it.

"Call Miss Margaret," she choked out. "She babysits Katie while I work."

He cuddled the blanket around Katie, wrapping them up together. "This Miss Margaret—how do I reach her?"

"The paramedics...friends of mine." Her voice broke off, weak. "They'll know."

"No, Mommy." Katie tugged at her face. "Don't leabe me!"

"Not leaving..." Sonya whispered. "Just have to sleep."

Katie tightened her arms around Sonya's neck and squeezed so hard Sonya coughed for air, but she cradled her daughter tighter, unable to release her for fear she would slip away forever.

Then Katie would be all alone with no one to love her.

THE MINUTES DRAGGED by while Brack waited on the ambulance.

He didn't like the fact that the woman had drifted

into unconsciousness. No telling how much blood she had lost. What if the attack had damaged internal organs?

Twenty minutes passed. Still no ambulance.

He had to check her wounds. He coaxed her to roll over to her side, and he carefully cut away the remainder of her flannel gown, leaving the blanket secure around her legs. Then he leaned close to study her wounds. Sharp claw marks remained where something had ripped away the flesh on her hands and back. Dirt, dead skin, leaves, and mangled tissue were matted together in an ugly maze. The wounds were deep, but not to the bone, so hopefully her internal organs weren't injured. But she needed stitches, antibiotics and painkillers. And the area had to be cleaned.

He rushed to the bathroom, grabbed the first aid kit he kept on hand, then cleaned the worst of the dirt and debris from her back. She moaned and he winced, hating to hurt her but knowing it had to be done.

In all the years he and his brothers had been rescuing birds of prey, he had seen vicious attacks by animals. But he'd never seen anything so awful as the tender skin on the beautiful woman—desecrated, clawed at as if her attacker wanted to literally taste her blood.

If a bird had done this, it was supersized. Maybe injured. Or what if it was diseased? Was it possible that his beloved creatures had contracted some kind of strange illness that caused them to attack humans?

Finally, a siren squealed outside, and the paramedics punched the gargoyle doorbell, causing a resounding lion's roar to moan throughout the house. Katie jerked her head up, startled.

He forced a small smile. "I've got a crazy doorbell, don't I?"

She nodded, a tiny smile lifting the corner of her mouth as if they shared a secret. Then she dropped her head back down against her mother's.

He hurried to let the rescue workers in and quickly explained what had happened. The woman's name was Sonya Silverstein. Apparently she worked with them as a paramedic. She and Katie had just moved into the old farmhouse just a mile away from Falcon Ridge. He could see the rambling wooden structure from the top of the ridge.

Katie climbed into his lap while the paramedics checked Sonya's vitals and started an IV, placed a temporary dressing on her wounds, moved her to a gurney and transported her to the ambulance.

"Check the little girl, too," Brack said. Although she appeared to be okay, he didn't know how long she'd been out in the snow or how weak her health was. "And Sonya said to call Miss Margaret."

A big barrel-chested guy who introduced himself as Van Richards nodded, then reached for Katie.

"We'll call her on the way. Come on, peewee, you can ride in the truck with your mama."

"But whats about Snowball?" Katie asked.

"Snowball will be happier staying at my house where it's warm tonight," Brack said in a low voice. "We can take him back to your house in the morning."

She scrunched her mouth in thought, but seemed to accept his offer.

Van nudged her arm. "We need to go, Katie."

Katie glanced up at Brack with those mesmerizing eyes, eyes full of terror. "Will you comes with us, Mister?"

"Brack," he said softly.

Van shot him a skeptical look that bordered on distrust, as if he suspected that Brack might have attacked Sonya. "There's not room."

Katie wrinkled up her nose. "I can squish over."

Brack silently cursed. All his life, he and his brothers had endured those condemning looks. They'd been dubbed murderer's sons. And then there was their strange affinity for the wild.

It was the very reason he hated this town. He still wasn't sure he'd stay.

To hell with these guys. He didn't have to prove himself to them or anyone else in this godforsaken place. He'd done all he could tonight. He'd saved the woman and kid. Now he could walk away.

Katie tugged at his hand, her chin quivering. "Pwease, Mr. Bwack," Katie pleaded.

Really, how could he refuse the poor little girl? He wanted to know more about the creature that had attacked the woman, anyway.

The younger guy, Joey Bates, climbed in the driver's seat while Van settled Katie into the back.

"I'll drive my SUV to the hospital and meet you there, sweetie, okay?"

She nodded, then pasted on a brave smile and huddled into the blanket beside her mother. Sonya was breathing steadily, but anxiety still tugged at Brack. He waved to Katie as the door shut behind them, then crawled into his Land Rover and cranked the engine. The wind beat at the windows, fresh snow swirling in a fog. More questions hammered through his head as he maneuvered the vehicle down the mountain toward town.

Didn't Sonya have any family to call? Where was her husband?

If he was alive, if they were divorced, did he ever see Katie?

If so, why wouldn't she have wanted him to call the man now? She'd need help with Katie while she healed.

They're not your problem, he silently reminded himself. *Don't get involved.*

But he had to find out exactly what had attacked Sonya. Was it one of his birds of prey or was it another kind of creature—a human one who not only killed animals but now had attacked an innocent woman?

BRACK PACED the hospital waiting room, sipping the stale, cold coffee from the vending machine as he waited on the doctors to check Katie and Sonya. A half hour later, one of the nurses finally appeared; he almost accosted her with questions, but at the last moment held himself in check.

"Sir, were you the man who found the Silverstein woman and child?"

He glanced at her name tag. Amy. She was youngish, maybe early thirties, blond hair, a kind smile. "Yes. Brack Falcon. How are they?"

"They're both going to be fine. They treated Sonya's injuries and have settled her into a room now. Her little girl is in there with her." She paused, studying him, her eyes narrowed. "We've called the babysitter, Margaret Mallady," she continued. "She said she'd be here as soon as possible to pick up Katie."

"Good." He could breathe now. Go home.

"Did you see the attack on Ms. Silverstein, Mr. Falcon?"

He shook his head. "No, I heard her screaming and found her on the ground."

A frown creased her forehead. "What were they doing outside in the blizzard?"

"The little girl snuck out looking for her kitten."

"That sounds like Katie." The woman's round cheeks ballooned out as she shook her head.

"Poor Sonya. She's had her hands full. She didn't need this."

He frowned, wanting to ask what she meant but warning himself not to.

Don't get involved, and you won't get hurt.

He was a loner. A man who needed no one. A man who didn't want anyone needing him.

"Doctor Waverman called the sheriff," Amy said. "To report the attacks."

Sheriff Cohen. Dammit. He was the last person in town Brack wanted to see. He hated the man for railroading his father into jail twenty years ago. And he'd tried to run Rex out of town when he'd first arrived, and he'd interfered with their investigation.

"Oh, there he is now." She rushed forward to greet the sheriff, then gestured toward Brack. Sheriff Cohen's jowls shook as he gave Brack a once-over. His look said it all. Why had the Falcon boys returned to Falcon Ridge—to cause trouble?

Cohen shifted, then jerked his pants up with his stubby thumbs and stalked toward Brack. "So, you're the other Falcon?"

Brack nodded. "Sheriff."

"You found the Silverstein woman?"

"Yes."

His bushy eyebrows climbed his forehead. "Mind telling me what you were doing out in the woods?"

"You know my family rescues injured birds.

Lately there have been several attacks on the animals. I heard a loud screeching sound, and was out checking on them."

"You were searching for wounded birds?" Suspicion laced the sheriff's gruff voice.

"Yes. Then I heard a scream and found the woman on the ground. She'd been attacked. But she told me to look for her little girl." He forced a steely calm to his voice although the memory of having to leave the woman alone haunted him. "I found Katie hiding in a cave, then carried them both to my house and phoned the paramedics." He finished matter-of-factly, glaring at the sheriff, willing him to defy his statement.

"You know what attacked the woman?" Cohen asked.

Brack shook his head. "I didn't see the actual attack."

A doctor appeared through a set of double doors, then introduced himself to Brack and the sheriff. "Is Ms. Silverstein awake yet?" Sheriff Cohen asked. "I'd like to get her statement."

Dr. Waverman shook his head. "She's pretty heavily sedated, but we can go in for just a moment. Her daughter is with her."

"Tell me about her injuries," Sheriff Cohen ordered.

Dr. Waverman winced, then described the claw marks on Sonya's back and hands. "I've never seen anything quite like it. The marks look like talons but some of them are so large…"

"Damn birds," Sheriff Cohen said. "This is you and your brothers' fault," he snapped. "We never had trouble with birds attacking people before, not till you moved back and started providing a refuge for them. Are you breeding some special kind that feeds on humans?"

Brack's blood ran cold at the man's accusations. "That's ridiculous. If the birds are attacking people, they must be sick."

"Then they need to be destroyed," Sheriff Cohen said.

Brack's jaw tightened, his control teetering on the edge. What kind of ignorant moron was Cohen? "What they need is medical treatment."

"Gentlemen, why don't we see what Sonya has to say before we do anything rash," Dr. Waverman suggested.

Brack and the sheriff exchanged silent, menacing looks, but followed quietly. The scent of antiseptic and medicines pervaded the halls; the beep of hospital machinery and rattling of medicine carts and gurneys added a layer of charged tension.

Brack's gut clenched when he stepped inside. Sonya lay against the stark white sheets, her dark curly hair spread across the pillow, her face pale in sleep. Long dark lashes curled against ivory skin dotted with the faintest row of freckles. Her lips were a natural ruby color, her chin slightly pointed, her face heart-shaped. He hadn't gotten a good look at her before, but she was stunning, like a real-life Sleeping Beauty. The childish story taunted him— if he kissed her, would she wake up and be healed?

Ridiculous.

His gaze landed on her bandaged hands and anger churned through him. A primitive surge of protective instincts swelled in his chest, as well.

The sheriff walked over and stared at Katie with a scowl. She looked impossibly small and fragile huddled in the chair beside her mother's hospital bed. Someone, probably the nurse, had helped her into fresh dry pajamas and socks, and had thought to give her a pad of paper and some crayons. She was drawing intently, her pug nose scrunched in concentration.

"Katie, did you see the animal that attacked your mother?" Sheriff Cohen asked.

So much for tact.

Katie slowly tipped her face upward, but she cowered into the chair away from the hulking sheriff.

Brack strode forward and knelt beside her chair. She automatically reached for his hand, and he slid it around her trembling shoulder. "It's all right, honey. We just need to know what happened to your mommy."

"It was one of those hawks, wasn't it?" Cohen asked. "They've been attacking each other, and tonight they attacked your mother, isn't that right?"

Katie's lower lip quivered. "I d-don't k-know what it was."

"What do you mean, honey?" Brack asked softly.

"It wooked wike a giant bird," she whispered, "but it w-was a monster."

Brack gritted his teeth, then glanced at the picture she'd drawn. Although it was crude, a four-year-old's handiwork, the definite shape of a winged creature filled the page. Maybe a large eagle or hawk. Black and brown, with long, sharp talons.

Except this bird had the head of a human.

HE LIFTED his talons in front of him, smiling at the torn flesh and blood lingering on the sharp edges. Tonight the animal inside him had emerged from the gray emptiness of the night, called to life by the scent of blood and fear.

First the eagle that he had ripped apart with his talons. Then the little girl's terrorized cry. The scent of her small body. Then the smell of a woman's.

Oh, but she had tasted sweet.

Her blood had only whetted his appetite for the hungers of the flesh. For her body. Her heart. Her soul.

She had been the first human.

But not the last.

The animals had served him well in the beginning. But as he fed the beast within him, the need for more sustenance grew.

From now on, the birds would be his appetizer.
   Then he'd feast on a human's blood and let the
two mingle together.

Chapter Four

Brack stared at the drawing of the winged monster, and his gut clenched. Katie was only a child, was tiny herself, and she'd been terrified—had she imagined the half bird-half man? Or could it really exist? Some kind of mutant...

No, it was impossible. He practically lived in those woods, knew the mountains. If such a creature existed, he would have seen it.

There are places to hide, a voice whispered inside his head. The old mines and tunnels. The dark edges of the forest...

The rumors about the epidemic of typhoid fever that had once destroyed half the town rose from the depths of his subconscious. The bodies had been burned, buried in a tunnel underground, the old mine blasted shut, hoping to contain the germs of the dead. He'd always wondered if somehow the ashes of those who'd died might filter into the land or water and rise to haunt them.

"Katie—" Sheriff Cohen leaned over, beefy hands on his knees "—was that what you saw, or are you getting the birds mixed up with this man here?" He pointed to Brack. "Are you sure he didn't attack your mother?"

Katie's eyes widened to saucer size, and Brack cursed silently. How dare Cohen suggest that he had attacked Sonya? The son of a...

Cold rage poured through him, but he stood ramrod straight, his pulse pounding as he waited on Katie's response. He didn't know what he'd do if she decided she should fear him, but the thought disturbed him more than he wanted to admit.

Sonya's eyelashes fluttered, then she opened her eyes and stared at him. Her eyes were the most unusual green he'd ever seen, somewhere between the lush green of the Colorado mountainside in spring and the dark, rich color of emeralds. And they were as bewitching as an animal's eyes in total darkness.

Again, he felt a deep connection, although a wariness flickered in her pain-filled expression, and he realized she had heard Cohen's accusations. Her skeptical gaze tore at him.

Hell, he didn't care. He was what he was, and he wouldn't change for anybody.

Katie clutched the sketchpad to her side with one hand and slid her other one around his own. "No, Mr. Bwack, he saves us. And the birds...they brings him to me."

Brack frowned. Did she have some kind of sixth sense when it came to animals as he did?

Whatever the reason, her gesture of unquestioning trust tugged at emotions long buried in his chest.

Emotions he didn't want to feel for her or her mother.

Emotions that whispered that maybe he didn't really want to be alone. That as much as he'd hardened himself to thinking that he could live without a woman in his life, he was wrong.

That Sonya Silverstein might fill some part of his soul that had been lost a long time ago.

He immediately jerked his gaze from hers, his instincts warning him to walk away. He could not forget who he was. Could not get involved with Sonya and lose himself in the process.

He had to discover the truth about these bizarre attacks and take care of the birds. Nothing else mattered.

He wouldn't let it.

EVERY BONE AND MUSCLE in Sonya's body ached, but she dragged herself from the effects of the medication and pain, and opened her eyes. Her daughter was frightened and needed her.

The scent of alcohol and hospital odors permeated the air. The rustle of the sheets as she twisted them in her fingers rattled over the blur of voices. Through the fog of drugs, Sheriff Cohen's accusations registered. She noticed the angry glint in Brack Falcon's powerful jaw as he'd clenched it. He could be formidable when crossed. Maybe even dangerous.

But her frail little daughter slid her small hand into his large one in blind trust.

The sight made her heart twist. Was Katie right to trust this stranger?

He had been in the woods when she was attacked. She'd heard the rumors about the Falcon men. Had been forewarned by some of the older women in town to stay away from them.

Could he have attacked her, then come back to rescue her to make himself look like a hero to the town?

His dark eyes shifted over her, and unease clawed at her chest. He didn't strike her as the type of man to want a hero's welcome or attention. Yet what did she know about him?

She'd certainly been wrong about her former husband.

But something had definitely transpired between her and Brack Falcon back in the woods, some moment of intense fear that had connected them. That, and another emotion she couldn't pinpoint at the moment.

Old insecurities and distrust from her marriage taunted her.

She couldn't trust any man. Especially where her daughter was concerned.

Yet Katie, in her innocence, seemed to like him.

On the other hand, Katie exhibited a wariness toward the other man, who looked like the sheriff, as if she immediately saw him as an enemy. Or maybe she just didn't like him belittling her new friend.

Whatever the reason, it was *her* job to protect Katie, not Brack Falcon's. She and Katie were a team and she couldn't allow anyone into their lives. Couldn't chance either of them growing too attached and getting hurt.

The sheriff turned to her then, as if he'd just noticed she was awake. "Ms. Silverstein, you're awake now?"

She nodded, although when she tried to speak her lips felt as if they were glued together.

"I'm Sheriff Cohen. Maybe you can clear this up. Did this man attack you in the woods?"

Brack Falcon's dark eyes pierced straight to her soul, and her stomach fluttered. Katie huddled closer to Brack, and Sonya wet her lips, the realization that her daughter was clinging to Brack sending a shiver of trepidation through her.

Yet hadn't she wanted to cling to him in the woods herself when she'd been terrified? Hadn't she begged him for help and felt comforted in his strong arms when he'd carried her and Katie to safety?

"No," she managed to whisper.

"Then what was it?" Sheriff Cohen asked.

Sonya searched her memory for details, for some way to explain, but she'd only glimpsed the shadow of a creature. She'd been too busy trying to fend off the attack.

"I'm not sure," she said in a strained voice. "Some kind of animal, maybe."

Cohen jammed his lips together. "I'm calling in someone from the state," he said. "They'll track down those damn birds and destroy them." He turned to Brack. "And if I find out that you and your brothers are raising some mutant attack birds or that you're responsible for these vicious attacks, I'll lock you up for attempted murder."

He turned back to Sonya. "If I were you, Ms. Silverstein, I'd stay away from this man, and keep your daughter away from him, too."

"I tolds you it was a m-monster," Katie cried. "He wooked wike that picture!"

Sheriff Cohen's laugh boomeranged through the room as he cut his eyes over Katie, then Sonya. "Honey, that creature is part animal, part man, just like the Falcon men. They don't belong in this town." He fisted his hands on his hips. "Now heed my warning, or I have a feeling next time you won't be so lucky."

Sonya clutched the sheet between her fingers again, the sheriff's cold tone sending a shiver through her. Brack stiffened and started to release

Katie's hand, but she gripped him tighter as she watched Sheriff Cohen stalk from the room.

Brack cleared his throat, his voice gruff when he spoke. "I'll leave if you want, Sonya."

The way his deep voice rumbled out her name made a tingle travel down her spine. His stiff posture suggested that he would understand if she said yes. That he was aware of his bad reputation.

Yet her daughter was smitten with Brack and afraid of the sheriff. Fatigue clawed at her again. She couldn't keep her eyes open. And she didn't want Katie to be alone while she waited on Margaret to arrive.

Still, Brack was big and tough, so intense that he exuded power. And with power came danger.

She should tell him to leave. She and Katie didn't need anyone but each other.

But Katie had been through so much already tonight. And she looked so small and vulnerable beside him....

"Please stay with Katie until Ms. Margie gets here," she whispered.

He shifted on the balls of his feet, looking uncomfortable for a moment. Then he gave a curt nod.

Uneasiness speared through her. She didn't want to trust him, didn't want him in her life.

And if she was wrong about him and he hurt her daughter in any way, she'd help the sheriff run him out of town and not think twice about it.

BRACK GRIMACED as Sonya slipped back into sleep. Dammit, she was in pain. And it bothered him on a level he didn't want to explore. Cohen's intimidation tactics disturbed him even more. Not because he was afraid of the man, but because Cohen had tried to scare the kid with them.

He might not want a family, but he wasn't a monster, either. And he sure as hell didn't make it a practice to go around terrifying children.

Katie clung to his hand, and he glanced down to see her yawn. The poor little girl had been through hell tonight and needed some rest. And that baby-sitter might not be able to drive through the storm for a while.

Dammit. He needed to get going. Itched to hike into the woods and hunt down the creature who'd attacked Sonya. But he'd promised Sonya he wouldn't leave Katie alone.

Katie's head lolled to the side against the chair arm, and he scooped her up, wrapped the blanket around her, then sat down and cradled her in his lap. Katie snuggled into his chest and fell asleep instantly. She was so teeny she barely weighed anything at all. So frail that the urge to protect her and slay all her demons hit him.

But he didn't need any complications right now. He wasn't Katie's father and refused to get involved with her or Sonya.

Sonya whimpered then and rolled to her side, her

dark hair falling across her bruised cheek, and he fought his baser instincts. Then, hell, he lost and brushed her hair from her cheek, trying to soothe her. She moaned and jerked her eyes open as if she'd been in the throes of a nightmare, and their gazes locked. She had been reliving the attack—he saw the terror in her expression.

Then she looked down at her daughter curled against him, and her expression softened. "Thank you for being so kind to Katie tonight," she whispered.

"How could anyone not be kind to her?" he asked gruffly.

Pain tightened her features. "The kids…they tease her, can be mean." Her voice broke. "And others…they don't understand."

His jaw went rigid, his body taut as tension vibrated between them. It was none of his business, but he had to ask. "Where's her father?"

A long second passed, and a chill swept through the room, as if a ghost had passed through. "He's not a part of our lives," she said quietly.

He wanted to ask more but bit back the temptation, and Sonya clamped her lips together as if she'd already said too much.

Better they left it that way. He didn't need to know personal information. Only that *something* had attacked her tonight, and he'd find out what it was.

Still, as she stared at him, the sadness in her eyes tore at him.

Her husband must have abandoned her and Katie. Bastard.

His gaze fell to her lips. They were so ripe and pink he wondered what they would feel like under his mouth. Would she taste as sweet as she looked?

Suddenly he wanted to soothe away her pain. Make her smile and forget about the man who'd hurt her.

But he barely knew her, or Katie. He didn't belong in their lives and could not replace the jerk who'd forsaken them.

Hell, his own family had been torn apart when he was small so it was natural that he'd feel compassion for her and her child. After all, he *wasn't* a monster.

But he wasn't a man who wanted a relationship with a woman now, either.

Tomorrow Sonya would go home. And he would return to Falcon Ridge. He'd hunt down her attacker, take care of his birds, and keep Cohen away from them.

And he'd live alone, just as he always intended.

SONYA SLEPT fitfully, waking every so often to search the darkness for her daughter. The nurse had called Margaret again to see what was keeping her. Margaret's husband had to clear the entrance to their drive before they could maneuver into town to get Katie, but she was finally on the way.

Brack had dozed off himself, but his body was so big he looked uncomfortable sleeping in the chair.

Dark beard stubble dotted his wide, strong jaw and his scraggly, shoulder-length hair brushed his collar, looking unkempt. He looked rugged and wild, as if he belonged out in the woods with the animals.

Yet with his head tilted sideways, his arm curved protectively around Katie, he also looked vulnerable. Tears pushed at the backs of her eyelids again, her chest hurting from the pressure. But she blinked back the moisture. The pain and medication were making her sappy. Making her read things that weren't there.

Brack Falcon was not a vulnerable man.

But God knows, she'd been terrified when she'd been attacked. More so for Katie than for herself, but still…the memory of that creature tearing into her flesh would haunt her forever. If Brack hadn't come along when he did, she might have died. And so might have her daughter.

Would Stan raise Katie if something happened to her?

A tremor rippled through her. Would he eventually accept her disability and love her unconditionally?

If not, would her mother want Katie?

Sonya choked back more tears at the thought of the chasm between her and her mother. Evelyn Simpson didn't even know she had a grandchild….

Not that that was entirely her mother's fault. No,

her own stubborn pride and guilt had kept her from turning to her mother after the divorce.

And from confiding about her handicapped baby.

Her mother's bitter warnings about Stan whispered in her ears. Evelyn had never liked him. She'd tried to convince Sonya that Stan was selfish, that underneath his charm lay the heart of a manipulative man who wanted to control every aspect of his life, including his wife and child.

A man who hated imperfections.

God, if she'd only listened to her mother…

But then she wouldn't have her daughter. And she couldn't imagine not having Katie in her life.

But in light of the attack tonight, she should rethink her silence. Katie would love Evelyn, and her mother…she sensed her mother would accept Katie and her limitations.

Brack shifted slightly, and she tensed as he opened his eyes and stared into hers.

"Are you all right?" he asked in a voice husky with sleep.

She nodded, well aware of how intimate the small, dark room seemed. His breathing rattled in the silence that followed, as if he, too, felt the sexual tension between them.

"Do you need something?" he said in a low voice. "Pain medication?"

She shook her head, her emotions ping-ponging

in her chest. Why did his soft, husky tone make her want to cling to him?

And why did the thought of doing so terrify her?

The door squeaked open, and Margaret and her husband came in. Sonya sighed in relief, knowing she needed a reality check and for Brack Falcon to leave. He was taking up too much of the room. His scent, his body, seemed to fill it.

Margaret worried her bottom lip when she saw Brack in the room and maintained her distance from him, as if he might bite. Sonya explained about the attack, and Margaret gasped, then hugged her arms around herself.

"I've heard about the ghosts that haunt the town," Margaret said, "and I knew wild animals lived in the woods, but this is awful."

Her husband frowned, looking worried, then scooped Katie into his arms, and they left, both dismissing Brack's offer of assistance.

A muscle twitched in his jaw as he stood and worked the kinks from his long legs. "I'll go now."

Sonya inhaled, wondering if she should have assured Margaret that Brack was safe. But she couldn't. "Thank you, Brack. For everything."

Anger glinted in his eyes. "No problem."

Sonya told herself it didn't matter what he thought of her. She didn't intend to apologize for her friends wanting to protect her daughter. It was better he leave now. Hopefully, they wouldn't have to cross paths again.

Because she had no intention of getting involved with him or any other man.

HIS HUNGER was mounting, growing more incessant, the need to feed more often throbbing within him.

He wanted to taste Sonya again. She had been so delicious the first time that he craved more. But he had to bide his time.

When he saw her, and he *would* see her, she must never know how he felt about her.

He would befriend her. Earn her trust. Become her confidant.

And hide his dark side.

Until then, he had to find prey elsewhere.

He dipped his talon in blood, drew out a white sheet of paper, and began to write.

> Some animals mate only once
> You are mine now, Sonya.
> You wear my markings
> and will for life.

Laughter and lust sang through his bloodstream as he drew a heart on the page with the blood. He wouldn't give her the note just yet. But one day he would.

Instead, he'd leave her a small present. A token to assure her that he hadn't forgotten her.

His animal instincts alive, he set off into the woods, eyes piercing the darkness, senses alert for the weak.

First the hunt.

Then the kill.

Then he would spread the blood of his victim on her door so she would know he hadn't deserted her. That he was coming back.

And that soon she would be his.

Chapter Five

Brack stalked outside, battling irritation at the wary look Sonya's babysitter had given him. Sonya had looked relieved to have him leave, as well.

Hell, what did he care?

He had a job to do, and he'd damn well do it. Someone or something was hurting the birds he loved, and he intended to put a stop to it.

He phoned Deke and Rex and filled them in while he drove back to the house. A half hour later, he met his brothers in the library to strategize.

"Sheriff Cohen thinks we're raising mutant attack birds up here," Brack said.

Deke gave a belly laugh and Rex cursed. "Sheriff Cohen is a moron."

Brack's sentiments exactly. "He's determined to pin these attacks on us, and to run us out of town."

"We're not scared kids anymore." Rex sipped his coffee. "And he's not running us or our families out of town again."

"I'd like to see him run out of office," Deke muttered.

Brack and Rex said amen to that comment.

"He threatened to bring someone in from the state agencies to check out the birds, but I don't trust him," Brack explained. "I think we should call in our own wildlife biologist, someone who can help us figure out what the hell's going on. If it's up to Cohen, he'll destroy the falcons and burn down Falcon Ridge."

"Over my dead body," Rex snapped.

"We'll get to the bottom of it first, get the animal rights activists on board if we have to," Deke assured him. "You were in the woods, Brack? What do you think happened to the woman?"

The memory of Sonya's terrified eyes haunted him. "I don't know. I heard a horrific attack cry that sounded half human, half animal. And you've both seen the injured falcons. Something is literally ripping out their talons and mauling them to death."

"I've never seen birds prey on each other like this, or on humans," Rex said. "We should have the remains of the mutilated birds tested."

"I'll talk to the vet, Doctor Priestly," Brack said. "In fact, I've been wondering how this predator catches the birds. We all know that's next to impossible with a healthy raptor."

"Which means he may injure them in some other way first," Deke said.

"We haven't found bullet wounds in them, though," Brack said.

"Maybe he's poisoning them somehow," Rex said. "Tainting their food source with something to make them ill. I'll get the EPA out here right away."

Brack hissed, "And I'll have Doctor Priestly run tests, look at tox screens."

"You said the little girl claimed a monster bird attacked her mother?" Deke asked.

Brack nodded.

The three men exchanged skeptical but worried looks. "There were talon marks on Sonya's back." Her wounds had looked odd, sadistic like an animal, but humans could be sadistic, as well. Often, psychopaths began their criminal activities by killing pets and other animals as children. Then their violence escalated. Perhaps that was the case here.

"Is the woman going to be all right?" Rex asked.

Brack nodded. "She'll heal, she seems tough. By the way, they're our neighbors. She and her daughter just moved in to that old farmhouse down the hill."

"The one built over the land that's supposedly possessed?" Rex asked.

Brack nodded. He didn't know if Sonya had known about the rumor when she'd bought the farmhouse or not. But bad things had happened there before. A murder years ago. Another questionable death in the woods last year. Some said the land was tainted, that it held evil itself because of the miners who'd died and been buried below ground.

"Maybe Elsie and Allison can stop by and see her," Deke suggested.

Brack nodded, remembering how difficult Elsie's life had been. Her father had kidnapped her from her mother when she was four, then abandoned her in an orphanage for unwed mothers when she was thirteen. She'd been abused and traumatized and had only recently reconnected with her mother—all thanks to Deke. Then Deke had married her, and now they planned to open a center for troubled teens in town.

"Hailey will probably want to go, too," Rex said. "She's joined this group in town where they deliver a basket of goodies to new residents."

Brack shook his head at his brothers. They were turning damn domestic on him.

But he felt for his brother's wife, Hailey. Hell, how could he not? Their lives had been intertwined since they were kids when his father had been accused of killing her parents. Hailey had witnessed the bloodbath the town called the Hatchet Murders when she was little, but she'd repressed the memory until she'd returned to Tin City. At the time, Rex had been trying to prove their father innocent of the crimes. Then someone had tried to kill Hailey to keep her from remembering, and Rex and Hailey had been thrown together.

Brack was happy for his brothers, but he had no

intention of giving up his freedom for a woman. No, he'd almost made that mistake two years ago in Arizona when he'd mixed business with pleasure.

Erica Evans had poleaxed him when she'd come looking for a bodyguard for her and her child. He'd fallen hard for her, had even considered asking her to marry him.

Then she'd hauled it back to her husband.

In the end, she'd claimed he was too dark and brooding for her. Said he didn't know how to socialize. Hell, she was right. He'd prefer a hike in the woods alone to a party any day.

But the thing that disturbed him most was her final dig—she claimed that he scared her kid.

Sonya Silverstein's beautiful face flashed into his mind, then her little girl's, and the mental wheels in his brain rolled like a freight train barreling ahead. But he refused to board that train again.

"I'm going into the woods now, see what I can find," Brack said. He strode from the room, needing to be alone.

Needing to blend into the woods with the animals and forget that Sonya's green eyes had momentarily made him want to bury himself in her and forget his vow of solitude.

NIGHTMARES of the attack tormented Sonya. Katie's terrified screams echoed in her head. Her own followed.

She jerked awake and stared at the clock, her body tense. The nightmare was over. Katie was safe. And she was in the hospital.

The clock read 6:00 p.m. She desperately wanted to go home.

She could not spend another hour in this room. The smells, sounds...they were a part of her job. Yet in the back of her mind, other memories stood out. The night she'd given birth to her daughter. The problems with the delivery. The horrifying realization that something was wrong.

The incubator where they'd placed her premature newborn. She'd been born six weeks early, and weighed only three pounds. She had struggled for days with her breathing. And then the tests...

Hours of endless waiting. Days of not knowing. Stan's denial.

Then his withdrawal.

As if only the perfect in society deserved love.

She'd fought against hating him then. Not for herself but for the infant who needed him. And last night she'd come so close to losing her baby again....

She had to go home. Tuck Katie into bed, touch her and know that they were both still alive.

She beeped the nurses' station and begged the RN to persuade the doctor to release her. Katie needed her tonight, and she needed to be with her in their own house.

Even though she was beginning to wonder if the

house was haunted. Had it had been built on tainted land as rumors in Tin City claimed? Land where evil bled through the ground and rose to leak a sinister danger in the walls.

Dr. Waverman, a physician she had worked with more than once when she'd worked the ER rotations, stepped into the room. He was midthirties, had sandy brown hair, hazel eyes, and had displayed more than a passing interest in her since she'd accepted a job with Tin City's only rescue squad unit.

And although he seemed nice, she hadn't felt any sexual sparks or interest in return.

Maybe she had cut herself off from men because she was afraid. Her parents' marriage had failed. Hers had ended bitterly.

Everyone she loved deserted her.

She'd even convinced herself that she was past feeling anything for any man.

Then why had she felt a connection with Brack Falcon? Why had her skin tingled and her body felt drawn to him?

Because he saved your life.

It was only natural.

"Sonya." Dr. Waverman looked up from her chart. "I think you need to rest at least twenty-four hours before going home. You lost a lot of blood."

"I'm fine, Doctor Waverman. I can't sleep here, especially since I would have to leave Katie all night."

"Sonya, please call me Aaron. And it won't hurt Katie to spend a night with Margaret." He paused, giving her a concerned look. "It's healthy for children and parents to spend time apart. You need, you deserve, to have a life. Even if it is to rest."

"But—"

"You don't want Katie to suffer from separation anxiety when she starts school, do you?"

The thought of Katie attending school, of facing the kids who might tease her, sent a shudder through her. Granted, she had enrolled Katie in a small pre-school program, but that was different. Only three hours at a time, two days a week.

Besides, she didn't need a parenting lecture right now. She would worry about separation anxiety when the time came. When Katie was ready.

When she was ready.

Not when some man ordered her to do so.

No, she'd never allow another male to make her decisions for her.

"Please, Aaron." Sonya detested the wobble in her voice, but maybe at home she could stop having nightmares, feel safe, forget the trauma of the past night and day.

"All right, I'll prepare the paperwork." He moved closer, reached up and brushed his hand down her arm. "Just promise me you will rest, that if you need help with Katie, you'll ask Margaret to watch her."

"We'll be fine," Sonya said, willing strength into her voice. "I've been on my own with my daughter for four years, Aaron. I can manage."

A flare of sexual interest sparked in his eyes. "You don't have to do everything alone," he said softly.

Sonya bit down on her lip. She wished she could reciprocate Aaron's attentions, but anything more than friendship was impossible. She wasn't ready for a personal entanglement with anyone.

Not Aaron or the mysterious falconer who'd saved her life. The one who'd heated her blood with his dark, brooding eyes and his gruff exterior.

She simply wanted to be at home where she and Katie could be together, safe, hidden away from the monsters in the woods.

And the ones who looked like men—the ones who could hurt her just the same.

A MURKY GRAY SKY hung heavy with clouds as Brack hiked through the dense woods. Winter echoed in the shrill sound of the wind whistling through the mountain of trees. Animals skittered and scurried, scrounging for food. A vulture soared above, obviously zeroing in on the carcass of a dead animal for his next meal.

Brack veered to the right, tracking its movements.

Normally, the forest offered him solace, a place to purge his physical energy and frustration with a run or hike. A place to find inner peace, the strength he needed to sustain his goals, to serve his only friends, the birds of prey, and live as God had intended him to—alone and free in the wild.

But turmoil tightened his every movement today, his senses honed for dissension in the animal kingdom.

Had something in the environment poisoned the animals? Maybe the smaller ones that the falcons preyed on? Were some of the birds sick, diseased, carrying an affliction that caused them to attack at random? Or was a human among them, ripping at their flesh and using them as an excuse for his vicious attacks?

The idea of mutants—half animal, half human— was another possibility he couldn't ignore, although the idea seemed far-fetched. But the ghost legends and tales of the miners trapped below the city were infamous. And random deaths over the years created suspicions, and had never been explained. Like the death in the woods behind the old farm- house Sonya had bought.

He hiked a few more feet, then paused near Vulture's Point. His stomach churned when he spotted two juvenile hawks slaughtered near the west end of the ridge. The vulture had honed in on them for dinner.

He'd have to find food from another source tonight. Brack stooped, yanked on gloves, then gathered their remains into boxes he had brought with him in his pack.

He'd send them to the vet for analysis. The blizzard dwindled into a light snow as he trekked back toward Falcon Ridge, but the roaring wind continued to shake the trees and howl incessantly, biting at his cheeks.

A half hour later, he packed the boxes in the trunk of his SUV and drove down the mountain to the vet. Dr. Phil Priestly, the town veterinarian, studied the animals with dismay. The vet was in his midforties, intelligent and had done an internship at Cornell University at its Veterinary School of Medicine. He had also been attacked by violent wild dogs once and had a special interest in animal behavior. His assistant, a young guy named Elmsworth, watched him from the lab.

"I'll look them over, take some samples and blood, and see what we can find." He frowned and pulled at his chin. "You say the woman had talon marks on her back?"

"Yes. Thankfully her heavy coat offered some protection, but the attack was pretty vicious. My brother is calling a wildlife biologist and the EPA to help us look into this matter. If the water or vegetation is contaminated, it could affect other creatures in the forest."

And eventually might trickle into the town's water source and affect humans. A danger Brack didn't want to face.

The vet nodded. "I'll run full tox screens and let you know what I find."

"Good. We need to solve this mystery ourselves before Cohen stirs up so much panic, the town goes on a wild bird hunt and destroys the wildlife."

He thanked Priestly, then climbed into his SUV and cranked the engine. He wondered what the doctors had determined about Sonya, if they'd discovered anything on the blood or hair fibers on her skin.

He punched in the hospital's number. It took a minute but the receptionist finally patched him through to Sonya's doctor.

"It's Brack Falcon, Doctor Waverman. I'm calling to check on Sonya Silverstein."

"She's fine. I'm preparing the paperwork for her release now." He paused. "Although I wish she'd stay the night. She's weak and needs rest, but she insists she wants to go home and be with her daughter."

The mother bear protecting her cub.

"What did you find on those tests? Anything unusual?"

"I can't discuss her medical records with you, Mr. Falcon."

"I'm not asking about personal information. But if I'm going to find out what attacked her, I need to know if you discovered anything unusual. I'll check with the CSI lab if I need to."

Waverman muttered something beneath his

breath. "There was something odd," Waverman admitted in a low voice. "I haven't told Sonya yet, but mixed with her blood, I found traces of another human's blood. What's even weirder, there were also traces of animal blood on her skin."

Brack's blood ran cold. "The blood of a bird?"

"That I don't know yet. We'll have to wait on more tests to verify the source."

Damn, Cohen would have a fit.

An image of Sonya wounded and bleeding, lying in that snow the night before, flashed back, and Brack pressed the accelerator.

If Sonya's attacker was part animal and part man, then they were dealing with a mutant creature of some sort.

But if it was human, the sicko might be afraid she would recognize him. Which meant that he might come after her again.

And she might still be in danger.

Chapter Six

The hint of danger tapped at Sonya's nerves as the minutes ticked by. Alarm niggled at her at the thought of returning to her house. Even before the attack, the house had begun to creak and groan, the eerie sounds sending pinpoints of fear through her each night. In the darkness, she thought she'd heard a ghost whispering in the eaves of the wooden boards, and she imagined the dead that had gone before her walking underground and sending tremors through the earth that shook the walls and made the pictures on her nightstand rattle.

She shivered, and slipped off the hospital gown, wondering if she was going crazy. All this talk of ghosts in Tin City, and now of a mutant birdman... Heaven help her. She had to have imagined the ghost sounds. And Katie had to have imagined the monster.

If her husband had any inclination to sue for custody and he caught wind that she suspected her house might be haunted, he'd have a good case to take her daughter from her.

But Stan wouldn't do such a thing. He didn't want her or Katie.

She swallowed back the hurt, then winced at the soreness in her limbs as she pulled on the sweats the nurse had brought her. Thankfully, the ER kept a stash of extra clothes in case of emergencies. At least the shapeless clothes were loose, warm and nonabrasive against her bandaged arms and back.

A knock sounded at the door just as she pulled on socks. "Come in."

The door squeaked open, and Dr. Waverman poked his head in. Behind him, Brack Falcon appeared. Surprise made her chest flutter. He'd pulled his hair back into a ponytail with a leather thong, and his bronzed cheeks looked chafed from the wind. Beneath the hospital lights, the dark beard stubble grazing his jaw stood out, making him look impossibly formidable and rough, as if he might have been out fighting wild animals in the wilderness.

She didn't like the heat that shot through her. Much preferred the numbness of a man who didn't make her feel anything, such as Aaron Waverman.

What was the mysterious falconer doing here?

"I have the paperwork ready," Aaron said. "But I wish you'd reconsider your decision to go home, Sonya."

"I told you I'm fine," she said simply. "I'll rest better in my own bed." At least she hoped she would.

He gave her a skeptical look but thankfully didn't argue. "I'll drop by and change your bandage tomorrow."

"No, thanks, Aaron." The idea of him in her house, physically touching her, triggered a stab of panic to her chest. "Margaret can do it for me, or I'll have Reesie come by." Reesie was one of her coworkers.

Aaron shifted restlessly, and Sonya saw Brack studying her. Anger radiated from his brooding face and well-honed, muscular body. But a raw hunger flickered in the depths of his bottomless eyes, a primal look that twisted her stomach.

He obviously didn't like the connection between them, this sexual chemistry that seemed to throb in the air. She could feel it in every second that passed, every time their eyes met. He had to also.

Or maybe she'd imagined it, just as she'd imagined the ghosts.

Maybe he just didn't like her. He probably saw her as weak, needy, imperfect. Like Stan had.

"I came by to see what the doctors found from the tests they ran," Brack said as if he needed to explain his visit.

So much for his concern or personal interest.

Not that she wanted a personal relationship—she didn't. And she certainly didn't want to pursue this chemistry herself…not with someone as dangerous as him.

She swiped a hand over her sweating forehead. The drugs must be making her delusional.

"What did you find?" Sonya asked.

Aaron cleared his throat. "There were traces of your blood, of course, and another human's blood, as well as human hair samples. But we also discovered blood from an animal." He shot Brack a suspicious look. "Bird feathers were also caught in the blood."

Sonya clenched her fingers together and leaned against the bed frame. "I don't understand."

"Neither do I, " Aaron admitted. "I've never seen anything quite like it."

"Then Katie might be right." Sonya slid down onto the bed. "It was some kind of mutant creature that attacked me?"

Brack moved closer to her as if to offer comfort, although he didn't touch her. "There's another possibility. Some psycho is doing this and wants us to think he's a mutant, so he smears an animal's blood and feathers on his victims."

Nausea rose to Sonya's throat. "What kind of person would do that?"

"A very disturbed one," Brack said in a clipped tone. "But don't worry. My brothers and I are investigating. We'll find him."

Aaron placed a hand on Sonya's arm and patted

her gently. "If he's right, you might still be in danger, Sonya. Let me take you back to my place for the night. I have a guest room where you'll be comfortable."

"No, I want to be with Katie."

"She can come, too," Aaron offered.

Irrational fear snaked through her at the idea of staying with him, in his house, with or without her daughter. "Thanks, Aaron. But there's no reason to think this psycho would attack me again."

"You escaped. Maybe he thinks you can recognize him," Aaron pointed out.

Brack's jaw went rigid with anger, and Sonya glared at Aaron. Was he intentionally trying to frighten her? "I told you, I'll be fine, Aaron. But thanks for your concern."

"I have to drive past your place on the way to Falcon Ridge. I'll give you a lift home," Brack offered. He angled his head toward Aaron. "Don't worry, Doctor. I'll make sure she and her daughter are safe, even if I have to stay there with them myself."

Sonya's breath hitched at his bold declaration.

"And who's going to protect her from you, Mr. Falcon?" Aaron hissed.

Brack balled his hands into fists by his side as if he might assault the doctor, but a second later a cold mask slid over his expression.

Sonya clenched her hands together and moved toward the door. She wanted to assure Aaron that she wasn't afraid of Brack, at least not physically. But she didn't like either man ordering her around, acting as if she didn't have a choice in the matter.

Besides, she was terrified of Brack. Terrified that he would hurt her emotionally.

He can't. Not unless you let him get close.

There, she had her answer.

She knew how to protect herself. She'd guard her heart. Because Brack couldn't hurt her unless she let him.

SONYA WAS afraid of him.

The realization felt like a hammer against Brack's skull. How many times did it take for him to realize that no woman was going to want him? Not the man he was.

And why did her distrust disturb him?

He hardened himself. He couldn't allow it to affect him.

Slapping his control back in place, he turned abruptly toward the door. But he would protect her and find her attacker in spite of how she felt about him.

After all, tracking animals was his specialty. And if he didn't find the psycho who'd attacked Sonya, Cohen would continue to blame the falcons and might put them in danger.

While the nurse wheeled Sonya to the hospital entrance, he retrieved his SUV and cranked up the heater. She was shaking when she climbed in, from fear or the cold he wasn't certain, so he removed his coat and tugged it around her shoulders.

Her gaze flew to his, and the car seemed to shrink in size. The air grew hot, sultry, the scent of her female essence permeating the air. And then her fear rattled between them. She wet her lips, making him itch to kiss her and assure her that he was her friend, not her enemy.

He let the moment pass, though, knowing he couldn't start something he didn't intend to finish. He wouldn't waste time trying to convince another woman that he wasn't a monster himself just because he preferred the company of falcons to humans.

Besides, Sonya came with a ready-made family. And a husband somewhere who one day might want to reconcile.

She sucked in a sharp breath as she fastened the seat belt, and he realized she had probably hidden her pain from the doctor in order to convince him to release her.

He pulled away, then eased onto the ice-crusted road and maneuvered the curvy road up the mountain. Tension hummed between them, as if the air between them was charged with electricity. In the confines of the car, he became hyperaware of her every breath. Of his own heart beating overtime. Of the spark of heat between them. Of her delicate fingers wrapped around the edge of his coat.

A sexual kind of longing surged inside him, more intense than anything he'd felt in years.

One he had to deny.

Finally, he steered the Land Rover down the long dirt drive to the farmhouse. The SUV bounced over the ruts in the road, snapping ice beneath the tires as he downshifted into low gear. Snow continued to fall, ice crystals caking on the windshield, and the wind crackled through the windowpanes like a ghost announcing its presence.

"I'll call Margaret about bringing Katie home when we get inside," Sonya said, breaking the silence.

"I have four-wheel drive. If you need me to pick her up, I will. I can stop by the house and retrieve her kitten first if you want."

She stiffened but shook her head, and he frowned. If she was afraid of him, she probably wouldn't trust him alone with her daughter.

Not that he could blame her. But the thought hammered at his heart.

"Thank you, Brack, but I'll have Margaret's husband drive her home later."

His gaze latched on to hers, and his pulse accelerated. God, he wanted to wipe the fear off her face. And he had a fierce desire to kiss her.

For a second, he sensed she wanted it, too. Then fear darkened her eyes, and he reached for the door. He climbed out, his back rigid, his determination setting in. He didn't have to prove himself to anybody.

They walked up to the porch in silence. But as

she ascended the last step, Sonya gasped, then halted beside him. "Oh, my God."

He glanced at the front door and fury knotted inside him.

There in the porch light, two dead hawks lay mauled on her doorstep, their necks slashed, heads severed, barely hanging on by a tendon. Whoever or whatever had killed them had smeared blood on the door and wall.

Its sickly, metallic odor filled the air with a death-like warning.

AARON WAVERMAN studied the newspaper article on Sonya's attack, his gut churning. The papers portrayed the brutal incident as a supernatural occurrence. An assault by wild, rabid birds, diseased animals or some new mutated strain that liked to feed on humans.

Just as Cohen suspected.

But Sheriff Cohen was an idiot.

Aaron had known it the first time he'd met the man.

Just as he'd known when the Falcon men returned to town there would be trouble.

They had disrupted the town's security with their arrival. First the revival of the Hatchet Murders case. Now that teen center, which would only draw derelicts and troublemakers to the town. That, and more crime. And now these damn bird attacks.

He hadn't agreed with Cohen over the years on

anything, but he agreed that the town didn't need men rescuing wild animals that would turn on humans and feed on them. And Brack Falcon was doing that, he was sure of it.

Just as he planned his subtle attack on Sonya.

First, he was gaining her trust. And now he was acting like some damn hero. But Brack Falcon was a predator of the worst kind. He had no intention of marrying Sonya and settling down into family life.

Aaron recognized the lust in the man's eyes, because the same strong feelings overcame him when Sonya was around. But lust had nothing to do with commitment.

Falcon simply wanted to take from her. Take her body and make it his. Then he'd leave her, her emotions in turmoil, her life in shreds. Because Falcon wasn't a commitment kind of man.

Commitment Aaron knew all too well.

He had suffered in his young life. And he had learned how to commit himself when he wanted something.

Just as he had with medical school, he'd set his goals and nothing—not fear, his lack of finances, his own abusive family or competitors—had stood in his way of obtaining them.

Just like he wouldn't let anything or anybody interfere with his plans or dreams.

He would have Sonya as his.

Even if there had to be casualties in the process.

Chapter Seven

Sonya stared in horror at the blood smeared on her door and the massacred animal at her feet. Who would do such a sadistic thing? And why?

The sound of a coyote howling in the distance bled through her consciousness. The wind swirled snow and dead leaves around her, and the shutter on the window flapped back and forth, resounding through the tension.

A shiver started deep inside her, resonating with fear and trepidation. She thought the attack had been random. That she had simply been in the wrong place at the wrong time.

But someone or some *thing* knew where she lived. And the bloody animal had been left as a message.

He wasn't through with her yet.

"Sonya…" Brack guided her away from the door with his hand braced to her back. "Go wait in the car."

A fog enveloped her, but she shook her head. Even with terror seizing her, anger suddenly surged through her. This farmhouse was her home now, her sanctuary, the place she planned to raise her daughter. How dare this creature invade their home and try to terrorize her?

"I'm okay," she managed to say, although her voice sounded brittle in the blustery wind whipping around them.

"Go to the car now and lock the doors. I'm going to check out the house."

"No, Brack, this is my battle—"

He gripped her arms and forced her to focus on his face. His expression was fierce, his mouth set in a grim line, his dark eyes piercing her with a dozen different emotions. "There's a psycho stalking you, and he might be inside. Now, please, just do as I asked."

Words lay unspoken in the thick tension stretching between them. The whispered promise that she could trust him underscored his gruffness. She almost leaned into him and begged him to hold her and make the nightmare disappear.

He shoved the keys in her hand. "If for some reason there's trouble, take the truck, get out of here, drive to town." Without another word, he released her, bent and retrieved a pistol from a strap inside the leg of his jeans. The sight of the weapon jerked her back to reality, reminding her of the violence that had invaded her life.

He didn't offer an explanation for the gun and she didn't ask. He simply flicked his thumb in a gesture indicating for her to do as he'd ordered.

She didn't normally take orders from men.

She didn't like it now, but the memory of her brutal attack was too fresh, and common sense overrode stubborn pride. She had no desire to tangle again with the creature who'd mauled her, not unarmed, anyway. As she rushed to his SUV, she contemplated for the first time since Stan had walked out the fact that she might need to buy a gun for protection.

She punched the locks on the doors and huddled inside, her neck bunched with nerves as she waited on Brack to check the house.

Who was this man who'd rescued her and her daughter last night in the woods when death had knocked at their doors? And why was he here now, acting as her protector again, putting his own life on the line to save her when he barely even knew her?

BRACK HAD TO drag himself away from the desperate look of need in Sonya's eyes and remind himself that he was here to protect her. Not to get involved with her.

Self-loathing kicked in for wanting her. He couldn't take advantage of a frightened, traumatized woman. Besides, he preferred the woods, the animals, to people. He liked to live on the edge, be free to go wherever a case took him.

And he had killed before. He would do so again if it meant saving an innocent life.

Whoever had hurt Sonya and had left this bloody warning had viciously slaughtered these animals in the name of his twisted killing game. It had to stop.

He slowly pushed open the door to Sonya's house. She'd obviously left it unlocked last night and the lights on when she'd ventured into the woods in search of Katie. No telling what he would find inside.

He held his breath as his gaze tracked the interior of the front room. A small den held a fireplace, a comfortable-looking denim sofa and an oversize chair. Throw pillows were scattered around, toys overflowed a wooden box, a coloring book and crayons lay on the pine coffee table. The house looked lived-in, but nothing seemed out of place.

Then he noticed the blood smeared on the walls.

Dammit.

Raw anger shot through him, primal and hot. What kind of sick bastard had done this?

He braced his gun in his hands, then skimmed the rest of the interior. No one was inside. At least no one visible. But he could be hiding, waiting for Sonya to return so he could strike.

Had the sadistic killer come to the house last night after the attack and painted her house with blood?

Brack inched silently through the den, his gaze

scanning the tiny bathroom and adjoining kitchen. More blood colored the linoleum and the walls.

One room lay to the right of the den, another to the left. The bedrooms. He veered left first, his gaze drawn to the tiny child-size white bed.

The room looked homey but not vandalized. Thankfully, no blood in there.

Did the killer have a heart after all? Some humanity left?

Relief hissed through him as he imagined Sonya's reaction if the monster had desecrated her daughter's room with his violence.

The wind whistled through the eaves, and the floor squeaked. He paused, recalling the stories of the ghosts haunting the land. His senses were honed sharp.

His throat tight, he inched back through the den to the opposite bedroom. There, an antique iron bed held a handmade quilt in blues and whites, and a wardrobe door hung open, revealing a satin robe and several pieces of silky lingerie.

His gut pinched, and he forced himself not to touch the lingerie. Then he spotted blood dotting the wood floor, and cursed. A bloody talon print marred the wall above Sonya's bed. He moved on into the room, scanned the corners, then the closet, and finally the bathroom. His chest expanded with air when he realized it was empty.

But he cursed again at the sight of the blood-streaked mirror. The intruder had been here, too. Crimson talon prints dotted Sonya's night cream jar and perfume as if he'd cradled them in his hands.

Or filthy paws.

The psycho had definitely wanted Sonya to see his handiwork, his signature. Like an animal marking his territory, this madman had marked Sonya as his.

The only question—when would he return to claim his quarry?

SONYA MASSAGED her neck where the tension knotted her shoulders. What was taking Brack so long? Had he found something or someone inside? Was he okay?

If there's trouble, take the truck, get out of here, go to town.

Could she desert him if the psycho who'd killed those birds was inside?

No. She was just about to open the door when he stalked outside. His jaw was rigid, his expression dark. Anger radiated from him in waves as he paused on the porch and stared at her.

Instead of immediately descending the stairs, though, he pivoted and scanned the area surrounding the house. The trees swayed with the violent wind, and fresh snow rained from the boughed branches. The sky rolled with more storm clouds, and she thought she detected movement at the edge of the woods. An animal or a person?

Her breath caught as she realized that the psycho might have been watching them when they'd found the bloody animals.

Brack climbed down the steps and walked toward the SUV, his expression grave. "He's not inside," he said as he opened the truck door. "But he's been there."

Sonya clutched her stomach, the realization that her home had been invaded triggering another streak of terror. She envisioned dead animals and blood strewn throughout the house and felt sick. In Katie's room…no, please, no. "What did he do?" she whispered.

Brack made a hissing sound. "He streaked blood on the floor and walls."

"Did he leave more dead animals inside?"

"Thankfully, no." He reached for his cell phone and punched in a number. His gaze latched on to hers. "It's gruesome, though. You don't want to see your home this way."

He cleared his throat, then spoke into the phone. "Sheriff Cohen, this is Brack Falcon. Sonya Silverstein had an intruder. Send a crime scene unit out here ASAP."

Sonya shivered, a knot of cold dread chilling her to the bone. Her house, the place she'd bought to offer her and Katie a sanctuary, was now a crime scene, not a home. Maybe she'd made a mistake in moving to Tin City. Maybe the mountains that she'd thought looked so peaceful and beautiful held too many dangers. Maybe the land really was haunted and the house should have been burned, as someone in town had suggested.

She'd told the real estate agent that she didn't believe in ghosts or evil tainting a place. Not until now....

"I...need to call Margaret and let her know what's going on."

Brack nodded and handed her his phone. "You should let Katie stay there. It will take hours to process the scene, then more to clean it all up."

Sonya frowned. She hated feeling helpless. Hated knowing this psycho had run her out of her home.

He reached in the back of his truck and grabbed a large metal box. "My brothers and I are private investigators. I'm going to take some pictures. Then when the crime unit finishes, I want my people to take samples."

The thought of him searching through her house, touching her things, invading her space, triggered more unease. But she wanted this guy caught.

And having Brack close by made her feel safer.

Don't get used to it, a voice whispered in her head. *He's only here because of the attack. When he leaves, you'll have to stand on your own.*

Margaret answered on the third ring. Sonya explained about the vandalism, and Margaret insisted that Katie spend the night. Her granddaughter was visiting, and the girls had built a fort to sleep in.

Sonya breathed a sigh of relief to hear her daughter's excited voice. More than anything, she wanted Katie to have playmates, friends, a normal life.

And she desperately wanted to spare her this horrible violence. Sonya told her goodbye and disconnected the call, then stepped onto the porch beside Brack. Nerves pinged inside her as she glanced inside the open doorway. All that blood...

Brack placed a hand on her back. "We can't go back in until the crime unit processes the scene."

She looked into his face, shocked at the intense anger in the depths of his eyes. The horror of this psycho's violence hit her, and she convulsed, trembling all over.

Suddenly Brack pulled her into his arms. She didn't argue, she simply fell against him, drained and shaking uncontrollably. He soothed her with his deep voice, stroked her back with a featherlight touch as if he remembered that she must be in pain from the attack.

"Who...did this?" she whispered brokenly. "And why?"

"I don't know." He pressed her face into the curve of his arms, and his chest rose and fell with his sharp intake of breath. He felt so strong and warm, so masculine that she breathed in his scent, letting it momentarily banish the scent of blood and death from her mind.

Brack was very much alive. Very much a man. In control. And so comforting and tempting that she buried herself deeper into his embrace.

Then her gaze met his. He pressed his lips together in a straight line. She stared at his mouth, saw the strength in his jaw, and her heart fluttered.

She wanted to kiss him. Let him make the terror go away.

He brushed his fingers along her cheek, tucked a strand of hair behind her ear. Murmured her name. He wanted it, too. All she had to do was tilt her head, close her eyes, relinquish control.

But Stan's bitter words about her being imperfect echoed in her head. She couldn't lose control again.

Control was all she had. The only way to protect herself. The only way she'd survive.

She pulled away, straightened her shoulders. Clamped down on her emotions. She had to rely on herself. No one else.

She couldn't risk getting hurt again.

And this man had the power to do it because he made her feel again. Tempted her to want things that she'd learned long ago were impossible.

FEAR DARKENED Sonya's eyes, replacing the hungry look Brack had detected only moments before. Dammit. One more second and he would have kissed her. Felt her soft lips beneath his. Tasted the hot passion he sensed she tried to squelch.

Hell, he did not need this complication. This attraction.

He silently cursed himself, and his jaw went rigid. Anger replaced desire. For a moment, she'd let him comfort her from the horror of the blood in her house, but then she realized who was holding her, and she'd pulled away and looked at him as if he were the enemy.

He couldn't let himself forget what the town thought of him. They would turn her against him with their gossip. Not that it should matter... dammit.

He didn't care what anyone thought.

He was here for one reason and one reason only—to find out what was attacking the birds, and now Sonya.

Then he'd hightail it back to Arizona and lose himself in the wilderness there.

The sound of an engine cut through the tense silence, and the sheriff's vehicle spit ice and snow as it careened to a stop. Cohen lumbered from his squad car, yanking up his pants with his thumbs. Brack grimaced, bracing himself for the man's brash and idiotic assertions.

A second later, a crime scene unit arrived, climbed out and strode up to the porch.

Cohen took one look at the mess and paled. "Mighty convenient that you found this, Falcon."

"Just do your job and collect some samples for

analysis." He glanced at Sonya, saw the questions in her eyes.

"Get to work, boys," Cohen told the CSI team. He stabbed a stubby finger at Brack. "You aren't going to interfere with my investigation," Cohen bellowed. "For all I know, you're doing this yourself."

"I don't get my kicks terrorizing women or animals," Brack snapped. "And consider my investigation as backup work. You don't know squat about wildlife. Even you have to admit that my brothers and I are the experts here."

His pudgy cheeks turned red. "How will I know if you're hiding something?"

Brack raised himself to his full six-three and glared down at the short, squatty man. "I want the truth as much as you do, if for no other reason than to protect the animals."

"At the risk of the citizens?" Cohen asked with a glare.

Sonya huddled her arms around her waist and stared at both of them as if she didn't like being caught in their ongoing war. And she didn't deserve to, either. His pride be damned.

"Listen, Cohen, for once, let's work together on this one." Brack lowered his voice, struggling to rein in his volatile temper. "The sooner we find this psycho, the sooner the town will be safe again. And if we discover that the birds are carrying a bird flu or some other disease, I'll call in specialists to treat them myself. My brother has phoned the EPA, and they are sending a wildlife biologist here to conduct some tests."

Cohen twisted his mouth sideways but gave a clipped nod. Then without a word, he set to work, collecting samples of blood and feathers left in the wake of the terrorizing culprit.

Sonya watched silently, her eyes darting across each room as they entered it, her emotions plain on her face. She felt violated. Terrorized.

And angry.

He was glad to see the anger surface. That meant she was a fighter. If his instincts proved right, she was going to need that toughness before it was over.

Because this psycho had just gotten started.

HE LICKED the blood from his talons as he watched from the deep shadows of the woods. He wanted Sonya to know he had marked her as his. Wanted to watch her face when she spotted the present he'd left at her door. The fruits of his labor.

The darkness in his soul.

Wanted her to know that he was close by. That he could have her when he wanted.

That he had the power to tear her apart just as he had the birds.

But what was that Falcon man doing with her? Trying to encroach on already spoken-for territory?

Another predator eyeing the same meal as him?

Fury raced through his veins, triggering a surge of animal instincts. Long ago, he'd recognized the beast inside him. He'd only been a kid when his taste for blood, for the hunt, had surfaced. He'd learned it from his father. The sick games he'd liked to play. First his father had taught him how to track a squirrel. A rabbit. A deer.

Then his father had upped the stakes. Invented a new twist on hide-and-seek. Forced him to play the role of the hunted. He'd left him in the woods and forced him to learn to survive off the land. Forced him to be the prey.

But in the end, *he* had turned the game around. He'd set the trap and lured his father into it. Then he had killed the SOB and watched the blood spill from his guts. He'd been mesmerized as the thick, sticky, red life had coated his hands. Had grown hard as the metallic odor had invaded his nostrils.

And he'd known that in a past life, he had not been a man.

But a raptor instead.

Since then, he fed off the hunt. The kill. The tearing of live flesh and skin. And now he had marked his territory. His ultimate prey.

Falcon had to recognize the signs, *his* markings. And he'd better back off, turn tail and find other ground to hunt.

He'd kill him if he didn't.

Chapter Eight

Brack pivoted from the porch and searched the darkness at the edge of the woods. Shadows flickered and danced through the trees, like creatures of the night stalking the ridges. Low clouds hung in the sky threatening more bad weather, and the wind railed through like a freight train at full speed, its wheels grinding and churning around the hills.

From the bowels of the forest, the growl of an animal in heat echoed off the mountains, one stalking its prey. Waiting to pounce.

He smelled the rage. The bloodlust. The need for the hunt.

The same animal who had left the blood for Sonya.

"Sonya, wait here with the sheriff."

She frowned and rubbed her hands up and down her arms. "Where are you going?"

"He's out there."

Sonya jerked around to study the thick rows of

trees flanking the mountainside. "Where is he? Did you see him?"

"No, but I can smell him." He held up a hand, warning her to be quiet. "He's been watching us. He feeds off of fear."

Unease flickered in her eyes, then she caught his arm. "Brack, please...don't go."

His heart clenched at the concern in her expression. Other than his mother, no one had ever worried about him before.

He didn't need it now. He could take care of himself.

And he didn't intend to allow this monster to get near Sonya again.

He squeezed her hand where it lay on his arm, felt the fine tremor of terror in her ice-cold fingers. "I'll be back."

She bit down on her lip, then moved inside the house by the doorway. But the crime scene techs wouldn't allow her any farther. He saw the fury in her eyes. Understood the helplessness. Had felt it when his own father had been falsely arrested.

This monster had caused her to be temporarily banned from her own house. She wouldn't be totally safe until he was caught.

He felt her watching him as he strode into the woods with a flashlight. But he couldn't dwell on her feelings. He had to focus on sniffing out the killer. He moved on padded feet, searching for disturbed brush, tracks in the snow and ice, broken limbs that might have been severed as the culprit had made his escape. Ahead, he sensed movement. The flutter of wings slicing through the bitter wind, the racing of the animal's heart as he picked up his pace, the scent of fear and excitement in the chase.

He paused, his gaze scanning the woods. The skin on his neck prickled. The killer was watching him. Engaging him in a sick, twisted game. Leading him on.

He had to play it smart.

Because this guy was setting a trap.

THE NEXT HOUR passed in agonizing slowness. The crime scene techs and the sheriff worked intently, scouring her house, taking prints and photographs.

Sonya checked the grandfather clock a thousand times.

Why was this happening to her now? She and Katie had just settled into the farmhouse. She'd thought the fresh, clean air and woods would offer a healthy place to walk and hike and strengthen Katie. They would both make friends and be a part of the town. They'd be free of the anonymity of the big city, of the noise, the hectic, demanding lifestyle and the crime. She'd finally felt as if she might recover from her failed marriage.

But then she'd learned the house she'd bought

was sitting on haunted land where a tragedy had occurred, where ghosts and evil spirits lingered.

And now this....

What would Stan say if he knew she was in danger? Would he think she was incompetent?

Would he want Katie to stay with him? Probably not. He'd barely been able to hold her when she was a baby. And when he'd seen her struggling with braces on her legs, then crutches, he hadn't been able to handle it.

Besides, he already had a new girlfriend, someone younger, prettier. A perfect woman.

She shut out the sound of his hurtful words echoing in her ears, and stared out the window, searching the dark for Brack or the creature, but a light snowfall and the thick aspens and firs along with the nighttime made seeing anything impossible. Ironically, the beauty of the mountainside struck her, the peaceful quiet that had drawn her here.

But Brack Falcon lived on the ridge above her. He posed a different kind of danger. Destroyed her equilibrium simply with one look.

Feeling antsy, she turned to face the front foyer, but the ugliness seeped back as she spotted the drying blood on the floor and walls. The vile creature who'd smeared the animal's insides had to be the same monster who'd assaulted her the night before.

What if he attacked Brack and hurt him? What if Brack didn't return at all?

How could she live with that on her conscience?

Sheriff Cohen cleared his throat, pushing himself up from his squatting position with his hands on his knees. His bones cracked and popped, his breath wheezed out. He was a heart attack waiting to happen.

"I've collected samples of the blood in each room and fibers that resemble bird feathers. I'll send them off for analysis." The crime team approached, told Cohen they had what they needed, then left.

The sheriff glanced around at the mess in her den with a scowl. The scent of blood and death permeated the room. How would she ever rid her walls of the vile odors?

Even if she did manage to erase it from the walls and floor, the image would be forever imprinted in her mind.

"My gut told me a bird attacked you, but ain't no bird doing this," Sheriff Cohen said. "I hate to say it, but Falcon may be right. This might be the work of a crazy man."

Sonya nodded. The attack the night before and the emotional strain had completely exhausted her.

But the place had to be cleaned, and she couldn't lie down and sleep in her bed with the remnants of this violence surrounding her.

Suddenly a loud screeching sound erupted in the darkness. The same inhuman attack sound that had caused her skin to crawl the night before. The same sound she'd heard right before the creature had mauled her. She ran to the window and searched the forest beyond.

Was Brack all right, or had the psycho attacked him?

SHADOWS HOVERED and floated above the spindly treetops. The screeching attack call resounded through the mountains like a warrior's call from another time.

Squirrels and rabbits scurried to find safety. A deer galloped through the thicket, a wild dog howled and somewhere in the distance a bear bellowed a warning of its own. The earth trembled, leaves raining down onto the icy ground.

Above him, several falcons lifted in flight, their wingspans fluid yet beating a rapid path as they fled. What in the hell was disturbing the forest like this?

He searched the limbs and brush for the source of the sound. Tension vibrated in the air as if the wildlife had telegraphed a warning that a terror had been unleashed among them. United, they teamed together to defend their homes and lives.

Another screeching cry raised the hair on the nape of Brack's neck. He removed his gun and spun around, expecting to see the winged creature pouncing toward him, but a tree limb cracked and splintered, shooting down to the ground. He jumped aside before it slammed into his head, then turned around. Leaves and bushes fluttered as if the culprit had slithered through the brush.

He lunged forward, shoving through the growth and tangled vines, certain he was on the culprit's tail. But his foot caught in a hole, and he stumbled onto a carpet of branches. A trap.

He cursed himself for falling for it.

Before he could stand, razor-sharp, knifelike talons dug into the back of his head. He reached for his gun and tried to roll sideways, using one hand to fend off the attack, but the blades ripped into his hair and skin. The scent of blood filled his nostrils. His own.

But fury spiked his adrenaline, and he lurched to his hands and knees. The impact threw his attacker off. But the world spun three hundred and sixty degrees, and his vision blurred. He blinked to focus and grappled for something to hold on to as he forced himself upright. By the time the world stopped spinning and he had wiped the blood from his eyes, his attacker had disappeared into the woods.

He staggered forward, searching the darkness, but the world had turned gray. Another screech, this time one of glory, echoed off the mountain nearby. Then the forest grew quiet again, as if the storm had ended.

His heart pounded, though, as he realized the creature had won this time.

He jerked a handkerchief from his coat pocket and pressed it to his head to help stop the bleeding, then raced through the woods, hunting again. The next half hour, Brack felt as if he were chasing his tail. He detected the flutter of movement in one direction and followed it, only to hear the screeching sound behind him from the opposite direction. His head throbbed, and he was growing dizzy again. So woozy he had to lean against a tree to keep from passing out.

He raised his hand to the back of his head. Blood seeped down his neck. The handkerchief was soaked. He wouldn't be any good to Sonya if he passed out, and the damn killer finished him off. Besides, it was nighttime, and he didn't trust Cohen to keep Sonya safe.

He had to admit defeat for now. Head back to the house and check on Sonya. Regroup.

But next time would be different. He would catch this SOB.

In an effort to steady himself, he leaned over with his hands on his knees and dragged in several deep breaths. Cold air filled his lungs, and the wind beat at his face. The chill was good. It might keep him conscious.

Questions assaulted him as he dragged himself back down the trail toward Sonya's house. Something about Sonya's attacker having both animal and human blood....

Was it possible that the killer had been attacked by an animal and carried some kind of strange bird disease that caused his bizarre behavior? Some disease that made him attack like an animal?

SONYA FIDGETED with her hands as she paced the porch. The wind whipped her hair around her face, adding to the chill of fear that settled in her bones. She was going out of her mind with worry. Brack had been gone over an hour. Where was he? Was he hurt? Injured? Did he need her to call a search and rescue team?

For God's sake, she was a paramedic herself. If he needed help, she had to find him.

But venturing into those woods alone with a psycho animal on the loose would be completely foolhardy. And the only time she'd been a fool was when she'd fallen for Stan.

No, one other time—when she'd ignored her mother's advice and married him.

Sheriff Cohen wheezed another breath, obviously anxious to leave. But even he had the decency not to desert her.

She considered getting out the bleach and starting to clean, just to give herself something to do. Cleaning would be a healthy diversion. Maybe if she scrubbed the violence away, it would disappear from her life forever.

But her body protested every movement she made now, and the smell of blood and the dead birds was nauseating. She couldn't face the task alone. Not tonight. And hadn't Brack said he wanted his own team to take samples?

The house moaned as if it were in pain, reminding her of the ghost legends surrounding the house and the people who'd died before on the rugged land behind her property. The night shadows streaking the woods beyond made the ridges look even more ominous, as if anything could be hiding out in the murky depths.

The psycho was out there. She felt his presence, his sick lust, his beady eyes. He was waiting to come back.

Tears pushed at her eyelids, but she fought them. She could not fall apart.

The brush parted, and she froze. Expected to see an animal. Or maybe the crazy person who'd painted her house in blood.

But Brack slowly staggered into the clearing and the light from the house. He was breathtaking in his size and power. Like a panther, he moved with fluid grace. A quiet, dangerous intensity underscored his every movement, yet he had the subtle grace of a beautiful kestrel in flight.

He stumbled slightly, and her pulse raced. Dear God. He had blood on his shirt. He was hurt.

She ran down the steps toward him, her heart beating frantically in her chest. Blood dotted his shirt and streaked his hands and neck. Behind him, the trees shivered with the wind's force, and the clouds grew darker. She choked back fear as her medical training kicked in. She couldn't panic. She had to treat his injuries, offer a steadying hand, call for help if necessary.

She hissed a breath. Back in control.

Now was not the time to be the simpering female. Brack needed her, and she wouldn't let him down. Not after he'd rescued her and Katie.

"Brack?"

Pain etched lines on his face though he tried to mask it. "He escaped, dammit."

She forced a smile although her lips felt glued together. "It's all right. You're hurt," she whispered. "Let's get you inside."

"I'll be fine." Disgust laced his voice as if he hated admitting failure. As if he'd let her down. "Is Cohen finished?"

She nodded. "We've been waiting on you."

His gaze met hers. "Pack an overnight bag."

"Brack—"

Anger flashed in his dark eyes. "Don't argue, Sonya. You can't sleep here tonight. It's too dangerous. I'll arrange for a team to clean your house tomorrow, then have my security guys install dead bolts on your doors and locks on the windows before you return."

She'd be a fool to argue with his logic. Besides, she wouldn't sleep a wink in her house tonight anyway. And she wanted to check his injuries. He might have a concussion and should go to the hospital, but she sensed he was too stubborn to admit he needed help.

He swayed slightly, and she slid her arm around his waist. He draped his arm around her shoulder, conceding slightly, and she cushioned his weight.

Cohen met them on the front steps, his look cautious. "Did you see anything?"

"No. He got away."

Cohen scowled, then turned to Sonya. "You want me to drive you to town to rent a room for the night?"

Sonya bit down on her lip. A hotel room would be the wisest place for her.

But Brack cleared his throat. "I'll take care of her."

Cohen glanced from her to Brack, then back to her again, and she nodded in agreement. "I have medical training. I need to clean up his wounds. And he'll drop me where I want to go."

Cohen shook his head. "I warned you, Ms. Silverstein."

Sonya frowned at him, irritated that he continued to harass Brack when Brack had been nothing but protective and kind. For God's sake, he'd nearly been killed chasing this psycho. She caught Brack's sideways look and heat rippled between them.

He'd said he was taking her back to his place. Was she really going to stay at Falcon Ridge with him?

With Katie away for the night, they would be all alone....

FOR A MINUTE, Brack had been certain Sonya would leave with the sheriff. Play it safe.

Unreasonable relief filled him when she didn't.

Damn. He didn't want to admit his weakness, his failure. Didn't want to admit that the thought of seeing her again, of protecting her, had driven him forward.

Cohen sped away, his distrust leaving a sour taste in Brack's mouth. His father had been right to return to Arizona. Cohen had cheated him out of twenty years of his life.

Brack also had the urge to leave, but he was too stubborn to let the man win again.

And now...the injury was taking its toll. He felt light-headed and mad as hell. He'd lost the SOB, and he had almost passed out on the way back to Sonya's house. But pain had been his friend for so long that he welcomed it. It reminded him that he was a survivor. That he had trained for extended periods of time and had survived in the wilderness under conditions more brutal than this.

That he would suffer if it meant catching this killer.

Sonya's hand pressed against his back sent a

shard of pleasure through him. An unwanted emotion and sense of coming home.

He wanted Sonya at his place as much for his own peace of mind as for her safety.

Not a good predicament for a man like him to find himself in. That meant he was allowing emotions into the game. Beginning to care about her.

Frustration gnawed at him. If he'd only caught the creature that had attacked him, he could have ended this mystery tonight. Then he could walk away from Sonya with a clean conscience and know that she wasn't in danger.

And he would be able to keep his resolve and stay uninvolved.

She took his keys, and he relented and climbed into the passenger side of his SUV. She quickly ran into the house to pack a bag. His head hurt like the dickens as he allowed Sonya to drive them to Falcon Ridge. Either he was hallucinating, or the silhouette of her slight frame looked ethereal in the sliver of moonlight that finally broke through the storm clouds, like some kind of angel of light that had appeared to ward off the angel of death.

He pointed to the turn-off for Falcon Ridge, set in the curve of a thicket of trees, and she maneuvered the SUV up the winding drive as if she'd driven through winding mountain roads all her life. Maybe she had.

His chest swelled with pride as his old homestead came into view. The huge stone structure with its turrets and arches resembled a gothic mansion from medieval times. Maybe an old castle. At least he saw it that way.

But his mother hadn't been comfortable in the cavernous stone walls. He understood her hesitation and knew the house held painful memories for her.

The walls also echoed with fond childhood memories for him. Playing with his brothers. Hiding in the corridors and basement. Inventing ghost stories to explain the haunting sounds echoing off the walls at night.

Climbing to the attic so he could be higher, closer to the sky as he studied the falcons in flight.

Anxiety rippled across Sonya's face. "This is your home?"

He nodded. "The house belonged to my parents, and my grandparents before that." He reached for the door handle, climbed out, then retrieved her overnight bag. She met him in front of the SUV. Relying on drilled-in instincts from security details, he surveyed the property, the outside of the house, scanning each nook and cranny, the stillness of the woods nearby, the dark shadows of the eaves and overhangs as they climbed the massive stone steps. Her sharp hiss of breath shattered the night as they stepped inside, as if she was gathering courage.

His protective instincts kicked in, along with anger.

"I know you're afraid of me," he said in a husky voice. "But I'm not going to hurt you, Sonya. I promise."

Her gaze locked with his, and emotions warred in her eyes. Need. Desire. Fear.

His gut clenched, and the same emotions ran roughshod over him. He wouldn't hurt her.

But she definitely had the power to hurt him....

SONYA WAS tired of being afraid.

Brack's quiet promise tempted her to trust him. But trusting a man completely was impossible.

The massive stone walls and high ceilings of Falcon Ridge seemed ominous as they entered. Woods surrounded the house, the floor and walls streaked with shadows from the towering trees, reminding her of the isolation of the mansion. At first sight, the rooms felt cold. But warm burgundy and green tones filled the den to the right, an oil painting of the mountainside hung above a sleek cherry table in the foyer and thick red velvet carpet inched up the steps.

Above the staircase, photos of falcons lined the paneled walls. All black-and-whites. Eagles, hawks, other raptors she didn't recognize. Some in flight, their beautiful wings spread wide. Others feeding or attacking their prey.

"We rescue and train the birds here," Brack said in a deep voice tinged with pride. "I can show you the garden outside, the cages..."

Fear careened through her. Irrational maybe, but memories of her attack still hovered at the edge of her mind. "No, thanks. Not right now. We need to look at your head wound."

When she glanced up, he was staring at her. His expression was etched in granite, but his eyes held questions. "They don't attack humans, not unless they're threatened," he said.

She shivered. "But you were attacked tonight."

"By a human. At least part human," he said in a husky voice.

Nervous tension rattled between them as he led her into the kitchen by the tall stone fireplace. She wrapped her arms around herself, still cold from standing outside her house while the crime scene team finished.

He frowned. "You're freezing. I'll start a fire."

"Do you have a first aid kit?"

He threw some wood into the massive fireplace and lit it. Seconds later, a fire blazed, the wood crackling as it caught. "Yes, but I'll take a shower and clean up myself."

"Brack, I'm a paramedic. Let me look at your head first. You might need stitches."

"No, no stitches." He remained intense, but he retrieved a first aid kit, then pulled out a kitchen chair, turned it backward and straddled it. Then he leaned forward, offering her access to the back of his head.

His raw masculinity overwhelmed her. His shoulders were so broad they filled the expanse of the chair, and he was so tall that even sitting, his head was at her breast level. She inhaled sharply, told herself she could touch him without responding. She had to think like a professional. She'd treated countless men before and hadn't fallen apart over touching them.

She slid her fingers gently into the long strands of his hair, and his breath hitched. His hair was tangled and clumped together with blood. She dampened a cloth and wiped away as much as possible, separating the strands of his hair with her fingers until she could check his scalp. "The talons punctured the skin, and ripped away the top layer in places," she said softly. "You probably should go to the ER."

"No. Just clean it and it'll be fine."

She'd known he would be stubborn, tough. Would refuse medical help unless it was forced on him. Deciding a butterfly bandage would do, she used the antiseptic and began methodically cleaning the wounds, grateful to see the bleeding had stopped.

"Do you remember being here last night?" he asked.

She frowned. "No…"

"After you were attacked, I brought you and Katie in here. I cleaned your back while we waited on the paramedics."

A frisson of unease skated up her back. Yes…the memory slipped into her consciousness. Fleeting seconds of feeling his hands on her. Gently touching her, wiping away blood. Soothing her with his quiet strength. Feeling safe and warm in his care.

So he had seen the wounds on her back. She would have scars.

Visible ones this time, although Stan had left emotional ones with his cutting words.

She was imperfect on the inside. And now on the outside, as well.

She gently pressed a piece of gauze over his neck and wiped away the dried blood. His breath hitched again, and fire shot through her fingertips. His masculine scent overrode the scent of blood and fear in the air. His quiet strength and powerful size robbed the room of air. The firelight painted a soft, golden glow around his solid form. And as she leaned forward to wipe his forehead, his arm brushed her breast.

"That's good enough." He stood abruptly, ending her medical attention, then faced her, towering over her. Dark emotions glittered in his black eyes. Eyes filled with a raw, primal hunger that sent fire through her belly.

Their gazes locked. She felt trapped, mesmerized. His breathing vibrated in the silence. Hers followed. Then he slid his hands up into her hair, angled her face in his hands as if he were molding her to fit him, lowered his head and claimed her mouth beneath his.

His lips were soft, but demanding, his kiss gentle yet powerful, his hands cradling her like a delicate china doll, yet insistent that she meet his hunger with her own.

She couldn't resist.

Once, she'd watched a movie called *Never Been Kissed*. As Brack took her lips below his, she melted in his arms and realized she had never truly been kissed by a man before, not as if he might starve without her taste. He slid his tongue over her lips, teased them apart, then swirled his tongue inside her mouth.

Desire speared her, and she moaned in response, then lifted her hands and gripped his muscular arms. If he let go, she would fall.

He deepened the kiss and released a guttural groan from deep in his chest.

Sonya whimpered, desperate for more. And terrified that she would disappoint the man.

That second of fear destroyed her confidence, and she stiffened in his arms.

He noticed immediately. Pulled away and stared into her eyes.

"Sonya…"

His voice sounded heady with passion, and her heart fluttered. But old insecurities rose to torture her.

"I can't do this, Brack," she whispered.

He dropped his hands to his side and squared his shoulders. Although heat still radiated from his body, a troubled look flickered in his eyes.

Then he stepped away from her, turned and removed a key from a hook on the wall. "Here. You can sleep in the wing at the top of the stairs. The room on the right." He folded his big hands around the counter edge with a white-knuckled grip. "Lock the room if you'll feel safer."

She stared at his hands, at his chest rising and falling with each rapid breath, at his mouth which had set hers on fire. The question of fear and trust lay between them, waiting to be answered. Tension scorched the air in heat waves.

God, she wanted him. And she almost relented and fell back into his arms.

But Brack was brooding. Mysterious. Strong. Physical.

Controlling.

And she had to maintain control.

So she took the key, ran up the stairs and closed the door. The bedroom seemed massive, the hollow walls echoing with her fears. Heaving for a steadying breath, she locked the door. Not because she thought he might come to her.

But to keep herself from going back to him.

Chapter Nine

Nightmares of giant birds of prey disturbed Sonya's sleep. The winged creatures swooped through her house, snatched Katie, and disappeared into the forest where she never saw her again. She lay awake in the predawn light, her body aching from the gut-wrenching fear.

Another kind of ache seared her as well. An ache to be held by Brack. Comforted by his strength. To feel his lips claiming hers again in a wild dance of passion.

What was she going to do?

She could not rely on Brack or give herself to him in any way and chance losing a part of her soul that had barely healed from Stan's rejection.

No. Focus on the present. Get through one day at a time. Today she had to rid her house of the blood. Add security.

Even then, should she take Katie back to the house?

While she wanted to be stubborn and prove she

could stand on her own, she'd be a fool to disregard the reality of her attack and the violence of the night before.

And what if she failed to protect her daughter?

Terror at the thought sent her climbing from the massive four-poster bed in Brack's guest room. She quickly showered, letting the warm water soothe her sore back, then turned to study the claw marks in the mirror. The skin looked puckered, red and purple and ugly beneath the light, a visible reminder of the danger surrounding her and the only reason Brack had befriended her.

Dismissing her troubled emotions, she dressed in jeans and a thick, warm sweater, then brushed her hair and tiptoed down the stairs. Inside the cavernous kitchen, coffee brewed, and a fire warmed the tiled room. A box next to the fireplace served as a bed for Katie's kitty, Snowball. A cat toy lay beside the kitten, and a bowl of water had been placed within reach. Katie would be relieved to know Brack had taken care of her new pet.

A sliver of sunlight streamed through the French doors, the snowy woods beyond painting a landscape that belonged in a postcard. A garden area with a trellis draped with rose vines filled a large area, the view of the cliffs and valley below stark.

She poured herself a mug of coffee, then walked to the window to look outside. Her stomach fluttered. Set against the primitive wilderness of the mountains behind him, Brack looked so powerful and big, so rough with his dark, unkempt hair and sheepskin jacket, that he took her breath away. He wore thick gloves and held a falcon perched on his forearm. She froze, gripping the cup with steely fingers, waiting for the animal to attack. She could feel its talons ripping at her flesh....

Instead of attacking, though, the hawk lowered his beak against Brack's arm, and Brack gently stroked the wing tip, an expression of intense concentration on his face as he spoke to the bird.

He was so mesmerizing she simply stared at him while she sipped her coffee, drawn to him in a way she didn't understand. Fearing him in a way that finally forced her to admit that she wanted him more than she'd wanted any man since her divorce.

Maybe since her marriage.

Sex with Stan had been less than satisfying. He had focused more on his own needs than hers. When she'd suggested couples counseling, he'd claimed any problems they'd had were her fault.

Finally she'd given up trying to talk to him. And then she'd stopped loving him....

The realization startled her, but she knew now that it was true. And that truth would help her heal.

Brack glanced through the window and saw her, and their gazes locked. Dear heavens, she had never lusted after a man before, but she wanted this man. After four years of being alone, feeling undesirable, his touch the night before had awakened a need in her she'd forgotten even existed.

His dark eyes flickered with the same heat sizzling through her veins. A heat that grew hotter with every look and touch. A touch she wanted so badly she couldn't tear herself away from him.

She sensed Brack would take his pleasure in bed, but she had no qualms that he would satisfy her first. But acting on the heat between them meant she might get hurt.

She itched to go to him, but ordered her feet to remain in place. She couldn't deal with the pain of failure again.

BRACK STARED at Sonya, his body rock-hard from a sleepless night of lying awake wanting her. One touch last night, one taste, had only whetted his appetite.

An appetite he feared would not be abated until he made her his in every way.

He cursed himself. Physically he craved her with a pain that throbbed in his loins. An ache that would have to remain unassauged.

And mentally, emotionally...no. He refused to go there.

He'd been weak with another woman and nearly lost his soul. Hadn't he learned his lesson then?

He tore his gaze from Sonya and spoke quietly to the hawk, grateful his injuries were healing. He wished he could erase Sonya's fear of the birds he loved so much. Wished she could see their beauty the way he did. Then maybe she could understand him. Trust him completely.

No sense wanting the impossible.

He stroked the falcon's wing tip again. Soon he'd turn the bird back to the wild where it belonged.

Just as *he* belonged there.

Time to get on with the day. He eased the falcon into the cage, removed his gloves, then strode back inside, forcing a blank expression on his face as he scrubbed his hands.

"I already arranged for the cleanup crew to take care of your house," he said, looking into the fire instead of Sonya's face. "They should be done by lunchtime. And my team is there installing dead bolts, new window locks and a security system."

"Brack, I'm not sure I can afford a security system."

He poured himself another cup of coffee, still avoiding facing her. Would his naked desires show in his eyes? "Don't worry about it."

She touched his arm, and his gaze swung to hers. "Then we'll work out a payment plan."

So independent. She had to stand on her own. He admired that about her. "Security work is my specialty, Sonya. I refuse to let you and Katie back in that house until it's completely safe."

Dissension settled in her eyes. She wanted to argue, but her daughter's safety took priority over pride. He'd known her motherly instincts would override her personal feelings about accepting help from him.

He removed pancake mix and eggs from the refrigerator. "I've been thinking," he said as he cracked the eggs into a bowl. "The gruesome blood and marks in your house, they resemble an animal's, but only a sick, deranged man would violate your house like that. This psycho may be someone you know."

Her startled expression made his gut pinch with guilt. She wouldn't like the rest of his questions, either, but they were a necessary evil in solving the case.

"Sit down and think about it. I want you to make a list of all the men in your life. Anyone you've been involved with the past year or so. An old boyfriend, lover that you broke up with. Someone at work who might have a crush on you. And I'd like contact information for your ex-husband."

Sonya gasped. "Stan wouldn't do this kind of thing."

His jaw tightened. "Does that mean you still love him?"

"No."

Her quick admission sent relief spiraling through him. Why, he didn't know. He shouldn't care about her relationship with her ex. "Maybe he's trying to scare you into running back to him?"

A pained look flashed into her eyes. "Stan isn't a violent man," Sonya said. "If anything, he's the opposite. He left emergency medicine because he didn't like the trauma cases."

Wimp. Had the man deserted his daughter because of her handicap?

Still, he didn't sound like he fit the profile of the killer. And a psycho stalker was the only culprit that made sense. Not a bird or mutant creature.

Birds wouldn't smear blood on the walls of Sonya's house and floor. That act had been done by a human, one who intentionally wanted to terrify her.

He handed her a piece of paper and pen, then turned to the stove and poured the pancake batter onto the griddle. "Write down any men you've been in contact with," he said in a low voice.

"Brack, I can't accuse the people I work with of trying to hurt me—"

"Just make the list, Sonya. I'll be discreet questioning them, I promise."

She gripped the pen and frowned, and his pulse pounded. Did she have a lover or boyfriend that she didn't want to tell him about?

SONYA NIBBLED on the hotcakes and sausages Brack had prepared, but her appetite had vanished. The thought of making a list of her friends and coworkers as suspects in her attack made her stomach churn.

Not that she had that many friends in town. She and Katie had only been in Tin City about four weeks.

And as far as lovers or boyfriends...there was no one. There hadn't been since her marriage ended.

"Can I see the list?" Brack asked.

She pushed the pad toward him warily. "I really don't think anyone I know would hurt me. And I haven't been in town long, Brack."

While Brack studied the names, Sonya mentally reviewed them herself. Stan Silverstein, her ex-husband. Brack's suggestion that he might try to scare her into running back to him was ridiculous.... He didn't want her back.

Aaron Waverman, the doctor who'd treated her—he had hinted at wanting a relationship and she'd blown him off. Would he be angry enough over her rejection to hurt her?

No...she didn't believe Aaron was dangerous. He was a healer, for God's sake.

Katie's pediatrician, Dr. Salinger—he was in his mid-fifties, happily married with grandchildren.

Van and Joey—the paramedics she partnered with. But neither one of them had expressed a personal interest in her or exhibited violent tendencies. And Joey had even had trouble passing the EMT class because in the beginning he had fainted at the sight of blood.

Dr. Phil Priestly, the vet she used, and his assistant, Jerry Elmsworth. Dr. Priestly had a distinct, intense manner but he'd never shown interest in her. And Jerry...he'd barely paid her any attention. He seemed slightly slow and had a nervous tic. She'd sympathized with him and felt connected because she realized he probably dealt with rude stares just as Katie did.

"I still don't want you talking to Stan," Sonya said.

Brack arched a dark eyebrow. "Why are you protecting him, Sonya?"

"I'm not. I…don't want to give him reason to think I can't take care of Katie."

His mouth hardened. "So you're worried he might sue for custody?"

"No, not really." He didn't even want visitation rights. "I just don't want him involved in our lives." *And thinking that I'm a failure as a mother.*

He placed his hand over hers, and heat shot through her. "I'm sorry he hurt you. He sounds like a real stand-up guy."

She pulled away, thumbed her fingers through her hair and sighed. "It doesn't matter anymore. But he's a dead end as far as these bizarre attacks go."

He studied the names again. "This list is short. Everyone on it is associated with you through work or Katie. How about old boyfriends?" He looked into her eyes, his expression a blank mask. "Who have you been involved with since your divorce?"

Embarrassment tinged her cheeks, but she didn't owe anyone an explanation for her choices. She liked being alone.

Or at least she had until Brack had touched her. "No one," she said matter-of-factly.

He sipped his coffee. "Really? You can't tell me there's been no interest."

She bit back a sardonic comment. She could confess that she hadn't been interested in anyone, that she'd been dead inside since Stan left her. Even before.

But her reaction to him the night before negated that argument.

"I've been focused on moving, getting settled in Tin City, Katie. She's all I need in my life now."

He lifted his brows in question, but she refused to reply. Need and want were two different issues. Besides, a temporary need could go unsatisfied.

"All right. How about someone else at the hospital or in town? Anyone pursue you who you turned down?"

Sonya massaged her temple where a headache pulsed behind her eyes.

"Sonya?"

"Aaron Waverman," she said quietly. "He…asked me to dinner a few times but I declined." She stretched her fingers in front of her on the table, stared at the nails she'd broken trying to claw her way to safety during the attack, then to the scratch marks on her hands. "But, good heavens, Brack, Aaron is a doctor, not some psycho killer who turns into a giant bird at night to prey on his victims."

Brack shrugged but didn't comment. "How about Doctor Priestly? How do you know him?"

"The vet?" Sonya smiled. "We got Snowball from the clinic, and he adminstered her shots. That's it."

"And his assistant, Elmsworth?"

"He's quiet, seems kind of shy." She hesitated, twisted her fingers together. "Katie didn't care for him, though, but there really wasn't a reason."

The wind howled outside, and the small amount of sunlight that had fought through the clouds earlier disappeared, cloaking the day in a murky gray.

The telephone trilled and Brack answered, a frown deepening the grooves in his forehead. "Yeah. All right, Sheriff. I'll be right there."

Sonya's pulse pounded as he ended the call and turned to her. "What's wrong, Brack?"

"There's been another attack."

"Oh, my God!" Sonya pressed her hand to her stomach. "Who was it?"

"Two teenagers were hiking this morning. They got separated. A few minutes later, one of the girls heard a scream about a mile away. She ran through the woods and found her friend mauled and bleeding in the snow."

The scene played out in Sonya's mind in vivid clarity. "Is the girl all right?"

Brack shook his head, his expression grave as

he placed his coffee cup into the sink. "I'm afraid not, Sonya. The girl is dead."

BRACK HATED the look of anguish on Sonya's face, but he wasn't a man to mince words and lying to her would serve no purpose. Besides, if she was scared, maybe he could convince her to leave town for a few days.

He wanted her safe. Away from the horror of this bizarre killer.

She stood shakily. "We have to talk to the girl who survived. She must be devastated."

He moved in front of her, blocking her exit. "No. I have to go, but you don't. Why don't you pick up Katie and go to Denver for a few days."

"Katie's father is in Denver. I don't want to go back there."

"Then go to a friend's, or a hotel in Boulder." He rubbed his thumb across the palm of her hand. His pulse pounded as he envisioned the dead girl, then saw Sonya in her place.

"Brack…" Her voice cracked. "I'm a trained paramedic. I'm not going to fall apart. I can handle seeing this girl's body."

"This crazy killer just murdered a girl, Sonya, not even twenty-four hours after smearing blood all over your house. I don't want you to end up like her."

She shuddered. "I don't want that, either, but I let

one man run me out of my home, Brack. I don't intend to give another man that kind of control over me."

Her declaration stood between them. A statement, not a question. He admired her courage, even if he didn't want to accept her response.

Besides, he didn't have time to argue. He wanted to see the crime scene before they moved the girl's body. Timing might mean the difference in tracking down this killer. He grabbed his gun, tucked it inside his jacket, then yanked on his coat. "Then let's go."

The ride passed in strained silence, the gray clouds hovering above the mountain peaks casting the world in a dismal gray. He mentally braced himself for the scene ahead and assumed Sonya was doing the same. As he maneuvered the icy roads, he checked the edges of the woods for signs of unrest. He hit a patch of ice, and the SUV started to skid, but he steered into it and maintained control. He'd be damned if he died in a freak car accident when he had a killer to catch.

A few minutes later, he and Sonya trekked through the woods together. She didn't complain about the cold or the hike, simply kept up beside him as if she'd regained her strength for the fight. His admiration for her rose another notch.

Voices echoed from a clearing ahead, Sheriff Cohen's and then that of his new deputy, Johnny

Wilkins. The young deputy was snapping photographs as Brack broke through the trees and spotted the girl.

Damn, she was young and had her entire life ahead of her. A skinny blonde. Her friend, he assumed, sat on a stump nearby crying, her head in her hands.

He paused to study the body, and Sonya stilled beside him, her breath hitching. The victim lay in the snow, her jacket ripped to shreds, her clothes torn and stained in blood. More blood had spilled onto the white snowpacked earth, painting crimson streaks that looked macabre. Her face was pale, her eyes wide with shock, the flesh on her hands torn and bloody. She'd obviously used her hands to shield her face in a desperate attempt to fend off the attack.

Bile rose in Brack's throat at the brutality of the crime.

Sonya staggered slightly, then leaned into him. For a brief moment, he squeezed her hand, then a silent look of understanding passed between them, and he released her to confer with the sheriff. Sonya stooped beside the girl's friend and spoke softly to her. A second later, the teenager collapsed into Sonya's arms sobbing.

"Thank you for phoning, Sheriff." His throat tightened as he spoke the words. "Did the girl's friend see anything?"

Cohen glanced at the surviving teenager and

shook his head. "Claims she was too far away. She heard a loud screeching cry, then her friend screamed. By the time she reached her, it was too late."

Just as it had almost been too late for Sonya the night he'd found her. His throat constricted at the realization that if he hadn't heard that cry, Sonya might have ended up dead, too. Then he would never have known her. Never known that Katie was out there, either, and she might have frozen to death.

Unwanted emotions crowded his chest. Thank God Sonya had fought so hard to survive.

Cohen shot him a sour look. "I don't like you and you know it, Falcon. But if you know who or what is doing this, now's the time to speak up. The town gets wind of these attacks and we're gonna have pure panic on our hands."

"I don't know who killed her," Brack said in a dark tone. "But I'll find out. And when I do, we'll put a stop to it."

He had to, before anyone else died.

THE THRILL of the hunt ignited pinpoints of excitement through his veins.

He licked the blood from the tips of his talons and inhaled the teenage girl's scent. She was so young. Innocent. Ripe.

And she'd tasted so sweet. Almost as sweet as Sonya.

Too bad the other girl had escaped.

He watched from his perch on the ledge above, his eyes piercing the shadows of the woods as that Falcon man and the sheriff studied his handiwork. Sonya was here, too. Cuddling the other girl. Witnessing the sorrow left in his wake.

The power he'd had over the girl's fate.

Her face had turned ashen when she'd first laid eyes on the bloody body, at the realization that it might have been her.

And one day soon it would. Unless she allowed him to become her lover first. Giving herself to him would be her only salvation.

The only way he'd let her live.

Chapter Ten

Sonya cradled the girl against her, and soothed her with nonsensical words. "My name is Sonya Silverstein. I'm a paramedic. Are you all right, sweetie? Are you hurt anywhere?"

"No, I'm okay." The girl gulped and rubbed at her swollen eyes while the wind tossed her tangled hair in her face. "I just…can't believe Debbie's dead."

"I know.…" Sonya situated herself in between the teen and her friend's body so she didn't have to look at her mangled corpse. "What's your name, honey?"

"Beverly…Wallace. We came up here to hike. But then I ran ahead because I thought I saw a peregrine, and we got separated." She gulped. "Oh, God, if we'd only stayed together, m-maybe she'd still be alive."

"It's beautiful country for hiking," Sonya admitted, knowing the comment sounded inane when grotesque violence colored the sight before them. "It's not your fault that your friend was attacked, Beverly. If you had been with her, he might have hurt you, too."

"But...maybe I could have saved her..."

Sonya understood all too well the power of guilt, rational or irrational. She suffered with the cold truth every day that her own body had given Katie the gene for her disorder. If she could have the muscular weakness, the physical limitations, she would lift them from her child and carry the weight herself.

"Shh, you can't blame yourself for some maniac's assault." She removed a tissue from her pocket and handed it to the girl, then paused a moment as she dried her eyes. "Can I call someone for you? Your parents? A friend?"

The girl clutched her arms. "Debbie's parents! They're going to be so upset." Her voice cracked and another round of sobs racked her frame. Sonya's heart squeezed. Debbie's parents would be devastated. No matter how old your child, parents weren't supposed to have to bury their own offspring.

"We'll take care of them," Sonya promised. "How about your mother and father?"

Beverly nodded against her and sniffed. "I already gave the sheriff their number. They're going to be so mad at me."

"Beverly, listen to me, your parents are going to be glad you're alive." Sonya tucked a strand of the girl's hair behind one ear and tipped up her chin. "Now, tell me about the attack. Did you see anything?"

"No…I was too far away. But I heard this awful sound. It was like a wild animal screeching, then Debbie screamed. I ran as fast as I could, but I lost my compass earlier, and I got turned around." She gasped for a breath. "When I finally found her, she was lying in the snow…and there was so much blood."

"She was already unconscious?"

Beverly nodded. "I didn't even get to tell her goodbye."

Sonya's heart broke for the girl. They had to stop this killer before he hurt anyone else.

But what in the world were they dealing with? She'd been attacked herself, and she still wasn't sure if it was an animal or a man.

Brack suspected that her attacker knew her personally. But which one of her acquaintances or friends could be so vile as to kill an innocent young girl?

The wind wailed through the tall trees, scattering dead leaves and snow, and the sound of a bird cawing broke the quiet. Suddenly Sonya felt as if someone was watching her.

Or some *thing*.

Was the person or animal who'd killed the girl nearby? Was he watching them scurry about in fear, trying to figure out his identity while he still carried the fresh scent of blood on his hands?

Sonya scanned the forest nearby, and her skin crawled. The flutter of wings broke through the wind, and she thought something moved on the ledge above them.

He *was* up there. Watching. Enjoying their fear.

And he would kill again.

ONCE AN ANIMAL or human developed the taste of the kill, he rarely turned back.

Brack grunted in frustration, saw Sonya staring at the ridge and turned to scan the horizon. If the predator enjoyed his hunt, had he lingered to guard his kill afterward? Or had he taken his fill and moved on to find more prey?

Dark clouds rolled across the tops of the trees, the shadows of impending bad weather casting a gray as dismal as the death hanging in the air. In the distance he spotted a lone hawk soaring in flight, then diving downward to hone in on its find.

Just as this killer had done.

Dammit. He didn't see anything, but the predator was out there now. Gloating over his success. Watching them react to his sick, twisted work.

Sonya pointed east. "Brack, I think he was up on that ledge."

He pivoted, searching. "I sensed his presence, too. I'll check it out."

She caught his arm. "Be careful."

He offered her a token smile and strode into the

woods, weaving through the dense foliage to climb the ledge. Minutes turned into half an hour as he hiked, looking for signs of the predator. Broken limbs, more injured animals, a dead squirrel, feathers, blood.

But if the killer had been watching, he had already fled.

Frustration knotted his muscles as he hiked back down the path from the ledge and returned to the scene of the crime. The medical examiner had arrived and completed his preliminary analysis, and a crime scene unit from the county was scouring the area for evidence.

Brack snapped several photos and questioned the surviving girl, Beverly Wallace, but she hadn't seen anything helpful.

So far, they had zilch.

Nothing more than what they already knew. The creature sounded like an animal and attacked like one, too, although the visit to Sonya's house indicated he was human, or at least he had the cognitive abilities of a human.

Brack cursed. He used the term loosely. No psycho who viciously ripped at a girl's throat and body until she bled to death was human.

He'd worked as a P.I. for years, had spent weeks and days in the woods, but he'd never encountered anything this bizarre.

He mentally ticked over various possibilities as

he and Sonya drove back to town, creating a profile of the killer in his mind. The killer must be familiar with the woods. He might have grown up here or maybe he lived nearby. He had studied the raptors. And he liked the power of attacking the weaker, maybe enjoyed playing the game. Perhaps he'd grown up hunting as a child.

He had to consider the obvious. Could the killer possibly be another falconer?

Some man so obsessed with studying wildlife, particularly the birds of prey, that he thought he'd turned into one? The thought sent a frisson of unease through him. Even without a psychology degree, Brack understood the birds' behavioral patterns. The mating game. The song and dance. The attack.

The hunger that had to be sated. The survival instincts that drove him to hunt and kill.

Only this killer hunted as much for sport as he did survival.

He needed to check into any hunting club or hunters in town. Jesus. That theory could open a big suspect pool. But if the killer was a hunter, why hadn't he used the typical weapon of choice—a rifle or shotgun? Why talons?

And where did he get them? A costume shop?

Adrenaline hummed through him, and he hoped he was on to something. He'd check the residents for anyone interested in wildlife biology, the environment perhaps, maybe a student from one of the local universities. Tin City didn't have a costume shop, but he'd research that possibility online and in Denver.

Following that logic, he had to consider the vet as a suspect and his assistant, as well. He'd also research bird-watching groups. Maybe the blood analysis would turn up something with the DNA.

He cut his gaze toward Sonya. She sat with her hands knotted, face ashen, seemingly lost in thought. She hadn't spoken a word since they'd gotten in the car.

He placed his hand over hers. "Are you all right?"

She nodded. "I was just thinking about Beverly. She may need counseling to overcome her guilt."

Brack entwined her fingers with his. He was surprised when she didn't pull away, and inordinately relieved that she trusted him. "Deke's wife is opening a teen center with a counselor on board. I'll mention it to her."

She squeezed his fingers. "Thank you, Brack."

The way she murmured his name twisted his insides. Seeing the dead girl had reminded him that life could be taken away in a heartbeat.

He silently vowed to protect Sonya. He couldn't stand the thought of her ending up like the teenage girl.

SONYA CLUNG to Brack's warm, strong hand, desperate to erase the chill of death that invaded her at the sight of the young teenager's mangled body.

Her job had forced her to face the inevitable cycle of life and death before, yet the girl's injuries seemed more horrid and stark because another person had cruelly and intentionally inflicted them.

She didn't want to analyze the reason she hadn't pulled away from Brack when he'd entwined his fingers with hers, but his quiet strength gave her strength, too.

He squeezed her hand and pulled into the parking lot of the country café. She and Katie had eaten here twice, although some of the decor disturbed her. In honor of the town name, Tin City, the new owner served dishes on tin plates, and the tables were topped with thin pieces of tin, which gave it an eclectic look. Punched tin art, as well as news articles about the ghosts that haunted the town, especially the ones chronicling the miners from the 1800s and some of the fallen mines, filled the walls. The owner, Minnie Weaver, confessed that she played up the town's history for the tourists, but that she didn't believe in ghosts herself.

Sonya wasn't so sure. Not after living in the old farmhouse. And the rumors at the hospital—sometimes in the morgue she sensed the tortured spirits of those who'd passed. Odd sounds, moans and groans, echoed from the walls, supposedly from the people who'd died in the typhoid epidemic. Their bodies had been buried underground, somewhere below the hospital's floor.

"Let's grab some lunch, then we'll swing by and retrieve Snowball before we get Katie," Brack said. "I promised her I'd bring her kitten back today."

Sonya's throat convulsed. She had no idea he'd made a promise to Katie, but the fact that he remembered and fully intended to keep it touched her deeply. How many times had Stan promised to come home at night to see Katie before Sonya tucked her into bed and never shown? How many times had Katie cried for him only to go to bed knowing that her father chose work over her?

Sonya had finally realized that her husband worked late to avoid having to see both of them. That he already had another woman in his bed.

The old pain stabbed at her again, reminding her to guard her heart.

As soon as they entered the café, tension rippled through the room. Patrons twisted, turned, whispered. Suspicious looks darted their way.

Brack instantly tensed, and she remembered the rumors about his family. The Falcon men were strange, spooky. They talked to the birds.

Their father had once been imprisoned, thought to have murdered a family called the Lyles in the worst bloodbath the town had ever seen. Last year, his sons had returned to Falcon Ridge to clear him of the crimes. And even though the real murderer had been caught, suspicion and distrust still tainted their name.

Ignorance. People were often afraid of what they didn't understand. Just as they were of Katie.

Because they didn't want to dig deeper and face their own flaws.

"You don't have to sit with me if you don't want," Brack said in a husky voice.

"Don't be ridiculous," Sonya muttered. "You're my friend. I don't care what anyone thinks."

And she didn't. Her indifference toward social status had separated her from Stan. He valued appearances, whereas Sonya committed solely to her own convictions and beliefs and didn't care one iota what anyone else said. She froze, her thoughts crashing in her head.

For the first time since she'd met Brack, a small smile tugged at the corner of his mouth. "You've got guts, Sonya. I like that about you."

A blush stained her cheeks. In spite of his intense, brooding manner, she was beginning to like a lot of things about him, too.

Suddenly she became aware of his breath feathering her neck. Of his scent and big, masculine presence beside her as they slid into a booth. Minnie approached, her eyes darting back and forth between them. "What can I bring you all?"

Sonya ordered the soup and sandwich, and Brack ordered stew and sweet iced tea. The air grew warmer, the room smaller. The scent of warm, homemade pies and Brack's musky odor suffused her. Sonya tried not to stare at his big hands as he accepted the glass of tea and glanced down at the newspaper on the table instead.

Her heart slammed into her ribs—a photo of the woods where she'd been attacked was on the front page. Beneath the headline, Mutant Bird Attacks Local Woman, Katie's crude drawing of the half bird, half man had been highlighted.

Brack muttered a curse. "Where did they get that?"

"I don't know," Sonya said. Good heavens, she didn't want the people in town ridiculing her daughter. And she didn't want her mother finding out she had a grandchild by reading it in the paper.

The hair on the back of Sonya's neck tingled, and suddenly she sensed someone was watching her. As if the creature who'd attacked her was actually nearby. Maybe in the diner.

BRACK'S TEMPER flared at the sight of the article. He wanted to find that damn reporter and tear off his head for mentioning Katie. Sonya's attack, of course, was news, as the girl's death would be today, but the fact that Sonya had survived meant the killer might return for her.

And Katie might get caught in the whole rotten mess. What if the killer tried to get to Sonya through her little girl?

Sweat broke out on his brow. He'd give Sonya a

day maybe, then he'd insist again that she leave town with Katie.

Sonya fidgeted and quickly glanced around the room, her body tensing.

"What's wrong?" Brack asked.

"I…I don't know. I have the oddest feeling that someone is watching me."

"Half the town is watching you because you're with me," Brack said in disgust.

"No, it's not that.…" She bit down on her lip, then rubbed at her neck. "Like *he's* here, watching me, just like I sensed he was in the woods."

Brack hitched a breath and squared his shoulders, mentally noting every male in the room. A teenage boy, but he was cuddled with his girlfriend in a corner booth. Two old geezers playing checkers in the back on a whiskey barrel that served as a table. Minnie's husband, Lewis, but he looked to be in his late sixties, too stricken with arthritis to attack anyone.

The vet, Phil Priestly, sat in the back booth, eating quail and licking his fingers. Brack frowned as the man's expression met his. Then Priestly flicked his thumb up in recognition and shrugged as if he was embarrassed to be caught eating the bird.

Or was that the reason he looked uncomfortable?

Could he possibly be the person who'd attacked Sonya?

Another man at the counter pivoted and stared at him, then stood and walked his way. Brack frowned.

"Mr. Falcon?"

"Yes."

"I'm Emerson Godfrey. You and your brothers work with the falcons in the area?"

Brack clenched the edge of the tabletop. "That's right. You're from the EPA, correct?"

"Yes. I'll need to test any injured birds that you've rescued."

"The local vet is handling that."

"Then we'll consult with him. But we have to determine if the falcons are diseased so we can decide how to handle the situation."

"The birds didn't cause these attacks," Brack stated.

"Maybe. Maybe not. But there were suspicious findings in some of the animal and plant life specimens your brother had analyzed. It's possible we're dealing with some kind of rare bird flu. If so... well, then it could be dangerous for the citizens of Tin City."

And dangerous for his falcons, Brack thought. And what if some of the birds *were* sick? It might explain how the killer was able to catch them and kill them. Perhaps he poisoned the smaller animals, set a trap to catch the birds, then zeroed in on them when they fell ill or weakened. Otherwise, a healthy bird could quickly escape a man's hands.

Dammit. He knew how destructive bird flu could be.

And what it would mean if it wasn't contained.

SONYA SENSED Brack was upset by Mr. Godfrey's appearance. His falcons were like his children, and he'd do anything to protect them, just as she'd do anything to shelter and protect Katie.

After eating, they stopped at Brack's, and he rushed in and retrieved Snowball, then drove her to Margaret's house. Katie hobbled toward her, grinning from ear to ear.

"Mommy!" She vaulted into Sonya's arms, and Sonya held her to her chest, tears pushing at the backs of her eyelids. God, she'd missed her. But seeing Katie so excited was worth a night away from her.

"Mommy, we made s'mores, and swept in the tent, and watched two movies."

Sonya ruffled her daughter's curly hair and laughed. "I'm glad you had fun." Sonya thanked Margaret. "I really appreciate your taking such good care of her."

Margaret smiled. "How are you feeling?"

"Stronger," Sonya admitted. Seeing Katie happy helped.

A few minutes later, Katie snuggled into the backseat of Brack's SUV and hugged the kitten, giggling when it licked her face.

When they arrived, Brack checked the new security system. Thankfully the blood and animal remains had been removed, although Sonya still pictured them in her mind. She thanked Brack and walked him to the door.

He hesitated, and her pulse pounded as she remembered the kiss the night before. How deeply she'd wanted more.

But Katie was here now, a reminder that the two of them were a package deal. A car rumbled up the drive, and Brack pivoted, his shoulders squared, the wind tousling his hair around his face.

The door to the Pathfinder closed, and a tall, thin man wearing wire-rimmed glasses approached, his shoulders hunched against the cold.

"Ms. Silverstein!" the man called.

Brack stepped in front of the stranger, between them. "Who are you, buddy, and what do you want?"

"My name is Darrien Tripp." His wiry hair stood out in different directions, and his beaklike nose wrinkled up. He removed the magazine he had tucked beneath his armpit. "I write for *The Tween Zone*—we feature articles about the occult. I'm chronicling stories of supernatural sightings across the States and want to interview you about the creature who attacked you, Ms. Silverstein."

"Ms. Silverstein has nothing to say," Brack barked.

Tripp bristled. "Why don't you let the lady speak for herself?"

"Mr. Tripp, I already told the sheriff what I saw, which was nothing," Sonya interjected. "So, Mr. Falcon is right. I can't help you."

He pinched his lips together, looking annoyed, then leaned over toward Katie. "How about you, little girl? You drew the picture of the bird-man in the paper, didn't you?"

Katie nodded, her eyes huge as she glared up at Sonya, then back at the man. "It was a big monster," she whispered. "Just like you!"

Sonya stared at her daughter, stunned. Katie had never been rude to an adult in her life.

Katie suddenly darted behind her and clutched Snowball to her chest as if she expected the stranger to swoop down, snatch the kitten and run.

BRACK CONTEMPLATED Darrien Tripp's timing as he let himself in Falcon Ridge. He didn't like the smarmy man and hoped to hell he didn't harass Sonya and Katie again. If he did, Brack's next warning wouldn't be so tame.

He checked on the two birds caged outside, grateful to see both healing, then headed to his office computer and punched in the name of that magazine. *The Tween Zone* was a new publication that featured stories of bizarre occurrences, everything from potential sightings of statues of the Virgin Mary crying to vampires and psychics.

He skimmed the last five issues and noted Tripp had written articles on the occult, on a possible devil possession, a vampire in north Georgia, and a shape-shifter several people had claimed they'd spotted in a small mountain town in Tennessee—a half man, half mountain lion.

The articles consisted of people's accounts, but offered no real proof or evidence that the stories held truth or that they hadn't been manufactured to get attention.

What if Tripp had invented this bird-man himself, then shown up to write about him and garner attention for himself and his magazine?

He accessed the man's personal information. A background check proved he'd had two confrontations with the police—both episodes where he'd reacted with physical force toward people who'd tried to discredit him.

Brack dug deeper and discovered Tripp had grown up in the hills of Tennessee, and that his father had belonged to a hunting club. Tripp had also joined the club at age eighteen.

Then Tripp's father had died a violent death in the woods on one of their hunting trips. He'd supposedly been mauled by a bear.

Hmm. Tripp knew how to hunt. He wrote about bizarre cases. And now he'd arrived in Tin City asking questions, nosing around, wanting to write a feature on Sonya's attack.

It sounded suspicious. He'd keep an eye on the man. He might just be their killer.

KATIE'S CRY OF TERROR pierced the night. Sonya's heart raced as she threw off the comforter and ran toward her daughter's room.

She stumbled in the darkness and reached for the den light, but when she hit the switch, nothing happened. Panic tore through her.

"Mommy!"

"Katie!" Sonya burst into her daughter's room, dizzy with fear. "Katie?"

"The monster, Mommy! He's at the window!"

Sonya's stomach clenched. Katie was right. A shadow loomed in front of the glass, dark and vile-looking. Then the glass pane rattled and crashed and the creature reached for Katie.

Chapter Eleven

Brack jerked upright from a deep sleep, his heart racing. Something was wrong.

The phone trilled a second later, and he snapped it up. "Sonya?"

"Brack! He's outside Katie's window! He's trying to break in!"

"I'm on my way!"

He pulled on a shirt, not bothering to button it, then yanked on his jeans and boots. As he ran for the door, he grabbed his keys and pistol, then raced to his SUV. Cold air assaulted him as he started the engine and veered down the drive. He had to hurry. If he could catch this guy tonight, Sonya would be safe again, and this crazy mess would finally end.

A deer trotted across the road, and he slammed on the brakes and skidded, barreling toward the embankment. Dammit. He steered the truck sideways, spun, then righted himself, inhaling to calm down. His hands clenched the steering wheel as he approached Sonya's drive, his gaze skimming the property. Not wanting to alert the psycho to his arrival, he flipped off his headlights and parked at the edge of the drive between two ancient oaks.

He slid out, pausing to adjust his vision to the murky darkness, then moved stealthily through the trees toward the house. The whisper of his own movements beat like a drum in his ear, reminding him that a surprise attack was the only way to catch this killer.

Let the predator become the prey. Stalk him, then swoop in for the kill, a human imitation of the raptors.

Darkness shrouded the farmhouse, the towering ridges casting ominous shadows above the land. He scanned the neighboring woods, searching for signs of someone lurking nearby, and spotted a wild dog digging in the carpet of ankle-deep snow. Ice and twigs snapped below his feet, crackling in the tension-laden air as he inched closer.

Piercing eyes watched him. The scent of an animal's bloodlust filled the air.

His body tight, he pivoted and searched the outer perimeter of the house from the front. Nothing. He circled to the right, slipping in between the brush and inching his way around to the side of the house, then back.

Then that bizarre screeching sound split the night.

The brush at the edge of the woods parted, and a shadowy silhouette disappeared into the woods.

He wanted to chase it. But what if Sonya or Katie were hurt?

And what if he was wrong and the shadow had just been a deer? Perhaps the killer had created a trap to lure him away....

He quickly circled the remaining footage around the yard, studying the back of the house. Muddy bird-like prints marked the white paint. A low branch had broken from where the intruder had climbed up to the window. The glass was cracked.

Furious, he hurried to the front door. His blood froze at the sight.

A note written in blood was stuck to the door.

You are mine, Sonya,
The others are only a substitute
until we can be together.

Rage tore at his composure. He pounded on the door.

"Sonya, it's me!"

Seconds later, Sonya peered through the sheer curtain, her face pale with fear. Katie latched her arms around Sonya's neck in a death grip. Sonya unlocked the door, and he stepped inside. "Oh, God, Brack…" She fell against him, shaking all over.

He pressed her and Katie into his arms and held them tight.

SONYA RELAXED into Brack's embrace, heaving with relief at the sight of him. The minutes between her phone call to him and his arrival had seemed like an eternity. The wind had beat the frame, and she swore she'd heard the moaning of a tortured soul wailing her name. Then she'd been certain the mutant was going to burst through the walls.

Katie shivered in her arms. "Shh, Katie, it's all right now. The monster's gone."

Brack coaxed them both into the den to the sofa, then wrapped a homemade afghan around her and Katie, tucking them into the blanket as if to secure them.

As her fear slowly subsided, anger took root. She didn't want to be victimized anymore. She had to regain control of her own life.

"What happened?" Brack asked.

Katie rubbed at her eyes. "I wokes up and the m-monster was tapping at my w-window!"

Sonya hugged Katie closer, hating the tremor in her daughter's voice.

"Did you see his face?" Brack asked.

Katie shook her head, tugging at the afghan. "Just his eyes. They was beady."

Brack patted Katie's arm. "How about you, Sonya?"

"It was so dark, he was just a bunch of big, blurry shadows," Sonya whispered.

Her fear for Katie almost paralyzed her as she replayed the scene in her head. She had to take her daughter away from Tin City until Brack and the police caught this maniac. She couldn't endanger her daughter any longer.

She considered phoning Margaret again. No. She didn't want to endanger the sweet woman, either, especially with her granddaughter visiting.

But she had to do something.

Her mother's face flashed into her mind, and Sonya's throat closed. She hadn't seen her in more than four years. Their parting words had been bitter.

But her pride no longer mattered. Nothing did except keeping her daughter safe and catching this killer before he hurt someone else.

FURY BLAZED through Brack. He itched to wrap his hands around the sick coward's neck for terrorizing Sonya and her daughter.

And the teenager's death needed to be avenged.

He stood and walked to the kitchen, retrieved a plastic bag then gathered the note from the front door.

Sonya paled and sank onto the sofa in shock when she read it. "That girl died because of me."

"Shh. Don't go there, Sonya," Brack said gruffly. "This is not your fault."

She was shaking with cold and fear. He had to warm her. Calm his own raging emotions. Sonya was all right for now. And he damn well wouldn't leave her alone again.

Knowing neither one of them would sleep anytime soon, he built a fire in her fireplace, made coffee, then poured himself a cup and brought Sonya a mug. Sonya rocked Katie back and forth in her arms, singing softly. She sounded like an angel.

His heart twisted. She didn't deserve this horror. He had to convince her to go into hiding.

Needing to do something concrete on the investigation, he decided to check the whereabouts of the men on the list she'd given him. He phoned the hospital and asked to speak with Dr. Waverman.

"I'm sorry but he's not here," the nurse said. "He left around 4:00 a.m."

Brack glanced at the grandfather clock in Sonya's foyer. Five-fifteen. Waverman could easily have driven from the hospital to Sonya's place.

The vet and his assistant were also listed. He had trusted Dr. Priestly with the injured birds, but the man was intense. Quiet. And Priestly had a special interest in the raptors, had written a thesis paper on them for a master's degree before he'd been admitted to vet school.

He punched in the vet's number. The phone rang a half dozen times, then finally Priestly picked up. He sounded out of breath.

From what? Running from Sonya's?

Brack scrubbed a hand over the back of his neck. What was he going to do now—ask Priestly if he'd been stalking Sonya?

"It's Falcon. You sound winded. Is something wrong?"

"I just returned from my morning run," Priestly said. "Eight miles a day."

"Didn't know you were a jogger."

"Have been since high school. Track team."

Which meant he had speed. Enough to escape Brack in the woods the night of the girl's attack.

"What's up?" Priestly asked. "You didn't call this early for a personal chat or to discuss my exercise regime."

Brack paused, trying to remember Priestly's home address. How far it was from Sonya's. His clinic was close, a couple of miles. No distance for a seasoned runner.

"I wanted to check on that hawk."

"He's fine. You can pick him up today if you want."

"Good. I'll see you later." Brack hung up and scowled. Priestly certainly had knowledge of the birds, and he would also know how to poison the small forest animals to trap the falcons. He could have fed a rabbit just enough to make it sick, just enough so when the bird preyed on the small creature, the bird would grow weak itself.

Weak enough to be attacked by a human.

BRACK HAD called the vet. And Aaron. Why? Did he suspect Dr. Waverman as the killer? Did he know something he wasn't telling her?

Sonya eased her sleeping daughter onto the sofa and tucked the blanket around her, then went to Brack. "What did you find out?"

"Not much. Waverman had already left the hospital. And Priestly sounded out of breath from a morning jog. He runs eight miles."

"His clinic is a couple of miles from here," Sonya said, following his logic.

Brack nodded. "I'm going to follow up."

Sonya bit down on her bottom lip, and Brack pulled her into his arms and held her. "You have to take Katie someplace safe. When you called, you scared the hell out of me."

His body shuddered against her, and she clenched his arms. "I'm sorry. You're right, though. I thought about where to take Katie while I rocked her to sleep."

She motioned him into the kitchen, then paced to the refrigerator, desperate for something to do with her hands. Being in Brack's arms felt too good. Too right.

Too tempting.

So she cooked him breakfast. An odd feeling settled in the pit of her stomach as she realized it was the second day in a row they had shared their morning meal. He accepted the plate of eggs and slathered butter and jam on one of her homemade biscuits. The situation seemed mundane, routine, but intimate with the fire blazing in the background and the snow lightly falling, as if they were cocooned in a cozy domestic family home.

But Brack wasn't family. And she couldn't harbor illusions that he and she shared anything more than the desire to stop this madman from killing again.

"I would offer my family's help and twenty-four hour protection, but Deke is dealing with vandalism at the teen center, and Rex's wife, Hailey, is expected to go into labor any minute."

"I would never impose on your family," Sonya said. *Especially when I have one of my own.* "I've decided to take Katie to my mother's."

He jerked his head up. "Does she live nearby?"

"In Denver." Where Stan also lived. Where bad memories dogged her. But she was over Stan. She knew it now. And being free of him gave her the power and confidence to accept that he couldn't hurt her any longer.

She wouldn't let him hurt Katie, either.

"All right. I'll drive you there after breakfast." He polished off another biscuit. "You'll both be safer, Sonya."

"I'm not staying, Brack," Sonya said. "I have to work tomorrow."

Brack's jaw tightened. "No. I want you away from Tin City."

"I refuse to allow this psycho to run me out of my home." She thumbed her fingers through her hair. "Besides, who's to say he won't follow me? And they need me at the hospital. We're already short of paramedics." She needed the money, too, but refrained from commenting. Stan had given her a decent settlement, but she'd spent part of it for the downpayment on the house and put the other in a savings fund for Katie's college education. And Katie always had medical expenses, physical therapy...

Brack opened his mouth to argue but the doorbell rang, and they both froze.

She stood and Brack followed her into the living area, then to the door. When she glanced out the window, she was surprised to see two women and a little girl on the porch, bundled in coats and scarves, their arms loaded down with something that looked like homemade goodies.

"Hailey and Elsie, my sisters-in-law, and niece," Brack said. He opened the door. "What are you doing here?"

"Us? What are *you* doing here so early?" The blonde teased.

Sonya blushed and realized how the situation might appear to an outsider. But their early morning rendezvous had been necessitated by danger, not romance.

Not that she hadn't had a daydream or two since he'd arrived, looking and playing the part of her hero.

Brack introduced Hailey, Elsie and Elsie's daughter, Allison.

"My mom says you have a little girl and a kitten."

Sonya laughed. "Yes, Katie's asleep on the couch with Snowball."

"Mommy." Katie looked up and rubbed her eyes, and Allison ran over. The girls quickly made friends, giggling as they played with the kitten.

"We were just having coffee and breakfast," Sonya said.

Brack shrugged, suddenly restless. "Sonya had an intruder earlier."

"Oh, my gosh," Hailey exclaimed. "Rex mentioned the attack the other night. Are you all right?"

Sonya nodded. "Thanks to Brack. He saved me a second time."

The women exchanged curious looks, and Brack shifted uncomfortably.

"There's a crazy guy on the loose," Brack explained. "He's already killed one teenage girl. You two don't go out alone, and don't let Allison in the woods until we catch him."

He spun away, leaving the women in the kitchen. His words had hammered home the realization that he had only come to her house because of the intruder. Getting involved with him on a deeper level was impossible.

So why did she feel disappointed? Why did she still want him to pull her into his arms and hold her?

BRACK HAD the sudden urge for a hike into the woods. He needed air. Space. Needed to bond with the wild.

Be free like the birds.

The panicky feeling seized him as he watched Sonya with his two sisters-in-law. He liked both women, was happy for his brothers, but had no desire for their domestic lives. Already their marriages were interfering with the P.I. business. Rex had refused a job last week because he didn't want to stray too far from Hailey during the last few weeks of her pregnancy. And his middle brother acted like a lovesick puppy. Instead of building cages now for their birds, he was building a playhouse for Allison. And now Sonya was talking to Hailey about her antiques store, about a new iron bed that would be perfect for Katie.

He didn't need homemade, cozy breakfasts, toys on the floor, a pregnant woman and a regular job to tie him down. He needed to be on his own.

Katie's small crutches made a thumping sound on the wooden floor as she struggled toward him. Allison stood beside her, holding the kitten.

"Mr. Bwack?" Katie said.

God, he wanted to flee this domestic scene, but

Katie's tiny voice twisted something deep inside him. He had connected with the munchkin ever since he'd first laid eyes on her. He recognized the fight in her and sympathized with her war against insensitive kids. Hadn't he and his brothers suffered the cruelty of being different? Of being labeled the devil's spawn because the other kids in town believed their father to be the Hatchet Killer?

"What is it, Katie?"

"Allison says she's seen the monster 'afore."

Brack frowned and the women's chatter died abruptly.

"What do you mean, Allie?" Elsie stooped down to Allie's eye level.

"The kids at school talk about him. He's the Talon Terror."

"You mean they've been talking about the attack on me and that teenage girl?" Sonya asked.

"No." Allison stroked Snowball's white fur. "There's a Web site with this cartoon, you know, like Spider-Man, but he's bad. The Talon Terror goes around attacking people. He's half bird, half man, just like in Katie's drawing."

Brack turned to Sonya. "Do you have a computer?"

Sonya nodded and stepped aside to reveal a laptop on the small desk in the corner. He moved past her, took a seat at the table, then booted up the computer and went to the Google site.

Seconds later, his pulse raced as he studied the cartoon character. The creature was vile, black, coated in feathers, with a beaklike nose, beady, piercing eyes, and five-inch-long talons.

He quickly skimmed several story lines, his gut churning at the violent portrayal of the raptors. Using both human and animal skills, the Talon Terror stalked his victims, watching, waiting for the right moment; then when the prey was most vulnerable, he seized the moment, and viciously swooped down and attacked.

First the Talon Terror had started out killing small animals: squirrels, rabbits, chipmunks. The detailed, vulgar sketches showed the mutant creature slurping the blood from the dead prey, licking his talons as he finished. As the series progressed, the violence escalated, as did the animal's progression. He became more animalistic and was losing his humanity all together.

In each of the last two story lines, an innocent woman had been killed, then left bloody and mauled for the vultures to finish.

HE STUDIED the array of photographs of the birds of prey on the wall, his mind vaulting back to childhood when he'd first become infatuated with the raptors. His obsession had begun after a local field trip when he'd spotted a sparrow hawk. The fact that the female had been larger than the male intrigued him, while the male condor was usually larger than the female, as in humans. He'd watched a hawk stalking its prey, his eyes intense as he formulated his attack plan, then swooped down, caught the animal in his talons, and ripped it apart.

With that attack, his first urge to taste the pleasure of the hunt had seized him.

So he studied the fabulous creatures, knowing he was connected to them in some way. The raptors weren't the only meat-eating birds, but they were the only birds that combined all the characteristics of hunting for food, meat eating, and flying well. The birds' lethal talons could snatch fish from the water, strike birds out of the air and rip open animal quarry. They were top predators, like lions and tigers, and although they hunted other creatures, nothing hunted them except for other raptors—and humans.

And they killed with their feet.

He had tried to imitate them. Had begun killing small animals himself, pouncing on the weaker, ripping them apart and watching the blood life flow onto the ground.

The more he attacked, the more he felt the animal's blood in his veins. The hunt and kill had excited him, and his urges and need had grown more potent every day.

He wanted their power.

Of course, the vultures were the exception. They

didn't hunt for their food, but ate carrion—the remains of dead animals.

What fun was that? No thrill of the hunt to whet his appetite. He pitied them. They didn't belong in the same class with the falcons.

He had left the girl for them the night before, but her body had been found before his friends had been able to feast.

The sight of the photographs stirred his animal instincts to life again. He wanted to soar above the sky as they did. Wanted their freedom, their keen senses, their hooked beaks. Wanted to watch the prey try to scamper to safety, only to realize they were trapped. That they could not escape the speed and flight of the falcon.

Sonya would realize that soon. Then she would be his.

And though the girl the night before had satisfied a temporary fix, he already craved the taste of more blood and flesh.

Tonight he would take another.

Chapter Twelve

"I have to talk to the guy who created this cartoon," Brack said. "He fits the profile of our killer." He punched in a few keys, waited, then in seconds, had the man's home address. Vulture's Point. Only a few miles from Tin City.

He stood and faced Sonya and his sisters-in-law. Both Katie and Allison were watching him with wide-eyed interest. "Sonya, I'm going to question this guy."

Wariness crossed her face. "Be careful."

He nodded, then made his sisters-in-law promise to stay with Sonya until he returned.

Hoping he'd hit on a good lead, he headed to the door. On the way, he'd call Rex and tell him to catch up with that environmental guy, Godfrey, and see if he'd discovered anything suspicious. And just to be on the safe side, he'd have him run a background check on the vet.

As soon as he stepped outside, a dark sedan

pulled up the drive. That overeager occult reporter again. The man climbed out, looking determined as he strode toward the front porch.

Brack blocked his path as he had the night before. "I thought Ms. Silverstein made it clear that she didn't want to talk to you."

"Listen," Darrien Tripp said, "I just want her account of what happened. I've been tracking strange occult and paranormal sightings like this all over the States."

"I researched your magazine, Tripp, and none of your stories have been substantiated with fact."

Tripp shrugged. "I believe the witnesses' accounts. And I've witnessed enough odd incidents myself, enough puzzling deaths over the years, to make me believe that anything is possible."

Again, Brack contemplated the possibility that this guy might be imitating a mutant bird-man to garner attention for his own articles. "Are birds of prey your specialty?"

"No. I've been to haunted houses, the raising of the dead ceremonies, even studied a possible werewolf once, but he turned out to be a fake."

Brack had no intention of leaving this man here with Sonya and the other women and children. "Ms. Silverstein and her daughter gave the police a full account of everything they saw. Now, if you don't leave them alone, she'll get a restraining order against you."

The man bristled. "Who the hell are you, buddy? Her keeper?"

"Damn right I am." Brack pushed his face into the thin man's and watched his pasty complexion turn a buttermilk color. "My research also revealed that you like to hunt. That your father died in a strange hunting accident."

Tripp's eyeballs bulged. "My father was mauled by a bear."

"And you were questioned about his death. You've also been arrested for violence."

"Those charges were dropped." Rage tightened his thin lips. "What are you getting at, Mister?

"Maybe you've turned your love of hunting toward bigger prey—like humans."

"That's crazy," Tripp said, but he backed away.

Brack gripped him by the collar. "Maybe, maybe not. But if you don't stay the hell away from Sonya and her daughter, I'll feed your skinny butt to the wild animals myself."

Fear, then a false bravado flared in the man's eyes, but he ran to his car and climbed inside. Just before he sped off, he raised a camera and snapped a picture of Brack.

Brack cursed. Dammit, now he'd end up in the *Tween Zone* magazine—no telling what kind of slant the reporter would give the story. He'd probably use Photoshop to paste his face onto the body of a beast.

Not that he cared.

The only thing that mattered was protecting Sonya. He'd break the little weasel in half if he had to in order to keep him away from her. And if he found out he'd attacked her, he'd kill him with his bare hands and let the vultures feed off his remains.

SONYA TRIED to relax with her visitors, but her mind strayed to Brack. What if this cartoonist had created the Talon Terror based on himself? What if he hurt Brack?

"Rex and Deke told us about the attack," Hailey said, dragging her from her silent reverie. "You and Katie must have been terrified."

Sonya's chest squeezed. "If Brack hadn't found us, and then Katie…" Her voice trailed off, and Elsie and Hailey offered sympathetic looks.

"That sounds like the Falcon brothers," Elsie said. "Always protecting everyone else instead of themselves."

Hailey sipped herbal tea. "It infuriates me that some small-minded folks in town still don't trust them."

"Old prejudices are hard to shake," Elsie agreed. "But Deke and Rex have both proven themselves. Unfortunately, since Deke and I are building this teen center, some residents are worried that we'll attract derelicts and troublemakers. There's also been some vandalism at the renovation."

"What you're doing is a good thing for the town,"

Hailey argued. "If you provide the kids with a viable place to hang out and socialize, they won't be as tempted to get into trouble."

"I've tried to convince the sheriff of the value of crime prevention, but he has reservations," Elsie said. "He was harassing Deke the other day."

"Sheriff Cohen seems to have it in for Brack, too," Sonya admitted.

"It all goes back to their father's arrest. Cohen is embarrassed that he screwed up." Hailey sighed and placed her hand on her protruding belly. "I guess Brack told you that my parents were murdered years ago, and that his dad was falsely convicted of the crime. If Rex hadn't pushed to clear his dad, I would never have known the truth about what happened to my family."

"What a shame that the Falcon family lost those years together," Sonya said. Just as she'd lost years now with her mother because of her own stubborn pride. Today she would try to make amends. "How did you two meet? Through the brothers?"

Hailey squeezed Elsie's hand. "Elsie and I were friends when I was little. The night my parents were murdered, her father kidnapped her. We only re-connected a few months ago."

"Thanks to Deke," Elsie said. "He saved my life, helped me slay old ghosts, and then he found Allison for me."

The house suddenly vibrated with the force of the

gusty wind outside, the wood floors and walls moaning, reminding Sonya of the ghost stories about the person who'd died on the property behind her farmhouse. Sometimes she wondered if his ghost lingered, wanting retribution for his death.

Sonya shifted uncomfortably. "You said Deke saved you?"

Elsie gave her daughter a long, doting, motherly look. "Yes. My dad claimed that my mother died, then he left me in an orphanage for unwed teen mothers. The man who ran the home was abusive." She paused and sipped her coffee, a faraway expression in her eyes. "I gave birth to Allison there, but the doctor told me she died at birth. I went back last year to turn the abandoned orphanage into a teen center, but the caretaker who'd run it years before tried to kill me. Deke helped me expose the truth about the man's abuse." Tears glistened in her eyes. "I can't tell you how much it means to have my family back together."

Sonya's cup rattled as she placed it on her saucer. She hoped her mother could forgive her, and that she could accept Katie as Elsie's mother had obviously accepted Allison.

She glanced up and both Hailey and Elsie were watching her. Had they come on a mission to convince her that the Falcon men were trustworthy?

She knotted her hands together. She'd already reached that conclusion on her own. But she didn't want to admit that she was starting to like Brack. Or that she was beginning to fantasize about more than his friendship.

No, she couldn't allow herself to want what they had with their husbands....

ANXIETY PLUCKED at Brack as he knocked on Jameson Viago's door. He hated leaving Sonya alone, but surely she'd be safe in the daylight with two visitors at her house.

The madman seemed to prefer to strike in the dark. He waited for his victims to be alone, until they were vulnerable, then attacked without conscience.

Exactly the way the Talon Terror did in Viago's comic strip.

The fact that the Web site had earned a huge following and attracted millions of readers unsettled him. Even if Viago wasn't their man, some lunatic might be imitating the character, copying the creature's MO.

Maybe that guy, Tripp. Or perhaps a fan of the Talon Terror.

He pounded on the door again, studying the man's home. Situated on the top of Vulture's Point at a central peak in one of the smaller mountain ranges, it was a contemporary *V*-shaped cabin with skylights and dozens of windows. Dense woods surrounded the property, the isolated location reminding him of his own house on Falcon Ridge. A perfect place for an outdoors person to commune with nature.

Or for a dangerous culprit to hide.

Footsteps sounded inside, and the door finally swung open. A tall, brawny man in his twenties dressed in all black appeared, a stony expression on his long, angular face. His skin was so pale it looked as if it had never seen the sun, his bloodless lips were pinched into a frown and his fingernails were jagged and painted black.

Heavy metal music blared in the background. Behind him, Brack noticed the dark brown walls, where devil worship symbols hung along with science fiction and horror movie posters. A life-size statue of an armored knight stood on one side of a stone table that held other science fiction memorabilia. *Star Wars* characters. *Deep Space Nine*.

"Jameson Viago?"

The man jerked his head to the side, then rolled his neck. "Yes, who are you?"

"Brack Falcon. I'd like to talk to you about your comic strip series."

"I don't invite fans to my home. You'll have to e-mail me."

"I'm *not* a fan." Brack stuck one foot in the door when Viago tried to shut it. Viago's gaze flew to his. Alarmed, he jerked his head again, and rolled his neck.

A nervous tic.

The guy's eyes were two different colors, as well—one a muddy brown, the other a pale green with yellow flecks. He looked like some kind of sci-fi or horror creature himself.

On the surface, Viago fit the profile Brack was piecing together in his head. And he had the physical strength to attack a woman and rip her to shreds the way the killer had mauled that teenager.

"We are going to talk," Brack said in a voice that brooked no argument. "We can do it here, or we can drive down to the police station."

"What are you? Some kind of cop?"

"A detective." Brack shouldered his way inside the door.

"What the hell is going on? You can't just barge into my house like this."

"Your Talon Terror stories," Brack declared, "are being used as blueprints for murders." He watched the young man's reaction. Nothing. "A woman was attacked, and a teenager is dead, both assaulted by a psycho who copies your Talon Terror's crimes. I want to know if you're responsible."

"Murder?" A flicker of excitement registered in Viago's odd eyes.

Disgust rippled through Brack. Viago actually sounded impressed. "This is not something to be proud of, Mr. Viago. Your series encourages graphic violence against women."

"My series is fiction," Viago argued in a grating, icy voice. He rolled his neck again.

Very telling. He was either guilty as hell, or he imagined his crimes on paper but didn't have the guts to carry them out. Not that killing took guts, but lack of morals. Sometimes psychotics were confused, warred with their own sick personalities, even experienced moments of lucidity and guilt.

Or he could be cold, calculating, lack any feelings of guilt, simply be anxious about getting caught.

"What the hell? You don't have any right to tell me what to think," Viago snapped. "You don't know anything about me, Mister."

Brack released a sarcastic chuckle. "Let me guess. You were a geeky kid. The teenagers in high school teased and tormented you, the bullies singled you out. They abused you. Hell, maybe your parents did, too. Maybe you've got some sob story, and your mother didn't love you. Or maybe your daddy locked you in a dark closet for days at a time."

"Shut up. My mother did too love me."

Good. He'd punched the guy's buttons. "You felt powerless all your life, so you've invented this superhuman animal to prove that you're not a wimp." The profile fit. He'd read about teen violence, school shootings, how the brutalized victims of bullies felt out of control. They internalized the pain and abuse, until their anger escalated to an insurmountable level. They finally broke and retaliated in a violent, brutal way, repeating the cycle, preying on the weaker.

"You're full of it, Mister. I simply draw the character and create his stories." Viago pointed to the door with a jagged black nail. "Now get out."

Brack spotted the guy's computer where his screen saver flashed a picture of a dead woman sprawled naked on a white sheet soaked in blood. His graphics and drawings of the Talon Terror were spread across a work table. All vile, degrading to women, each scene growing bloodier and more gory.

On the walls of the large, vaulted-ceilinged room, pictures of birds filled the white space. Dozens of photos of rare species, the falcons hunting their prey, closeup shots of the raptor as it ripped into the flesh of a live animal. Others showed carcasses of dead animals, their insides exposed, blood covering the ground.

Other photos included a white-tailed kite, a bald eagle, a northern goshawk, an adult gyrfalcon, an aplomado falcon and a eurasian hobby. Brack was drawn to the photo of a peregrine falcon. It was such an awe-inspiring raptor to watch because of its power, grace and speed in flight. One photograph captured the falcon as it performed a vertical dive from atop a cliff, striking at a bird in midair and capturing it with his feet.

But Brack saw the beauty in the animal, whereas Viago saw the violence.

"You've obviously studied the habits of the falcons in great detail," Brack said.

Viago shrugged. "Yeah, I did my research."

"Do you know Sonya Silverstein?" Brack asked.

"Who?"

"Sonya Silverstein."

"Never heard of her. I told you, I'm not this killer. I make up my stories to entertain and that's all there is to it." He gestured toward the door. "Now, do I need to call the cops and tell them you're harassing me?"

Brack glanced around the room, looking for signs that Viago might be lying. Maybe a falcon costume or talons he'd ripped from the birds and kept for himself. But the place appeared orderly, monochromatic, all blacks and whites.

Frustration knotted his neck. He wanted to search the house, the hidden corners, the man's bedroom for something to incriminate Viago. Maybe he had taken pictures of his victims, stalked them in advance. And he needed a sample of the guy's DNA.

But all he had was supposition. And no authority.

"I'll leave for now, but if you aren't the Talon Terror, then maybe one of your fans is." Brack paused, his voice hardening, "Go through your mail. He might have written you, sent you some kind of message. He'd want to brag about the fact that he was acting out your fiction in real life."

Viago scratched a ragged nail down his neck as he eyed the overflowing bin of mail on the table.

Brack removed a card from his wallet and slapped it on the desk. "If you find something, call me. You might be able to help us stop this guy from killing again and be a real hero."

Viago simply stared at him as he walked to the door. Brack cursed as he climbed in his SUV. He wanted to read that mail. Go through Viago's house and computer and look for a lead.

But he needed the police on his side with a warrant to do so. He'd talk to Cohen. But what if he refused to help?

Then he'd go above his head. Cohen wouldn't like it, but Brack didn't give a damn. He had to find this guy before he tried to hurt Sonya again. And he didn't care who he pissed off or offended in the process.

Lives were at stake. And this psycho had just gotten started with his game of hunt and kill. He had an obsessive personality.

Now his appetite was whetted, he'd hunt again.

And each kill would get more vicious until he was caught.

JAMESON VIAGO paced the confines of his den, battling an onslaught of the tics. He hated that he couldn't control the stupid nervous habit he'd developed over the years.

The doctors, countless ones that he'd seen, had told him he needed medication. And he'd taken it for a while, but drugs made him lethargic. Made him sleep all the time. And they caused sexual side effects.

Killed his drive so he couldn't perform.

And he needed sex. Just like he needed the Talon Terror and the blood and guts to give him life.

He paced from the corner to his desk, wondering how that Falcon man had found him. How had he sensed that Jameson had a violent side? That his bloodlust ran to animals and the hunt.

That he had been abused.

And that he had created the Talon Terror to prove to the world that he was somebody. Now he was finally gaining the attention he deserved. Finally building a following.

That Falcon man couldn't ruin it for him. He wouldn't let him.

The young boys and men…they admired his imagination. Liked the power the Talon Terror held. The total control.

And the women…some of them wrote him, as well. They thought he was a genius. A creative saint.

A few had even confessed they liked rough sex. That he could have them anytime he wanted. That if he wanted to rake his talons across them, that they would welcome the pain. They liked the game.

He jerked his head sideways. Rolled his neck.

Stared at his hands. Then the latest story line of the Talon Terror came to him.

In this version, he would add a twist.

The prey the Talon Terror had chosen—another falcon had also chosen as his mate.

They would have to engage in battle. There would be pain and bloodshed as they fought.

He picked up his charcoal and began to draw, detailing the Talon's intensity as he stalked his mate from the ridge, then his movements as he swooped down for the attack.

He could already taste the sweet blood on his fingertips.

Then the violence as the other falcon battled for the mate. But the opposing falcon would lose in the end.

And *he* would win. Then the prey would be his.

Chapter Thirteen

As Brack drove them toward Denver, Sonya wrestled with her thoughts and her conscience. Katie's reaction to the fact that she was going to see a grandmother she'd never met had been excitement, so like Katie to accept whatever Sonya told her with the quiet wisdom of a child older than her age.

But Katie had no idea what she'd been missing. That her own mother had robbed her of a relationship that might have given her an abundance of love and support.

Sonya ran her hands through her hair. It was a mess just like she was. How selfish had she been? How insecure?

She'd played right into Stan's hands, let him undermine her confidence, as if she were some weak, malleable puppet that he could dance on a string. No more.

Would her mother be as judgmental about Katie's condition as Stan had been? Would she blame her for her poor choice in a husband, for the flaws that she'd passed on to her daughter?

Would she be angry at her for not telling her about Katie sooner?

Katie had curled up with Snowball for a nap in the backseat, and Sonya stared out the window at the passing scenery, wishing she could will the answers, but the dismal gray storm clouds mirrored her life. One storm had passed through, but another loomed on the horizon.

If something happened to her, if this crazy madman succeeded and killed her, she'd want Katie to be taken care of and loved.

"Your mother hasn't ever seen Katie?" Brack asked.

She fidgeted with the threads of her sweater, noting one thread had slipped loose from the weave. Pull on it and the entire garment might unravel— much as she felt.

"No."

Brack arched a brow. "Your ex's doing?"

Sonya wanted to hoist all the blame on Stan, but even she couldn't do that. She'd always accepted responsibility for her own choices and actions. "No. I...was stubborn."

"Did you two have a falling out?"

"That's putting it mildly. She didn't think I should marry Stan." Sonya sighed, huddling into her coat, suddenly cold as she remembered their bitter argument the night she'd left.

And then the night Stan had come home smelling of another woman's perfume—the night she'd realized her mother was right about him. The same night Katie had been sick and she'd rushed her to the ER alone. She'd been terrified she might lose Katie, and she'd needed him. But he claimed he needed someone else, more of a woman than her.

Her voice reverberated with disgust when she finally spoke again. "I was young, impressionable, I believed everything Stan said. That we'd have a perfect life together."

"What went wrong?" Brack asked.

Everything. She was flawed. "When he said *perfect* life, he'd meant it literally. And Katie and I weren't."

His mouth flattened into a thin line.

She thought back, wondering why she'd hadn't recognized *his* flaws sooner. He'd had them, only she'd been blindly in love, thought they could overcome any obstacle.

"What about Katie? Does he see her?"

"No. He actually didn't want children. I was in paramedic school," she said, remembering back. "He was in med school. We married and I finished the program, although I'd contemplated continuing my education and studying pediatrics."

"What stopped you?"

"My pregnancy."

He gave her a questioning look, and she shook

her head. "Don't think I regret Katie for a moment. She's the best part of my life."

"But the cretin couldn't accept her impairment."

"Stan couldn't accept any kind of flaw. After we were married, he switched from internal medicine to plastic surgery. Now he makes a fortune performing breast augmentations and face-lifts."

Brack hissed in disgust. "Sounds like a saint."

"He was charismatic, but I realized later that he was a snake charmer." She rubbed her arms, so cold. "My mother warned me. By the time I got pregnant, I realized she was right. I couldn't bear to hear her I-told-you-so's. It was easier to stay out of touch."

"It must have been difficult to raise Katie alone," Brack said in a gravelly voice.

He had no idea. But she'd managed, and she valued her independence. Only now this crazy man had shattered her newfound peace.

She shivered, and he cradled her hand into his. She felt warmer, safer, humbled by his lack of judgment.

"What happened with that comic strip guy?" Sonya asked, determined to steer the subject away from her personal life. She felt raw. Exposed. Too vulnerable.

"He's odd, could be the guy." Brack's jaw tensed. "On the way back to your house, I called Cohen to request a warrant to search Viago's house and confiscate his files. If he isn't the killer, one of his fans may be. Whoever it is, he's copying Viago's Talon Terror, imitating his crimes."

Sonya huddled closer to Brack, grateful to have him on her side. She only hoped they found out the truth before another girl died.

They reached the street leading to her mother's house, and Sonya tensed as the familiar landscape and modest houses appeared. A pang of longing swelled inside her so deep that tears sprang to her eyes. Memories of her father teaching her to ride a bike in the cul-de-sac. Her mother and her planting impatiens around the mailbox. The beagle puppy they'd adopted when she was five.

Her father deserting them when she was twelve.

Her devastation. Her mother's.

Then the teenage years, when she'd been searching and her mother had been lost. Both grieving but unable to discuss the one subject that mattered most—the man they'd both loved who'd left them without once looking back.

Brack parked and turned to her, then pulled her into his arms. "Talk to your mother, Sonya. She probably needs you as much as you need her."

Sonya gulped back tears and forced a smile, praying Brack was right.

Katie yawned and stretched from the backseat, and Snowball meowed. Brack jumped into motion and helped Katie out, his silent look of understanding offering her courage as they maneuvered their way up the snow-crusted sidewalk. Seconds later, she knocked on her old front door, hesitant to open it and burst in as she would have done ten years ago.

It seemed like an eternity before her mother finally answered. Five years of pain, misunderstanding, loneliness and regret mingled as her mother's surprised expression turned to delight. "Sonya?"

Her tone sounded hesitant, but accepting.

"Mom, there's someone I want you to meet. Someone you should have met a while back."

Her mother had aged. Graying hair now shadowed the bobbed brown layers. Laugh lines crinkled beside her mouth, but sadness and hope tinged her eyes.

Sonya stepped aside and pulled Katie in front of her, Snowball, crutches and all. "This is your granddaughter, Katie."

"Oh, my heavens." Her mother choked back a sob, looked from Sonya to Katie. Disappointment, confusion, anger, then a deep sadness colored her expression.

Sonya's heart wrenched. "I'm so sorry, Mom. I wish we'd come sooner…."

"Shh. You're home now, that's all that matters." Tears glistened in her mother's eyes, then she knelt and cupped her hands on the sides of Katie's face. "Hi, Katie. You are the most beautiful angel I've ever seen."

Sonya's throat clogged with emotions, then her mother swept both her and Katie into her arms. Relief filled Sonya—she was finally home.

DÉJÀ VU STRUCK Brack as he remembered his own family's emotional reunion when his father had been released from prison.

He hated emotional scenes. Had struggled all his life to force a blankness to his soul, but somehow Katie and Sonya had tiptoed in and woven a spell around his heart when he hadn't been looking.

Finally Sonya pulled away and introduced him. He felt like a voyeur and wanted to leave. He didn't belong here, not now during their reunion.

They exchanged pleasantries, then he promised Sonya he'd return. At least she and Katie were safe for now.

Meanwhile he had research to do.

The library and county courthouse proved helpful. He checked into each aspect of Stan Silverstein's life, from the nature of his job to his reputation to his finances. After searching the county public records and library, he booted up his computer. Seconds later, he accessed the man's financial records, investments and insurance information.

Silverstein was a respected doctor in his field, although Sonya was right—he performed cosmetic work for the elite of Denver. No pro bono work for charities, no seriously deformed or injured patients.

The man made money off the rich and hadn't chosen the medical field to better mankind.

He'd given Sonya a meager settlement and paid child support directly into an account established for Katie. The minimal payment under law, Brack was sure.

He couldn't imagine Sonya marrying the type of man who could dismiss a child with a payoff like Silverstein obviously had.

He searched further, and discovered Silverstein had accumulated some major debt. He'd purchased a pricey country club estate, drove a Mercedes and bought expensive gifts for the women in his life.

At least his lovers.

Not his ex-wife or child.

Silverstein covered Katie's insurance, probably another court requirement. And oddly he still held a sizable life insurance policy on Sonya.

Greed was a powerful motive for murder. If he was the benefactor and Sonya died, then he'd inherit more than enough money to dig himself out of debt.

Another possibility reared its head. What if the man regretted his divorce? What if he wanted control over Sonya? Would he try to scare her into running back to him?

Or perhaps he simply wanted to drive her crazy out of revenge for forcing him to pay for Katie. Other possibilities also rambled through his head. Maybe she'd recently pushed him for more money or for him to spend time with his daughter, and he'd felt cornered and panicked. It was a long shot, but he had to pursue every angle and every man involved in her life.

Knowing the only way he could eliminate him or find out the truth was to face Silverstein, he shut down his computer and drove to Silverstein's office. The building that housed his medical practice was located in the downtown area, a modern skyscraper that held dozens of prestigious businesses, lofts and retail stores. High-dollar rent for professionals on the rise.

He entered the outer office, a plush room with steel-gray carpet, burgundy-and-green sofas and so many plants it looked like a jungle. The waiting room was empty, and he hoped that Silverstein was in, not off for some long martini lunch with a bimbo he'd picked to replace Sonya.

Fool.

The receptionist, a perky blonde with humongous boobs who had undoubtedly enjoyed Silverstein's handiwork firsthand, beamed up at him. "Can I help you, sir?"

"I'm here to see Stan Silverstein."

"Let me make you an appointment, Mister...?"

"Falcon. And I don't want an appointment. This is urgent." Brack cleared his throat. "I need to talk to him about his wife and child."

The blonde's plastic smile wilted. "Oh. Why, did something happen to them?"

He frowned, wondering if her question was rhetorical or if she might have an inkling that Silverstein had tried something nefarious. "I'd rather discuss the matter with him."

She chewed her ruby-red lip, then stood, her sweater revealing cleavage that would make some men drool. Even so, she was not nearly as beautiful as Sonya. And she was fake, whereas Sonya was real.

A second later she returned, then asked him to wait in the outer office. Apparently Silverstein was in the middle of a consult. Brack claimed a seat, his temper rising as the minutes ticked by. Ten. Fifteen. Thirty.

Finally, his patience snapped. He strode back to the girl, ready to battle his way into Silverstein's office, when the inner office door opened, a woman wearing a big floppy hat and sunglasses slid by, and the blonde motioned him in.

Silverstein's office was every bit as elegant as the front waiting room. Plush leather furniture, expensive cherry desk, a wet bar... The extravagant interior made Sonya's farmhouse look shabby at best, inciting his anger.

He braced himself to meet the man who'd won Sonya's heart. But when he appeared, Brack scowled. Silverstein was one of those yuppie types. Clipped, sandy-blond hair. Around five-ten. Fit, as if he worked out in a gym daily, and dressed in

designer clothes. His damn nails were even manicured, his shoes spit-polished, and a diamond-
studded band that looked like a college class ring
glittered on his right hand. Nothing on the left. His
diplomas and degrees hung on the wall, framed in
elegant brass frames, as if to shout his ivy-league
education.

"What is this about, Mr. Falcon? How do you
know my ex-wife?"

Brack detected a hint of jealousy in his tone and
clamped a lid on his temper. "I'm a private investi-
gator." He explained about the attacks in Tin City
and the one on Sonya.

Silverstein dropped into his desk chair and
pulled his hand down his face. "Dear God, is she
all right?"

So the man did care about her after all. He
should be relieved, yet unease speared him. "She's
safe, for now."

"Good. Then what can I do for you?"

"I think the man who attacked Sonya and killed
this teenage girl knows Sonya."

A drop of sweat trickled down his cheek. "You
mean Sonya is involved with someone?"

"I'm investigating her coworkers and acquaintances."

Silverstein straightened, his cheeks growing
ruddy as the implication finally sank in. "There-
fore, you're checking into *me?*"

"I'm thorough." Brack's tone hardened. "You and Sonya had an amicable divorce?"

Silverstein drummed his nails on his desk. "My relationship with my wife is none of your business."

"Your ex-wife," Brack clarified. The man had no claims on her now.

Or did he? He was Katie's father.

And Brack had traveled that route and gotten sideswiped once before.

"You wanted the divorce," he pointed out.

"At the time, yes. But…it might have been a mistake." Silverstein's voice softened. "Sonya is a special woman."

Unreasonable anger riffled through Brack. "So you're interested in a reconciliation?"

Silverstein hedged. "Whatever happens between myself and Sonya is our business, not yours."

The hell it wasn't. He intended to make it his business. "Maybe you regret the divorce, but don't want to admit it, so you hired someone to scare Sonya into running back to you."

The vein in Silverstein's neck throbbed. "That's ridiculous."

Brack gritted his teeth. "You haven't mentioned your daughter. You do remember Katie, don't you?"

Silverstein stood, pain grated on his face. "My relationship with my child is not your concern."

"I'm making it my concern."

"Why exactly are you here, Mr. Falcon?" Silverstein crossed his arms. "I thought you were a P.I. Your questions sound like you have a personal interest in my wife."

"She's not your wife anymore." And maybe he did have a personal interest in her. He sure as hell would respect and love her more than this pretentious weasel.

Love her? Dammit. Where had that thought come from?

He dismissed the ludicrous possibility. He was here simply out of concern, working an investigation. "Then why do you still carry a life insurance policy on her?"

"Sonya insisted on that for Katie's sake." Silverstein's cheeks reddened with anger. "Why? You aren't actually suggesting I'd kill my wife for money, are you?"

"It happens all the time, Mr. Silverstein."

"I'm a doctor, Mr. Falcon. I loved my wife and would never do anything to harm her." He gestured around the office. "And I certainly don't need the money."

"My research says differently. You earn a big salary, but you're in debt up to your eyeballs."

Silverstein stormed around the side of his desk, grabbed the door and flung it open. But not before Brack saw a split second of guilt flash into Silverstein's gray eyes. "Get out, Mr. Falcon. This conversation is over."

Brack shot him a cold stare. He didn't know if the

man was guilty or not, but he sure as hell didn't like him. He shoved his face into Silverstein's. "If I find out you tried to hurt Sonya, I'll be back." He clutched him by the lapel of his designer suit. "And money will be the least of your problems."

"Let me go or I'll call the police, Mr. Falcon. And stay away from my wife."

"You have no claims on Sonya now," Brack snapped. "You hurt her before, and I don't intend to let you do it again."

He released him with such force that Silverstein stumbled back into the wall with a thud, then Brack stormed out.

On some level, Silverstein obviously still cared about Sonya. Did he want a reconciliation with her?

And would she take him back if he asked?

ON HIS WAY BACK to Sonya's mother's house, Brack phoned Rex to check in.

"Brack, there was another woman attacked today," Rex said. "Reesie Lunsford, a paramedic. She worked with Sonya Silverstein."

Damn. He'd expected this predator to attack again, but so soon? And Silverstein had an alibi, although his theory of paying someone else still fit. "Is the woman all right?"

"No. She was DOA. And Tripp, the reporter for that occult magazine, has been all over town—he passed out fliers with a drawing of a creature who resembles that Talon Terror, and now half the community is convinced that there is a mutant creature stalking the women. The citizens are all in a panic."

"I'm sure they think we're involved."

"Tripp implied that, yes." Rex hissed a breath. "We're dealing with a serial killer, Brack. Unfortunately, I can't help much, either. Hailey started having mild contractions, and the doctor ordered her on bed rest until the baby comes. I have to stay with her."

"Of course you do." Brack silently cursed, though. Another death, panic in the town. All the more reason for him to get the cops on his side and push that warrant through.

He just hoped Cohen saw it that way.

Because as much as he wanted to blame Silverstein, Viago was their best lead yet. And as tempted as he was to break into the guy's house and look around for himself, he couldn't chance the guy getting off on some technicality. Neither did he want to end up in jail for interfering with an investigation and leave Sonya alone and vulnerable.

An image of the Talon Terror attacking another woman flashed in his head, and guilt assaulted him. If he'd caught this guy sooner, that woman might not be dead.

How would Sonya feel when she learned the killer had struck again and that he'd killed her friend?

Chapter Fourteen

Reesie—dead? No.

Sonya doubled over in shock, then sank onto the kitchen chair, grateful Brack had insisted they meet in private away from Katie. She couldn't believe that her friend and coworker was dead.

Guilt assailed her. The Talon Terror had become obsessed with her and had chosen her friend to flaunt the fact that he knew her friends and would murder them to hurt her.

But why?

"Brack, this is so unfair," she whispered. "Reesie was a good woman. She'd just finished earning her paramedic license, she was engaged... She had her entire life ahead of her...." A sob caught in her throat and Brack soothed her with soft whispered words.

"Who hates me so much that they would want to destroy me by killing my friends?" she cried.

He rubbed slow circles on her back. "I don't

know, Sonya. But we'll find him, I swear we will, and we'll stop him."

She wanted desperately to believe him. She also wanted to stay here and hide out, but she'd never been a coward and she refused to be one now. Besides, if she stayed here with her mother and this madman tracked her down, he might hurt Katie or her mother to get to her. "Thank you for not telling me in front of Katie, Brack. I don't want her touched any more by this violence than she already has been."

He nodded. "I know. She doesn't deserve it, and neither do you."

"I'm alive, Brack. Poor Reesie...." Tears trickled down her cheeks. She had to go back to Tin City, had to see her friend, do something to stop this lunatic before he killed someone else.

He leaned his chin against the top of her head, and she breathed in his scent. His courage. His masculine power and determination.

He was everything she needed right now. Only she wanted more.

She wanted to burrow herself in his arms, let him soothe her with his words and hands. Take away the pain of having Reesie's death on her conscience.

Make love to him until she forgot about death, until all she could think about was living....

"Sonya, don't blame yourself," Brack said in a gruff voice. "Just stay here, take care of Katie. Be safe and let me handle this investigation."

She clenched his arms and looked up into his eyes. "I have to go back with you, Brack."

His molten eyes turned to steel. "No."

She inhaled a deep breath. Considered all the options. "Yes. First of all, the paramedic team will be short now without Reesie. She was covering for me since my attack." Her voice cracked, emotions pummeling her. "And I refuse to let this killer win by running me out of my house and town. Besides, who's to say he wouldn't find me here?" She glanced at the closed kitchen door. "I won't risk the chance of him hurting my mother or Katie."

Brack looked torn for a moment, but she saw the moment her logic registered in his eyes.

"Then you stay with me until he's arrested," he said.

Sonya nodded, the idea of spending another night in Brack's house sending a ripple of unease through her. But staying alone was even more terrifying.

BRACK CRADLED Sonya close, his body humming with tension as he inhaled the scent of her feminine shampoo and felt her curves pressed against him. He admired her courage. Admired the fact that she refused to let this psycho intimidate her.

She was a strong, gutsy woman.

His hunger for her grew with each passing moment. Knowing she might be in danger intensified it, as well. And liking her only complicated that need.

Because need meant that he was beginning to feel for her, something he couldn't allow himself to do.

Caring about people meant the possibility of getting hurt. A possibility that he couldn't risk.

They'd just have to work through the next few days, find this killer. Then they could part ways as friends.

At least she hadn't argued about staying with him. He tried to suppress the frisson of excitement that skated through him at the thought. They would be alone. Sharing close quarters.

His body hardened as her breasts brushed his chest. Would he be able to keep his hands off of her?

Yes, he'd have to. He couldn't take advantage of her. She was only letting him hold her now because she needed comfort. Not because she wanted *him*.

But she felt so soft and fit perfectly in his arms. And it had been a long time since he'd been with a woman.

Hell, that was a lie. But the last woman and the one before had meant nothing. They hadn't stirred anything inside him other than a physical heat that had burned out within minutes after being with them and left him feeling oddly empty.

Sonya made him want more. Made him realize that meaningless lovemaking had been the reason he'd never returned to any of his former one-night stands.

Voices rumbled from the living room, and the kitchen door burst open. Katie stumbled in, Sonya's mother on her heels. Her eyes crinkled with a smile and questions when she saw them together.

Sonya instantly pulled away, and he straightened.

"Mr. Bwack," Katie said. "Snowball can do a trick. Wants to see?"

He grinned. He wanted to return to Tin City and push that warrant through, but how could he deny the kid? God, he was a sucker for her big brown eyes. "Sure."

Seconds later, he laughed as Katie dragged a ball of string around and watched the kitten chase it. A few minutes led to an hour as Sonya's mother insisted they stay for dinner.

Brack struggled to relax during the meal, but anxiety gnawed at him, and he couldn't stop thinking about the attacks. He wanted to search Jameson Viago's place *yesterday*. Wanted to look at those fan letters. But that moron, Cohen, hadn't returned his call, and he contemplated again going over his head. If Viago wasn't the killer, then one of his fans might be.

Then again, the timing of that occult reporter's appearance raised suspicion. What if Tripp went from town to town creating trouble, superstition, panic among the residents about something paranormal, then wrote up the story to draw attention to his magazine column? There were all kinds of crazies in the world. He had to check him out further.

By the time they finished eating, tension knotted his shoulders. He finished his ice cream with Katie while Sonya slipped into the kitchen to talk to her mother about leaving Katie with her. A few minutes later, she finally returned, then sat down and pulled Katie into her lap. "Honey, how would you feel about staying here with your grandmother for a few days?"

Katie's face lit up, then fear darkened her eyes. "Are you gonna stay, too?"

Sonya tucked a strand of Katie's hair behind her ear. "No, sweetie, Mommy needs to go to work. And a friend of mine, well, honey, she died today, and I need to go to her funeral."

"Did that monster hurts her?" Katie asked.

Brack's stomach clenched. Katie was too smart sometimes. He half expected Sonya to lie, but she didn't.

"I'm afraid so, sweetie."

Katie scrunched her nose. "Buts I don't want him to gets you, Mommy."

"He's not going to, Katie. I swear to you I'll be back to pick you up." Sonya hugged her daughter and rocked her in her arms.

Brack knelt in front of Katie and tipped up her chin. "I promise to take care of your mother, lamb chop. You trust me, don't you?"

Katie studied him for a long moment, and his heart pounded in his ears. He didn't know why her answer was so important, but it would pain him if she said no.

Then she nodded. "You'll brings her back to gets me?"

Her trust touched him deeply, and he brushed a kiss on her forehead. "Yes, I will. And when we return, that monster will be gone forever."

As he and Sonya walked to the car, he wondered if she trusted him as much as her daughter did. Then again, if she'd known what he was thinking earlier, if she sensed how much he wanted her, maybe she shouldn't.

A THICK SEXUAL AWARENESS vibrated through the car as Sonya and Brack drove back to Tin City. Sonya studied the passing scenery, wishing she could enjoy the majestic landscape, the snow-capped mountaintops and jutting ridges, but the flutter of nerves taking flight inside her destroyed the peaceful picture.

The yawning distance between her and her mother had finally been crossed. Katie was safe. And Evelyn had accepted Katie with open and loving arms.

But now she was alone with Brack Falcon.

A man she was very much attracted to. A man she admired but one who stirred her deepest fears at the same time. He tempted her to forget that she'd vowed to live the rest of her life alone. That she'd failed at her first marriage, had been a disappointment to the man who'd promised to love her, and that her daughter was crippled because of her.

She couldn't chance having more children only to see them suffer.

And she couldn't surrender her heart without fearing it might be broken again. She'd survived once. Could she survive a second failure or rejection?

In the distance, a hawk soared above the treetops, its shadow silhouetted against the ensuing darkness, and her heart thrashed. Brack and the animals bonded.

Yet those very same animals elicited fear in her now that she'd been attacked.

An image of her friend flashed in front of her. Poor Reesie.

"I'm going to investigate that reporter," Brack said, breaking the silence. "And I called Cohen about a warrant for that cartoonist's house and his fan mail, but he hasn't responded yet." His cell phone rang, and he unfolded it, connecting the call. "Falcon here."

She gnawed on her lower lip while he spoke in hushed tones. She should phone the paramedic unit, see if they needed her tonight. Check on her house.

What if the psycho stalking her had left her another present? Another dead animal? More blood?

Brack disconnected the call and turned to her. "That was Dr. Priestly, the vet I work with. He found some oddities in the blood work for two of the birds I rescued. Traces of poison."

"Poison?"

He nodded. "I suspected as much. The raptors are so incredibly agile and fast, and they have keen senses. It's impossible for a person to sneak up on them on the ground, not unless they're already weak or injured."

"You think he's somehow poisoning them so they'll be more vulnerable?"

"It makes sense. He probably poisons their food sources, setting traps with a small rabbit. I talked to Rex earlier, and he said that Godfrey, the specialist from the EPA, found some environmental disturbances. He's running tests now."

Sonya shivered and burrowed deeper into her jacket. "This guy is really crazy, isn't he, Brack?"

Brack slid a hand over hers, and she felt instantly warmer, calmer. "Yeah, he is. But we're getting closer to figuring out his identity. I can feel it."

Sonya stared at their entwined hands, her body tingling from his touch. She'd forgotten how much she missed a simple connection with a man. Forgotten how comforting it was to lean on someone else. "I have to see Reesie, Brack. And I need to call about work."

"You aren't going to work, Sonya. Not until this guy is behind bars."

She clenched her jaw. "The paramedic unit is short now, Brack. We barely had enough rescue workers to cover the shifts as it was, and I won't be working alone. We always travel in pairs."

His dark gaze cut to her, then back to the road as he maneuvered into the parking lot of the hospital. "I don't like it, Sonya. It's too dangerous."

Sonya sighed and climbed from the car, bracing herself to see her friend's dead body. She didn't like it, either, but she couldn't let her friend's death count for nothing.

A few minutes later, she stood in the cold room, her heart in her throat as the ghostly voices that she always heard in the morgue whispered through the eaves of the old building. Sounds rattled below. Almost like footsteps...

Someone had told her that the hospital, especially this wing, had been built above the old mining tunnels, the ones where the victims of the typhoid epidemic had been buried. At night, sometimes she'd imagined shadowy silhouettes, spirits rising and slipping through the concrete walls, their echoes of pain and cries for help forever trapped in the pit of death.

The medical examiner, Will Snyder, strode in, wiping sweat from his brow in spite of the frigid temperature.

The palms of Sonya's own hands grew clammy as he moved the sheet to reveal her friend's pale face, her eyes glazed in death, her face frozen in shock at the horror of her assailant's brutality.

"Did she suffer much?" Sonya asked.

Snyder gave her an odd look but didn't reply. She noted the viciousness of the attack wounds and understood his hesitant response—Reesie had died a terrible death.

The Talon Terror had ripped at her flesh, through muscle, tissue, all the way down to the bone. And this time he had gone straight for her heart, as if he'd intended to rip it out completely.

She fought nausea, battling it down, willing herself to be strong and not lose her composure in front of the medical examiner.

"I haven't completed the autopsy yet," he said in a low voice. "I was just getting ready to start it."

"Can I have a few minutes alone with her?" Sonya asked.

He gave her a concerned look over his glasses, then nodded. "I'll be in my office if you need me. I believe that Falcon man wants to talk to me."

"Yes, he does."

Snyder slipped out the door, and she sucked in a breath for courage. Brack had wanted to come with her, but she'd insisted on facing her friend alone. She couldn't risk growing too dependent on him, although doing so was so tempting....

She pulled on rubber gloves, knowing that preserving any trace evidence left on her friend was imperative, then lifted the sheet and cradled Reesie's hand in hers. Her skin felt cold, stiff, and bloody talon marks marred the tops of her hands. Defense wounds. Just like her own.

Only she had been lucky. She'd escaped alive.

She shivered, a cold horror seeping through her at the viciousness of the killer's attack.

Suddenly a whisper of icy air touched her neck, as if a ghost's fingers had brushed her skin. She spun round, half expecting to see a spirit floating toward her, but someone clamped a rag over her mouth and grabbed her around the neck. She flailed her arms, trying to jab her assailant with her elbow, then tried to scream, but she inhaled a gassy odor instead and gagged.

She grasped for something, anything, a scalpel from the metal table nearby, but missed. The steel table rolled and slammed into the wall with a grating crash, and the metal tools hit the floor with a resounding clatter.

Her attacker tightened his hold on her neck, and she tried to kick backward, to connect with bone, but felt her energy draining, felt the world spiraling into a gray abyss of nothingness.

Her legs sagged, and somewhere in the distance feet pounded. Someone shouted. The world went black, twirling sickeningly as she fought to focus. But she lost the battle and collapsed onto the cold floor as darkness engulfed her.

Chapter Fifteen

Brack heard the loud crash of metal from inside the morgue and took off running. He pushed past Snyder and barreled through the door, his heart pumping ninety miles an hour.

Then he saw Sonya lying on the floor and his heartbeat crashed to a stop.

Panic nearly seized him, but he pushed it aside, knelt and checked for a pulse. "Sonya, come on, baby, breathe, dammit."

A second passed. Two. Five. His own erratic breathing rattled in the air.

Finally he felt her pulse in her throat. Low and reedy, but indicating that she was alive.

The door swung open behind him. Footsteps pounded. "Good God almighty. What's going on?" Snyder bellowed.

"Someone attacked her. Get help! Then call security and tell them to block all the exits and to look for anyone suspicious."

Snyder grabbed the wall phone and called for a doctor. Brack traced a finger over Sonya's pale cheek, willing her to open her eyes, but they remained closed. Her breathing was unsteady.

He wanted to pick her up and move her, hold her and rub the life back into her, but decided it was best for the doctors to check her first. Although he saw no signs of neck or spinal injuries, he didn't want to risk hurting her worse in case she'd sustained a head injury.

Dr. Waverman raced in, followed by a nurse. A shocked look darkened Waverman's face when he spotted Sonya on the floor.

Or was he acting? Had he attacked her, then slipped out the door and returned to play her hero?

The nurse knelt to check her vitals.

"What happened?" Waverman asked.

"Someone attacked her. Doctor Snyder and I were talking in the other room. Sonya wanted a moment alone to say goodbye to her friend." Brack gestured toward the body on the table.

Waverman frowned and ran his fingers over her head, checking for injuries. "Let's get her to the ER. Grab a gurney, Snyder."

Brack turned to the nurse. "Don't leave her alone for a minute. Make sure a second person is with her at all times, too."

Waverman glared at him with animosity in his eyes. "You aren't suggesting that I would hurt Sonya?"

"I don't trust anyone right now," Brack snapped. Waverman started to lift Sonya, but Brack slid his arms beneath her first, and carried her to the gurney instead.

Waverman's snarl hissed between them as he grabbed Brack's arm. "That's ridiculous. I care about her, Mister Falcon."

Brack's jaw tightened. He'd guessed as much. But she'd blown him off so he might be desperate for attention. He jerked his arm free from Waverman. "If you really care about her, then make sure she's all right." He pointed toward the door on the opposite wall of the room. "Where does that lead?"

"It's a walk-through," Snyder explained. "It goes into a hall that leads to X-rays and radiology."

Brack headed toward the door, his mind spinning. What if Sonya wasn't okay?

No, she'd been breathing.... The nurses and doctors would treat her injuries. He had to hunt her attacker. The guy could be anywhere in the hospital by now. He could be disguised, too. Maybe as a surgeon, orderly, one of the cleaning staff or a repairman.

Dammit. He'd been in the other room—if only he'd come in sooner, he might have caught the bastard.

SONYA'S LIFE flashed before her eyes as she stirred from unconsciousness. Her childhood. Her mother sewing dresses for her when she was a little girl. Her father teaching her to ride a bike. The Christmas picture of the three of them all in red and white.

The day he'd walked out and never come back.

Then meeting Stan. Falling hard and fast. Her wedding day when her mother had looked so sad. Their terrible fight.

The day she'd found out she was expecting a baby. Stan's shocking anger at the revelation. Her own excitement. The distance that had dawned between them after that day.

Then giving birth to Katie. The pain. The fear that she wouldn't make it. Then holding her precious little girl in her arms.

Tears trickled down her cheeks as she realized she'd almost died earlier and might have never seen Katie again.

"Sonya?"

She frowned and blinked through the fog coating her brain, then found Aaron Waverman staring down at her with concern. A nurse stood beside him, her head angled, studying her.

"How are you feeling?" Aaron asked.

"My head hurts," she said in a croaky voice.

"Chloroform. But you're going to be fine."

She nodded, and he wiped the tears from her cheeks with a tissue. "Are you hurting anywhere else?"

She shook her head.

"Did you see the person who attacked you?" the nurse asked.

Sonya gulped back a sob. "No, he grabbed me from behind."

The nurse frowned and checked the IV, and Sonya cleared her throat. "Where's Brack?"

Aaron's expression turned pinched. "He went to check with security. They're searching the hospital now." He squeezed her hands in his, and a sliver of unease tickled her spine.

"Don't worry, Sonya, I'll stay with you."

Sonya bit down on her lip, praying Brack would hurry. She didn't feel safe now, knowing that her attacker was on the loose. And she didn't like Aaron touching her, didn't want to give him the wrong idea.

Because the only man she wanted to be with right now, the only man she wanted to hold and comfort her, was Brack Falcon.

BRACK CONSULTED with the head security guard, who immediately issued a hospital alert and lockdown. Then he and the chief of security, Gladdon, searched several restricted corridors, service entrances and exits reserved for hospital staff.

Unfortunately they found nothing.

Finally Gladdon led Brack to their central surveillance room so they could view the security cameras. They studied the elevators and all entrances and exits, scrutinizing orderlies, doctors, nurses, delivery- and servicemen, along with paramedic teams and visitors. Unfortunately, no one stuck out as suspicious.

Damn.

"He had to leave the hospital some way," Brack said.

"He could have hidden inside a linen cart or under a gurney," another guard said as he viewed the tapes. "Or hell, maybe he climbed under a sheet and is pretending to be a dead body."

Brack froze, contemplating the possibility. "We didn't check all the body bags."

Gladdon ordered the guard to continue watching the tapes, then they hurried back to the morgue. First they checked the body receiving room, then the neighboring one where the bodies were stored after autopsies.

"They're transported from here to the funeral homes," Gladdon explained. He turned to Snyder. "Is there any other exit?"

"How about the vent system?" Brack asked.

The men glanced up, but the vents were bolted by thick screws. A possibility for escape, but all the screws were clearly still in place.

The medical examiner, Snyder, tugged at his glasses. "You know there used to be an underground exit in here," Snyder said. "It was installed as an escape route into the underground tunnels in case of a nuclear attack or leak of some kind."

"Where is it?" Brack asked.

Snyder motioned them to one end of the morgue room where he conducted the autopsies. In the corner, a metal grate covered the floor. Brack knelt and noticed that the bolts had been removed.

He silently cursed. "You're right. Look at his." He snapped the metal grate off. "The attacker used it to escape. Get me a flashlight. I'm going to crawl down and look around."

Snyder fidgeted. "The tunnels are supposedly haunted by the ghosts of those people who died from typhoid."

Brack grimaced. He'd heard the rumors. But he refused to let gossip keep him from chasing a killer. Especially the man who'd attacked Sonya.

Gladdon handed him a small flashlight and a two-way radio, and Brack lowered himself into the hole.

As he descended the metal stairs leading downward into the tunnels, acrid smells of wastes and sewage, along with odors of decay and blood, filled his nostrils. Brack sucked in a sharp breath, forcing himself to adjust to the vile odors, then canvassed the dark space with the flashlight. His senses honed, he paused to listen for sounds of footsteps, an animal, man, anything to alert him that the tunnel was occupied.

Nothing except the hollow echo of something pinging against stone. And maybe in the far recesses, a low moan.

Ghosts of the dead? Or was someone trapped down here? Maybe the killer had left another victim in the tunnel?

Fearing the worst, he strode through the narrow tunnel of steel and stone, padding slowly so as not to alert the killer of his presence if he'd hidden inside.

He followed the hallway about a mile, then noticed a walled-off section, as if someone had blasted the room closed. Perhaps to hide or trap the bodies of the dead the town spoke of.

Left or right? He wasn't sure which way to go. He listened and thought he detected a noise to the right, so he veered in that direction. The darkness was blinding, the odors suffocating, the small, narrow space claustrophobic.

Mice skittered through the black interior. The hiss of a snake. The pinging of water cascading down rock. He came to several more turnoffs and corners, other areas blasted shut, and realized that the tunnels were more intricate and far-reaching than he'd first thought. They comprised a maze of streets, virtually like a city underground. He also passed several rooms which held remnants of trash, food wrappers, ragged blankets and a metal barrel that looked as if it had been used for a fire. Some of the indigent and homeless must have discovered the rooms and had sought shelter in the tunnels. The people lived like moles....

An hour later, he had to face the fact that he'd lost the killer. He could be anywhere in the maze. Or already above ground. He'd discovered two—no, three—openings to the outside, all which dumped a person on the edge of the town into heavily wooded areas.

He turned to head back the other way when the flutter of wings caught his eye. Suddenly a bat dove toward him. He shined the light at it and managed to fend it off, then began to jog back through the labyrinth of dark tunnels, anxious to return to Sonya.

But a sound behind him jarred him, and he pivoted. Something slammed into the back of his head—the butt of a gun, maybe? He spit out a curse and sank to his knees, fighting to stay conscious as the world disappeared into darkness.

THREE HOURS had passed. Sonya stared at the clock on the hospital wall of the ER, her throat tight with worry. She'd been treated and had insisted that she was ready to go home.

But where was Brack?

He'd been gone way too long simply to have checked the hospital. Something had happened to him. Aaron Waverman had offered to drive her to his house for the night and take care of her. But she'd declined, certain Brack would return any moment. Certain they would leave the hospital together. She'd almost died, and she wanted to hold him, forget her reservations and kiss him tonight.

Maybe even more....

Tears pricked at the backs of her eyelids. What if

he was hurt? What if he needed her? What if she'd
made a mistake and lost a chance to be close to
someone who might really matter in her life? The
heat between them had been combustible, the need
she'd felt intense.

But she'd grown so accustomed to denying
herself any pleasure that she'd been a martyr in a
ridiculous attempt to protect herself.

Ironically, she'd fallen for him anyway.

She paced the small ER cubicle, her heart
thumping wildly. There, she'd admitted it. Finally
been honest with herself. She had feelings for Brack
Falcon. A brooding loner who related to the very
animals she'd first thought had attacked her.

The door creaked open and Brack suddenly
stumbled in. He looked bleary-eyed, disoriented,
and reeked of sewage and body stench. "Sonya?"

A nurse appeared and grabbed him on one side.
Sonya raced to him, and braced him with her arm
around his waist. "What happened?"

"I tracked him in the tunnels below the hospital.
But he hit me over the head with the butt of a gun."

"Here, sit down," Sonya ordered.

The nurse helped her guide him to an exam table.

"Get a doctor in here, stat!" Sonya cried.

The nurse rushed to call a doctor while she
coaxed Brack to lie down, then leaned over to
examine the back of his head. A deep, bloody gash
marked the back of his skull.

"You need stitches," she said quietly. She brushed a strand of his hair from his forehead and their gazes locked.

"Are you okay?" he asked.

She nodded. "And you're going to be fine, too, Brack, but you may have a concussion. Just relax, and let me do my job."

He grunted in pain or frustration, she wasn't sure, but did as she said.

Dr. Waverman rushed into the room, and her stomach knotted, but she followed his command as he administered meds, cleaned and stitched Brack's head wound.

How could she do anything else? After all, she had to trust him this time.

But for some reason, she sensed Aaron was less than happy at Brack's return.

He wouldn't have followed Brack into the tunnel and assaulted him because he sensed they were getting close, would he?

No, he had been in the ER. But then he had left for a while, and she hadn't seen him the last hour....

BRACK'S HEAD hurt like the devil, but his pride smarted even more. He couldn't believe this killer had gotten the drop on him once again. And now having Waverman treat him was like another slap in his face.

Sonya squeezed his hand as Waverman focused on the last stitch, and he pressed her hand to his thigh, feeling connected in a way that made his chest tighten. He'd been pissed when he'd regained consciousness in that tunnel, but his fear for Sonya had forced him to drag himself up and slog the mile back to the hospital.

Dr. Waverman finished the last suture. "You should spend the night, let us watch you for a concussion."

"No way." Brack dropped his feet to the floor and stood, determined to prove he'd regained control.

Sonya gripped him by the arm. "Brack, maybe you should listen."

He angled his head toward her. "No. But if you need to rest, I'll stay here and guard your door."

"I'm fine," Sonya insisted.

Waverman made a disgusted sound. Sonya thanked him, and the tension thickened as she assisted Brack out the door. "You didn't get a look at him?" Sonya asked as they wove their way to his SUV.

"No. It was too dark." He pulled away and unlocked the door, but she insisted on driving again. He didn't argue. His head was still swimming, and he felt disoriented from the meds.

Inside, the vehicle seemed small and steamy as she cranked up the heater and guided the SUV from the hospital parking lot.

"What did you find underground?" Sonya asked.

"A whole series of tunnels." Brack leaned against the back of the seat. "They're spread underground like a small city. Some areas have been blasted shut. I'm assuming that's where those bodies were buried years ago. And there were a couple of areas where it appears that the homeless have taken up residence."

Sonya gaped at him. "Maybe the sounds we've heard aren't ghosts but people walking around down there."

"It's possible. I found a couple of openings leading above ground, too. They dump you out at the edge of wooded areas."

"You think this guy probably escaped through one of those?"

Brack nodded. "Stop by your house and pack some things, Sonya. You're staying with me until we catch this guy."

The fact that she didn't argue made him realize she must be truly scared this time. She should be. This psycho had come too close to killing them both.

Anger surged through Brack at the thought.

The tires churned on the icy asphalt but Sonya managed the turns with ease, then parked in front of her house. He checked the exterior, then strode inside and scoped out the house before he allowed her entry. She rushed inside and packed a bag, and within minutes, they arrived at Falcon Ridge.

Knowing she had been attacked earlier made him hyperaware of his surroundings, and he scanned the perimeter of Falcon Ridge as he climbed from the SUV. Thankful for the state-of-the-art security system Rex had installed, he opened the door and they entered together.

He built a fire, then turned to her, the fear he'd experienced when he'd first found her on the floor of the morgue clawing at his sanity. But he couldn't touch her. He smelled like sewage and sweat and blood. "I'm going to clean up. If you want to do the same, you can use the extra room where you stayed the other night." He removed the key from the hook on the wall and laid it on the table between them. The last time he'd done so, she'd locked the door, shutting him out.

She stared at it for a long minute, then left it lying on the table and walked up the stairs. He watched her, his heart pumping wildly at the realization that she trusted him now.

But what would she say if he came to her bedroom? Would she welcome his touch? Would she turn him away?

His body knotted with turmoil, he stripped, climbed into the shower and scrubbed his body, careful of the fresh stitches, then stood and let the hot water beat away the tension throbbing through him. The adrenaline that had driven him through the tunnel until he found Sonya safe in the hospital had waned, and in its place desire for her simmered below the surface.

Temptation ripped at his nerve endings. She had left the key on the table. He'd seen a second of hunger flare in her eyes. Would she let him love her tonight?

He closed his eyes and envisioned her standing next to him. Saw her naked body with water cascading over her curves. The subtle play of light and shadow dancing off her soft skin. His body hardened and pulsed with need.

He wanted her so badly he physically ached. Wanted to hold her and love her and make her his in every way.

"Brack?"

He jerked his eyes open. Through the frosted shower door, he saw her standing inside the bathroom doorway. She wore a long silky robe, and her hair lay in loose waves around her shoulders. God...she was so damn sexy. "Sonya?"

"I was worried about you," she said softly. "You've been in here a long time."

His tongue felt too thick to talk. Desire raged inside his blood as he contemplated dragging her into the shower with him.

It took every ounce of his willpower to resist.

He rinsed the soap from his body, then grabbed a towel and dried off quickly. Willing himself to move with caution, he wrapped the towel around his waist, then stepped onto the bath mat. Unfortunately, he inhaled her scent, and his sex thickened and jutted below the towel.

He tensed, hoping he wouldn't frighten her with his obvious desire, but they both might have died tonight and he desperately wanted to touch her.

NERVES PINGED inside Sonya as Brack stepped from the shower. Water droplets clung to his dark hair, and the moisture glistening on his chest painted his bronzed skin in a golden glow. His eyes skated over her, and beneath her thin robe her body responded as if he'd touched her with his bare hands. He was so tall, imposing, darkly handsome—irresistible.

He wanted her, too. Raw hunger and heat darkened his eyes, and his arousal pulsed thick and big beneath the towel. Her nipples budded to stiff peaks, begging for his touch. His mouth. Warmth pooled in her belly, and her legs wobbled as if they might buckle. She'd never craved a man as she did him.

"Sonya?" He stalked toward her, dragged her into his arms, and molded her mouth to his.

She sank against him, gripped his bare arms with shaky fingers and opened to him, savoring the potent hunger firing his kiss.

He tasted like man, wild and primitive, solid and comforting, bold yet tender. He ran his fingers through her hair, then lower over her shoulders, then he slid one palm over her breast. She whimpered and clung to him, a desperate need building inside her as he traced a finger over her aching nipple. His low moan stirred her passion, and she raked her hands over his broad back, pulling him closer, urging him to take more. He groaned and slid the robe down her shoulders then let it fall into a puddle at her feet. His hands roamed over her back, her waist. Then he cupped her hips and pulled her into him so his erection brushed her thighs. Erotic sensations zinged through her, mind-numbing and exhilarating. He felt thick, hard, strong, powerful, needy. She wanted him inside her.

She made a low catlike sound, and he thumbed her other nipple, running his fingers over it until she threw her head back and practically begged him to taste her. He pressed featherlight kisses along her throat, then nipped at her sensitive flesh as he pushed her gown down her shoulders. Aching for him, she thrust herself forward, pulling him closer, and he licked his way down her torso, lowered his head and closed his mouth over one turgid nipple.

She clung to him, her legs weak, her body on fire as he suckled first one breast, then the other. Licking, tasting, pulling her into his mouth as if he savored her pleasure. She whispered his name in a throaty voice that didn't sound like her own, thought she might explode from the heady sensations rippling through her.

She wanted to touch him, too, but he angled her sideways, and her reflection caught in the mirror. The talon marks still looked red and puckered, the ugly scars reminding her that she was less than perfect. That she had not been enough woman to satisfy her former husband.

Then the vile face of the comic Talon Terror flashed behind her eyes, and terror streaked through her. Brack had almost died tonight because of her. Another girl and Reesie had already lost their lives.

She pulled away, looked into Brack's eyes. Heat, hunger, and questions flared in his gaze as he studied her. He was the most perfect male specimen she'd ever seen. Like a god among men, a hero in her eyes. She didn't want to disappoint him, didn't want him to see her many flaws.

Didn't want to care so much. To know that if he hadn't returned tonight, she'd never forgive herself. That she would have fallen apart.

Because she was falling in love with him.

The terror that had seized her during her earlier attack, and the helplessness she'd experienced when her husband left her, rushed back, and she pulled away, grabbed her robe and fled to the other room.

She was a coward. She knew it. But she closed the door to the extra bedroom, afraid to go back.

SONYA SILVERSTEIN'S face haunted him.

He sharpened his talons, his blood sizzling with thoughts of making her his mate. He had been so close to having her tonight. A minute longer and he could have escaped with her. Carried her through the tunnels. Into the darkness below. Back to the land where he belonged. Where he'd first learned to love the hunt. To give chase. To take whatever he wanted as his.

But he'd missed his opportunity tonight.

And now he had to settle for another.

The dark cape shrouded his face, the night sounds of the traffic in the distance fading as he combed the edges of the forest park. Even during winter, the running path stayed busy during the day. But at night, it was virtually empty.

Yet tonight, one lone jogger circled the park. One woman who thought herself completely alone.

He'd watched her before. She was long and lean. A woman with no fear of the dark. A blonde with a body to die for.

And no fear of the Talon Terror who'd already terrorized and murdered two women.

A chuckle rumbled from his belly.

Fool.

Dressed in her designer running clothes, her iPod earphones jammed in her ears, she pumped her legs and arms, threw her head up into the wind, and sang along with her iTunes. The wind tossed her blond ponytail back and forth as her running shoes pounded the salted asphalt.

She thought she was invincible. That her speed, her long legs and lithe body could outrun a man.

She hadn't met a raptor before. Had no idea that

his agility far exceeded her puny efforts. He'd trained for the hunt well. Had honed his skills for years. Knew exactly how long to stalk, then when to swoop down for the kill.

He crept into the shadows to watch her circle around and around the track. She usually ran about forty laps. About the tenth one, she would become exhilarated. By the twentieth, she'd start to grow winded. By the thirtieth, she'd be so lost in thought she wouldn't notice that her stride was growing shorter. By the fortieth, her heart would be racing, her muscles straining, her energy waning.

Then he would pounce.

Chapter Sixteen

Naked, hard, still wanting Sonya, Brack leaned forward and braced both hands on the bathroom sink. He inhaled several calming breaths in an effort to control his turbulent emotions.

What the hell had just happened?

One minute Sonya had been whispering his name, moaning in pleasure, and the next minute she'd run. What had he done wrong?

His last girlfriend's caustic words about him being an animal reverberated in his head. Dammit, was that what Sonya thought? Had he frightened her with his intense desire?

He'd noticed the shimmer of tears in her eyes before she'd disappeared from the room.

He yanked on a pair of sweats and strode down the hall. He should leave her alone for the night. Let her sleep. Get some rest himself.

But an ache to understand her drove him forward anyway. He knocked on the door, preparing himself in case she told him to go away. "Sonya, can I come in?" He cleared his throat. "Please."

A strained heartbeat passed before she answered the door. When she opened it, darkness cloaked the room, but tears lingered on her cheeks. "I'm sorry, Brack."

He narrowed his eyes, his gut clenching. "Sorry for what?"

"F-for leading you on like that." She bit down on her lip. "I...shouldn't have started that, then run out."

"I don't understand." Emotions thickened his voice. Emotions he hated to reveal, but he'd felt such a strong connection to her that he couldn't help himself. And he'd thought she'd felt it, too. He reached out, gently brushed her cheek with the pad of his thumb. "What did I do wrong?"

Surprise flickered in her eyes, then regret, and he dropped his hand, thinking his touch repulsed her.

"You didn't do anything wrong," she said in a hoarse whisper. She turned away, walked across the room, stared out the window at the woods beyond through the sheer curtain. "It's me."

He finally released the breath he'd been holding, then followed her and stood behind her. She was so close. His hands shook with the effort not to touch her. "What do you mean? If you changed your mind, if I was too rough, tell me."

"No. God, no." She dropped her head forward, pain lacing her voice. "It's me, Brack. Old insecurities." Her voice broke. "I would only disappoint you."

Anger slammed into him. But he fought it and gently placed his hands on her arms. "What makes you think a foolish thing like that?"

"My ex…"

"You still love him?" Brack's heart pounded as he waited on her response.

"No." She turned around, vulnerability shadowing her eyes, sending his heart into a tailspin.

"I don't love him anymore, Brack. Not at all. But he said things…" She let the words trail off, and the truth dawned on him. The bastard had hurt her, had made her feel as if she were at fault.

He wanted to tear him apart limb by limb.

But a display of his temper would only send her running again, and prove Erica right. And when he made love to Sonya, he wanted her to know he could be gentle. Loving. Caring.

He also wanted to erase any lingering memory of her former husband from her mind.

Tamping down his rage, he lifted his hand and brushed his fingers across the side of her cheek. "Sonya, I want you so bad it hurts. There's no way on earth you could disappoint me. And if, when, we decide to go further, you can stop at any time. I would never force you."

Her lips parted, and she sighed, a soft, needy sound that ignited fire in his blood. But fear darkened her eyes again, and he warned himself to hold back. He had to go slow. Earn her trust.

Sonya needed time. And they had both been physically hurt today. She must be exhausted.

"It's been a long day," he said in a low voice. "You've been through a lot. And I won't push you or do anything until you're ready."

She pressed her hand over his. "You have a concussion, you were hurt because of me, Brack. You could have d-died."

Emotions warbled in her voice. He was patient with the birds he trained when they were injured. He could be patient with the woman he cared for, too.

The thought made him momentarily stiffen, tempted him to flee into the woods again. To find his solace. Be alone.

But he didn't want to be alone tonight. He didn't think Sonya did, either.

He laced his hand through hers. "Come on, lie down, Sonya." Tenderness underscored his words. "You need to rest and so do I."

Questions registered on her face. Uncertainty. Desire.

He felt them all inside him, too.

"I just want to hold you," he said softly. "We'll sleep in each other's arms. Nothing more."

A smile slowly tilted the corner of her mouth, and she nodded, then let him lead her to bed.

SONYA CURLED into Brack's arms and savored the feel of his strong, big body pressed up to hers. He was the most masculine man she'd ever met. And although she knew people in town feared him, she trusted him with her life.

But her heart?

What would he think if he knew that she was falling in love with him? That she hadn't only held back from making love to him because of her insecurities about her scars, but because once she gave herself completely to him, her heart would belong to him as well.

You're kidding yourself, a tiny voice whispered inside her head. *He already stole your heart.*

But would he want it? Brack liked his freedom. The woods. He would travel around in his job. And Katie needed security in her life. Not for Sonya to parade men through their life, men that would never stay and be a part of their tight-knit family.

He tightened his arms around her, and she forgot her reservations and fell asleep in his arms. At least tonight, she would let him chase her nightmares away.

And when she closed her eyes, she could pretend that they had a future.

SONYA HAD THOUGHT that sleeping with Brack would create an awkward morning, but instead, she felt an intimacy with him that she'd never felt with

Stan. They'd crossed some invisible barrier of trust, had given silent voice to their need for closeness and, in the darkness of the night, had managed to become more intimate even without the physical act of sex.

But as they sipped their morning coffee, the telephone trilled, dispelling the cozy domestic atmosphere. Seconds later, Brack disconnected the call, the haunted expression darkening his face again.

"Another woman was killed last night."

Sonya's heart fell. "Who was it?"

"A jogger named Sue Peterson." He scrubbed a hand over the back of his neck. "He left a note this time, Sonya."

Her heartbeat accelerated. "What kind of note?"

"Cohen said it was addressed to you."

"Dear God." She lowered her head into her hands, and he cradled her in his arms. A shudder tore through her. "He wants me to know he killed her because he missed his opportunity with me."

Brack pressed his head against the top of hers and nodded. "I'm afraid so."

Tears caught in her throat. "This has to stop, Brack. I don't know how much more I can take."

"Shh." He stroked her back gently. "Don't worry. It is going to end, Sonya. I'm going to find this guy and take him down myself."

A HALF HOUR LATER, Brack and Sonya met Cohen at the crime scene. Brack stared at the note the killer had left on the mangled girl's body in disgust. Sonya shuddered in horror next to him as she read the message.

> You made me do it, Sonya.
> You can stop me any time.
> All you have to do is be mine.

"Do you have any idea who's doing this?" Sheriff Cohen asked.

Sonya shook her head, her voice filled with remorse. "No. I wish I did."

"Did you get that search warrant for Jameson Viago's place?" Brack asked.

Cohen nodded. "I'm on my way there next."

"I want to go with you," Brack said.

Cohen surprised him with a nod. "All right, I can use your help. This maniac is terrorizing the town. Half the citizens won't even come out of their houses now. And that guy, Tripp, is adding to the problems."

"Does he have an alibi for last night?" Brack asked.

"I don't know yet. I'm going to pick him up for questioning." Cohen headed to his car and Brack followed, leading Sonya by the hand.

Tension filled the SUV as they drove in silence to Viago's place. When they arrived, Brack let Cohen lead the way up to the man's door. Brack contemplated insisting that Sonya stay in the car, but he wanted to see Viago's reaction to her, and she insisted she could handle the situation.

Viago answered, rumpled and half asleep, once again clad in all black. His hair was uncombed, his beard fuller, his eyes gluey as if he was high on drugs. Oddly, he merely stared at Sonya with no reaction at all.

"Mr. Viago, can you tell me where you were last night around midnight?" Sheriff Cohen asked.

Viago's eyes shifted to the bedroom, then his computer. "I was here. Working. Then I went to bed."

"Can anyone verify your whereabouts?" Cohen asked.

Viago flipped his computer around and indicated the time log. "I was working on updates for my Web site. See for yourself."

Cohen gestured toward Brack, and he studied the man's files. It looked legit. Unless someone else had logged in as him and completed the updates…

"I have a search warrant for your house and the contents of your fan mail and Web site." Cohen stuffed the paper into the man's hands.

Viago clawed his hand through his hair. "Listen, like I told Falcon here, I only write this cartoon. I'm not your guy."

Brack pointed to the overloaded box of fan mail. "Then it's possible that one of your fans could be. Maybe the answers are in there."

Sonya's face paled at the sight of the devil-worshiping posters and dozens of macabre photos of the falcons. Viago protested again, and Cohen snarled that he'd lock him up for impeding an investigation if he didn't cooperate, and the man shut up.

Brack and Cohen uncovered several science fiction magazines, some with violence as themes, other sci-fi memorabilia that he'd collected, a sword that he'd bought off eBay from a movie set, photos of old classics including *Dracula* and several low-budget horror flicks, as well as replicas of two falcons that had died and been preserved. Granted, the guy had some sick obsessions, but they didn't find containers of talons or a costume or trophies from any of the victims. Neither did he find any photos of Sonya that would fit a stalker's profile.

Brack checked the man's e-mails while Cohen and Sonya started skimming through fan mail.

"What are we looking for?" Cohen asked.

"Anything strange," Brack said.

"They're all strange," Cohen said in disgust as he gestured toward one letter. "They talk about raping and slaughtering women, loving the way the bird kills."

"He's right," Sonya said, a strained look on her pale face. "But this guy probably wrote Viago to brag about his actions. He would have wanted Viago to know he was the real Talon Terror."

"We need to take them back to the station. I'll have my deputy help us," Cohen said.

Viago stared glumly from his sofa, drumming his pen on a sketchpad as if he was contemplating his work. Brack wondered if he was planning his next story, but noticed a sketched outline of his next issue on the computer and frowned.

In this episode, two falcons had chosen the same mate. As the story line progressed, they engaged in a horrific battle for the female, a battle that ended in one falcon's death. The other won the mate.

The face on the dead bird looked strikingly like Brack.

SONYA'S STOMACH roiled at the violence in the letters. This sadistic cartoon character had drawn millions of fans. The ages of the kids writing in disturbed her even more. Adolescents in their early and late teens and twenties comprised the fan base list. Kids at impressionable ages who should be focusing on school, on healthier choices like church or sports or volunteer work.

The town desperately needed Elsie's teen center. She silently vowed to volunteer there as much as possible.

She skimmed several crude letters from girls who fantasized about romance with this terrorizing hawk. What kinds of abnormal relationships had these girls witnessed? Were they in abusive homes now? If not, they might be headed for relationships that were doomed to fail.

Reminders of her own divorce taunted her. Sighing, she glanced up and caught Brack watching her, concern on his face, and her heart fluttered. He'd been nothing but kind, protective, gentle, patient. He hadn't asked for anything in return.

She was completely in love with him at this point. There was no turning back. No guarding her heart or denying her feelings.

But she couldn't demand commitment from a man who thrived on his freedom.

Another letter caught her eyes, this one dotted in a dark red substance that resembled blood. With a rubber glove, she picked up the letter, then began to read.

Thank you for your amazing creature The Talon Terror. I knew when I was small that I was different. That I was an animal in another life.

When I read the stalking techniques of the Talon Terror, I recognized them as my own. My bloodlust runs thick, my need to feed on the creatures of the forest stronger each day. And now human blood has wet my lips, I realize that I was meant to prey on the weakest of them—the females.

I have chosen one as my mate. I will have her soon.

Until then, I stalk my prey, swoop in and snatch up the creatures with my sharp talons and rip them apart as you do.

Sonya cleared her throat and stood. "This may be our guy. He even signs the letter with bloody talon prints."

Brack placed a hand at the back of her waist in a soothing gesture. "Let's get it to a lab for analysis. If we can match the writing, fingerprints, blood with our killer and put a name to him, we can catch him and end this terror."

THE NEXT TWO DAYS passed in excruciating slowness. Brack checked constantly on the lab analysis but DNA testing took time. So did the writing analysis. They had located a costume shop online and were checking into the client base but so far nothing had popped up.

He urged Cohen to collect samples from Stan Silverstein, Viago, Tripp, Dr. Waverman, Dr. Priestly and Priestly's assistant, along with the paramedics, Van and Joey, who worked with Sonya. He'd made enemies of all of them, but he didn't care.

Each night he slept beside Sonya, but he didn't push for more. Although it was growing more difficult not to strip her out of her clothes and make love to her. But he was determined not to press her. To wait until she came to him. Until she wanted him as much as he wanted her.

Against his better judgment, she had worked the past two days, but she'd never worked alone. Unfortunately, two more women had been killed. Both on her shifts.

She had taken the 911 calls. The sicko was taunting her. Playing with her mind. Torturing her with guilt. Forcing her to view his brutality firsthand, to be the first one to witness the evidence of his sick, twisted desires.

His plan was working, too. He saw the pain in Sonya's eyes and her agony became his own. He hated the Talon Terror more with each vicious attack.

Sonya was out on call now, this time working with Van. So far, the man had proven himself clean. His writing didn't match the sample from the letter, and he had no history of violence, had never hunted or shot a rifle, didn't own a gun, and had a wife and two-year-old at home.

Brack would never forgive himself if he'd misjudged the guy and he turned out to be their culprit.

Godfrey met him at the edge of the woods, and they combed the property between Falcon Ridge and Sonya's farmhouse. "Someone has been poisoning small animals through food they've put out. He also sprinkled chemicals on the plants to poison them."

"Can we get a cleanup crew in?" Brack asked.

"Sure, but we have to find out who's causing the damage before the wildlife will be safe again."

The thought of losing the falcons, of them dying

and becoming extinct in the area, cut like a knife to Brack's chest.

Brack spent the next two hours scouring the woods, searching for injured animals, for the villain poisoning them and using them as bait to trap the falcons. Finally feeling defeated and frustrated, he headed back to Falcon Ridge. Knowing Sonya would return from work any minute, he showered and lit a fire in the fireplace, then went outside to check on the hawk he'd rescued the day before.

But the cage was open, and the bird was dead on the ground, its guts spilled across the patio. The killer had left a message for him.

He bowed his head and leaned against the table, hands bracing himself as emotions churned through him. Dammit, he felt like a failure. He'd let the birds down. And Sonya and all those other women…

"Brack?"

He pinched the bridge of his nose, battling the pain in his chest. Aching to hold Sonya and soothe his guilt.

Sonya moved up behind him, and gasped at the mauled bird. "Oh, God, Brack, I'm so sorry."

Fear and pain laced her voice. He swallowed back emotions, turned and pulled her into the kitchen away from the sight.

Inside, he blinked to clear his vision, then looked into her eyes.

Her tormented expression humbled him. He traced a finger along her cheek, and something else flickered... raw, hot desire.

"Brack..."

His sex hardened, and his body trembled with need at the sound of her sultry voice.

He shook his head. Realized his emotions, his hunger must be written on his face. He hated his loss of control. All the reasons he shouldn't kiss her warred with the intense need to have her.

She wasn't ready. She was vulnerable. She was afraid.

And he could not commit.

He strode past her and moved to the cabinet. For the first time in weeks, allowed himself to use something to assuage his pain. Even if it was a scotch.

He tossed down the drink, then poured another. The trickle of the amber liquid filling the glass shattered the silence. Wood crackled in the air as the fire popped.

Suddenly, Sonya's breath bathed his neck. He felt her hand slide over his. Remove the glass from his hand.

"You don't need that," she whispered. Her hands trailed to his shoulders where she began to massage the tension from his neck. He leaned his head forward, moaned out her name. Turmoil riddled the sound.

She pressed a kiss to his back, then reached around him and began to unbutton his shirt. The sound of the buttons being unfastened sent his pulse racing. He wanted to feel her hands on his bare skin. Wanted to touch her and hold her and sink himself deep inside her, to know she was his now, and that she would be in the end.

Her lips touched his bare neck as she lowered his shirt and pulled it off. His shoulders stiffened again. He wanted her so much that he dared not ask.

"Sonya…" His voice cracked. "I can't take much more."

She traced her fingers over his back, then kissed his shoulders, and he snapped. He swung around, yanked her hands away from his burning body, held them at her sides. Passion glazed her eyes, the need in his own burning hot and bright, like dry kindling beneath a lit match.

"I told you I can't take much more tonight." He choked out the warning, knowing he had to while he still possessed some semblance of control.

"I don't want to lose the birds, Sonya, and I don't want to lose you."

He hesitated, had to give her the choice, even if it would be agony right now if she walked away. "And if that means waiting until you're ready, then we wait."

Chapter Seventeen

"I want you, Brack," she whispered. "Right here, right now."

"Sonya?"

His gruff whisper heated her blood, incited her courage. He was hurting, and she wanted to soothe his pain. He had done everything for her so far and had asked nothing in return. He'd held her each night. Comforted her when she needed it. Talked to Katie and assured her that her mother was safe. Kept her company when she missed her little girl.

The day's events traipsed through her mind. Another woman dead. Another note. More blood on her hands.

She couldn't think about it tonight. Had to find some pleasure in being alive.

"Please, Brack. I need you." She trailed her fingers over his bare chest, felt his muscles flex beneath her fingertips. His skin felt hot to the touch, rough yet soft, just like Brack. She loved him more than words could say.

Her lips followed her fingers, and she pressed kisses along his chest, then his neck. With a soft sigh, she threaded her hands into his hair and drew his mouth down to hers. He tasted like fire and man and raging desire.

His low, throaty moan of acquiescence spurred her forward. Firelight flickered off his bronzed, corded, muscular chest as he pulled slightly away and gazed into her eyes.

"You are beautiful," he whispered.

"Brack—"

"Shh, you're perfect."

Her stomach tightened, but he lowered his mouth and kissed her again, this time so deeply that warmth pooled in her belly. For the first time in her life, she believed that she *was* beautiful, perfect.

But only in his arms.

His tongue swirled over her lips, begging for her to part them, and she did, allowing him entry and welcoming him inside. Her body screamed for more. She sucked his tongue into her mouth, met his passionate response with one of her own. Ran her hands over his nipples, then down his arms to his waist, and yanked at his belt buckle.

He shed it in one deft movement. Flung it to the floor. His pants and boots went next. She wanted him naked in the firelight.

She didn't realize she'd said the request aloud, until his eyebrows lifted. Then he complied with a smile. He looked so starkly beautiful, his tall, broad body glowing in the dancing flames. Dark black hair covered his chest and tapered to a *V* southward to his sex, which surged thick and long, jutting toward her as if begging to be inside her.

She reached out and wrapped her hand around him, and he groaned and tore at her clothes. Tenderness underlay his touches, yet a raw hunger that drove them both into a frenzy urged her to forget caution. They both needed this wild animal coupling, needed to touch and hold and stroke and pet and suckle.

He stripped her bare, then held her arms to her sides when she shied away.

"Please let me look," he whispered. "You can't imagine how many nights I've dreamed about this."

She smiled, his words eliciting a heady lightness in her soul. Her heart surged with love. She raked her hands over his chest again, and he lowered his head and claimed her lips again, thrusting his tongue in and out of her mouth in erotic strokes that heated her blood to a boil. His lips moved to her breasts, and he cupped her into his hands, flicked his fingers over her nipples, tortured her with his tongue. His hands dipped lower to tease her legs apart.

Any trace of shyness fled as he lay her down on

the rug in front of the fire, dipped his fingers inside her and sucked her nipples until she cried out as sensations splintered through her. He sheathed himself with a condom, then his thick erection replaced his hand and he stroked her center until she begged him to enter her.

Instead of thrusting inside her though, he cupped her face in his hands. Sweat-soaked skin rasped against skin. "Sonya, I want you now. All of you."

"I want you, too," she whispered. "I love you, Brack."

For a moment, his gaze locked with hers. Emotions flickered in his eyes, dark ones, troubled ones. Then a smile softened his mouth, and he thrust himself inside her. He stretched her, filled her with his length until she thought she might break apart.

A low, throaty moan tore from his chest, and he rose above her and whispered for her to watch. She glanced down and saw the two of them connect, watched as he drew in and out of her body, saw the raw hunger in his eyes as he loved her. They sank into a heated rhythm, bold, passionate, taking, giving, each movement of his hips, each bold, deep thrust building lightning-like sensations inside her.

When she thought she couldn't stand the pleasure any longer, he lowered his head and pulled her nipple between his teeth, sucked it deep and hard. Euphoria crashed through her with waves of pleasure that sent her free-falling over the edge. He caught her cry of ecstasy with another powerful kiss.

She clung to his arms, sensations splintering through her, as he moved deeper and faster, harder, with such force that her body trembled. Tremors of excitement rocked through her, and she spread her legs wider, wanting him as far inside her as he could get. Seconds later, he threw his head back, pushed himself even deeper, lifted her hips and angled her so that he touched her very soul.

Then he roared out a sound of pleasure as his own release ripped through him.

THEY MADE LOVE again and again during the night. Each time more primal. Raw. Passionate.

Brack had no idea how he had lived without Sonya before, but he never wanted to do so again. She was everything he'd ever wanted in a woman. Loving. Kind. Strong. Courageous.

A generous and sensational lover.

She gave, but she took. Offered herself to him without holding back. And he did the same. Found himself licking and tasting between her legs. Loving the feel of her sweet release on his lips.

And groveling when she took him in her mouth.

She humbled him. Made him feel things he'd never thought he'd feel.

Made him want to confess his love and whisper promises in the dark.

But something held him back.

She had said she loved him. The first time he'd taken her on the floor. And then numerous times in the bed since.

If only he had the courage to do the same.

But a killer still roamed Tin City. Destroying the wildlife. Killing innocent women.

And the killer wanted Sonya.

His arms tightened around her as she curled against his chest. He couldn't let this sicko take her from him. Not now when he'd just found her.

SONYA'S CELL PHONE trilled, jarring her from a deep sleep. She stirred, not wanting to leave the contentment and warmth of Brack's arms. But what if the call was about Katie?

She pushed her hair from her eyes, kissed him on the forehead, and retrieved her phone from the nightstand. Brack rolled over and threw his hand over his eyes, watching her, his hooded look of desire stirring her senses to life again.

She checked the caller log. Stan? She started not to answer, but panic clutched her. What if something had happened to her daughter, and for some reason he was calling to tell her?

"Hello."

"Sonya, I'm sorry to call you so early."

"What is it, Stan?"

Brack sat up and leaned against the headboard,

and she reached for her robe. Naked, she felt exposed. But Brack grabbed it and pushed it out of her reach, then folded his arms, leaned against the headboard and watched her beneath hooded eyes.

"I need to see you," he said. "There's something I have to tell you. About us."

"Stan…" She bit down on her lip. Did not want to have this conversation with Brack in the room, especially with him in her bed, with the scent of his lovemaking lingering on her skin. "I can't talk now."

"Then meet me later." His voice sounded troubled, emotional. Not like Stan. Or maybe it was—like the man she'd first met, the caring one she'd married.

"Please. It's important."

"Is this about Katie?" she asked. "She's at my mother's. You haven't heard from her, have you?"

"No, I haven't talked to her. But… Sonya, you have to see me. I…I made a mistake. I have to talk to you."

She reluctantly agreed, then hung up, curious as to what Stan could possibly want to say to her.

"What was that all about?" Brack asked quietly. The brooding, intense look hardened his eyes again. He had loved every inch of her during the night, and she had returned the favor. She'd even whispered her love in the dark. Now as daylight slipped through, she questioned her openness. Had she spoken too soon? Sounded too needy?

"I don't know," she said honestly. "He said he

wants to meet me, that we have to talk. That he made a mistake."

A muscle twitched in his jaw, but she couldn't read the expression in his eyes. "Are you going to see him?"

The question hung in the air while she considered her answer. She wanted Brack to say something, tell her that he didn't want her talking to her ex. That he loved her and wanted her to be with him.

"It's all right, Sonya," he said, his voice brittle. "You were married to him. You don't owe me anything just because we slept together."

His cold tone felt like a slap in her face. She grabbed her robe and slid it on, hugged her arms around her, suddenly feeling chilled and alone. She'd given him her heart and body, yet he didn't care if she went from his bed to see her ex?

And what did Stan want? He'd sounded so odd. Emotional. Like he had when they'd first met. When she'd thought he was a loving, kind man. Before she'd gotten pregnant.

He couldn't possibly want a reconciliation, could he? And if he did, what would she tell him?

BRACK CLIMBED from the bed and strode from the room, trying desperately to bottle up the jealousy that had shattered his euphoria. This could not be happening. He'd finally given in to his need for Sonya. Finally earned her trust.

Finally allowed himself to feel for a woman again.

And now what? Did her ex want her back?

He was Katie's father. Katie needed her dad. And Sonya might have whispered her love to him last night in the throes of passion, but in daylight, how would she feel? Would she realize that she had no future with a man like Brack? A man half the town scorned?

A man who couldn't commit to her now and had vowed no promises to her while he'd made love to her during the night.

Self-loathing filled him, and he went to his room, yanked on jeans, a shirt, socks and boots, and strode outside. The alarm was set. Sonya would be safe.

He needed to be alone for a few minutes. Commune with the wild.

Taste freedom again.

Decide if he could possibly fight Sonya's ex for her hand.

He jogged to the edge of the woods, then searched the perimeter. Daylight streaked the sky, although the mottled gray clouds still hung heavy and thick. Just like his mood.

Daylight brought reality. Sonya had only fallen in bed with him because she was afraid. She'd been terrorized.

Today she might realize that her future lay with the man she'd loved enough to marry. To share a child with.

And he wasn't that man.

Emotions churned through him, edgy and painful,

as he jogged into the woods. One mile. Two. Three. Four. He needed to get away. Needed to find his solace the only place that calmed him.

Hell, he thought he'd found it last night in Sonya's arms.

But he should have known that it had simply been an illusion brought on by lust and a primal need on both their parts.

That the Talon Terror had driven Sonya into his arms. Nothing more.

And now her ex-husband had called, she might go running back to him.

SONYA PACED the bedroom, her body aching for Brack, her heart breaking from knowing that he'd left her with no word about when he'd return.

And with the feeling that he didn't care if she reconciled with Stan if he asked.

She swiped at the tears streaking her cheeks, struggling over what to do. She couldn't beg Brack to love her, but she couldn't go back to Stan even if he did want a reconciliation.

And he might not. Maybe he'd phoned for another reason. Maybe he simply wanted to forge a relationship with his daughter. She couldn't deny him or Katie that.

The phone on the nightstand trilled again, and she raced to it and snatched it up. Her mother's number. "Mom?"

"Sonya…" Her mother's voice broke, a sob escaping. "Honey, it's Katie…she's gone!"

"What?" Cold terror seized Sonya, and she squeezed the phone between clenched fingers. "What do you mean, *gone?*"

"It was dark, and he came in the window and attacked me," she sobbed. "He knocked me out and took Katie! Oh, baby, I called the police and they're on their way now!"

Sonya slid down onto the bed, trembling from the inside out. "Mom, did you see the person who attacked you?"

"No…I'm so sorry, honey, Oh, God, Katie… she's out there with him. No telling what he might do.…"

Her mother sounded hysterical. "Mom, are you alone? Did you call someone?"

"The EMT just arrived."

"Good, have them check you out. Then phone a friend to stay with you. I don't want you to be alone."

"But the police—"

"Give them my number. I'm going to hang up, Mom. This guy wants me. He probably took Katie to lure me to him."

At least that was what she hoped.

She disconnected the call, then threw off her robe and dragged on clothes. Jeans. A sweater. Socks. Her heart raced. Where were her boots?

And where was Brack?

The phone trilled a second later, and she knew who it would be before she answered. She snatched the phone. "Hello."

"I have your daughter."

"Listen to me, you hurt one hair on her head, I'll rip out your throat."

A nasty chuckle rumbled over the line, then a wheezed-out breath. Next came his muffled voice. "You're the one who should listen. If you want to see your daughter again, then you'll do as I say."

"Anything," Sonya whispered. Terrified and desperate, she dropped her head into her hands.

"You have to come alone. You tell anyone, you bring that Falcon man, and you'll never see your little girl again."

Tears poured down her face, nearly choking her, but she gulped them back and summoned her courage.

Katie needed her, and she couldn't let her down.

Time for her to put an end to this terror and the deaths.

"Just tell me where to meet you, and I'll be there alone." She took a deep breath and pushed to her feet, then reached inside the nightstand and grabbed Brack's gun. "If you release Katie and she's safe, I'm all yours."

A BAD PREMONITION hit Brack in the gut, and he turned and saw a falcon soaring over the ridge near

Sonya's house. Two more hawks took flight, gliding toward Falcon Ridge.

A good three miles away from the house now, he broke into a jog. He had to get back. Check on Sonya. Apologize for leaving her bed like a jealous lover.

What the hell had he been thinking? He'd left Sonya alone and a killer was out here. Although Falcon Ridge's security was top-notch, any security could be breached.

Dammit. He'd let his emotions get the better of him and hadn't been thinking rationally. No, he'd been thinking about Sonya's touch on his body and the memory of their lovemaking on his skin, and he hadn't been able to stand the fact that her ex had called while he'd been in her bed. He'd wanted her to tell Silverstein that she'd replaced him.

But why would she? She'd whispered her love in the dark, yet he'd said nothing in response. Made no promises.

No, he'd been terrified, so he'd turned sullen and had left her without a word. Except to first mutter that she didn't owe him anything since they'd just slept together. As if their coupling had just been raw sex.

But their night together hadn't been simple sex, and he'd known it.

The emotional connection had scared the hell out of him.

He increased his pace, his heart racing as he

noticed another falcon taking flight over the drive. The wind burned his cheeks and whistled through the low branches of the trees. A storm cloud rolled above, obliterating any remnant of the sun trying to peek through. He ran faster, his heart roaring in his ears as he broke through the clearing. Sonya's car was not in the drive.

Where was she? Had he hurt her so badly she'd gone back to Silverstein?

He raced inside to see if she'd left a note. The downstairs was empty. No coffee brewing on the counter. Just the dead embers of the cozy fire they'd built the night before. And the imprint of her body on the rug where they'd made love. Where'd she'd given herself to him.

And whispered her love.

He sprinted up the steps, hoping she'd left a note in the bedroom. But there was nothing. Her suitcase looked as if she'd torn things from it in a hurry. Her cell phone was gone.

He glanced at the caller ID log on his phone, and checked it for recent calls. An unknown.

Then Sonya's mother. Maybe Sonya had decided to spend a few days with her mom and Katie after all. God, he hoped that was where she'd gone.

He grabbed the phone and punched in her number.

"Detective Cyrus Gladstone, Denver Police Department."

Brack's gut knotted, and he identified himself. "What's going on?"

"Mrs. Simpson's granddaughter has been kidnapped," the officer said.

Brack's blood ran cold. The unknown call. It was from the lunatic who'd taken Katie. The one obsessed with Sonya.

He jerked the drawer to the nightstand open to get his gun. He had to find her. But his weapon was gone.

Sonya must have taken it. And she'd left to meet this madman and rescue her daughter, alone.

Chapter Eighteen

Tears nearly blinded Sonya as she drove toward Vulture's Point. Images of her daughter played through her head, spurring her forward. Katie when she was just a tiny baby. So sweet, so small, so fragile. Katie growing inch by inch, laughing when she played peekaboo. Katie learning to crawl. Her development had been delayed, but it had been a magical day when she'd pushed her tiny body up on all fours and crawled across the room.

Katie's first birthday. She'd smashed her fingers in the cake and icing and smeared it on her chin. Sonya had laughed and taken a dozen photographs.

She gulped back a sob, battling the wind as its force banged the car and tried to drive it off the road. She hit an icy patch and slowed, her breath tightening in her chest as the mountain ridge dropped off to the side. Go over it and she'd never rescue her daughter.

More snippets of Katie flashed back. Katie

speaking her first word. Mama. Katie learning to eat solid food, hating peas, loving homemade applesauce. Katie learning to color. The two of them decorating sugar cookies for Christmas. Katie's first ornament, the baby doll she'd loved so much when she was two, Katie giggling as Snowball licked her cheek. The tea party they had planned to have…all the things that they hadn't yet done…

On the heels of her memories, an image of the mangled dead women's bodies materialized, and she fought the panic. She needed her composure to confront the maniac who had her daughter, had to remain calm for Katie.

The clouds opened up and began dumping more snow, making the visibility a foggy mess. She blinked and turned on the defroster, then downshifted, taking the curves slowly, winding around the mountain as she climbed toward the ridge. Finally, she spotted the point where she was supposed to meet the caller.

She shoved Brack's gun in the pocket of her coat, then careened over the bumpy road and parked at the curve overlooking the mountain. He'd told her there was an abandoned mine shaft about seventy feet away, and she hit the trail toward it in a dead run, anxious to make sure Katie was still alive.

Then she'd shoot the lunatic who'd kidnapped Katie and take her daughter home. Maybe they'd leave Tin City, go someplace new. Start over.

Someplace where she could forget Brack. Forget that she'd confessed her love and he hadn't reciprocated. Forget that this violence had tainted her little girl's life.

Her feet skidded on the ice, and she grabbed a tree limb to maintain her balance, then jogged down the hilly embankment. Her pulse hammered when she spotted the entrance to the mine shaft. She tightened her fingers around the gun and summoned her courage, then descended the last twenty feet with more caution.

She scanned the woods surrounding the mine shaft for signs of Katie's kidnapper. Katie had to be alive. She had to be. If she wasn't, Sonya would die herself.

The wind whistled shrilly; the sound of a coyote howling boomeranged off the mountain. She bit back a sob and leaned her head into the entrance. "Katie?"

Nothing.

Panic clawed at her, but she tiptoed inside. The mine was so dark, she couldn't see a foot in front of her. The stench of rotting vegetation, maybe a dead animal, assaulted her. She moved deeper into the shaft, heard the ping of water trickling down rock, of pebbles hitting stone, then spotted a small figure lying on the ground, curled and wrapped inside half a dozen blankets.

Her daughter.

She froze, for a moment afraid to move forward. "Katie?"

But Katie didn't respond, and Sonya hurled herself forward, then dropped to her knees beside her in pure panic.

God, please, no. Katie had to be alive. She couldn't lose her daughter....

ANGUISH FILLED Brack. What if this maniac killed Katie and Sonya? He'd never forgive himself.

He had to do something to find them, but he didn't know the psycho's identity yet.

Rage tightening his throat, he forced himself to pick up the phone, to call Deke and explain the situation. While he and Deke talked, Brack retrieved an extra weapon from his office, stuffed it in his jacket pocket, then strapped on his ankle holster and slipped his small revolver into it. A knife went into a strap on the other ankle.

"Meet me at Cohen's office. We have to get all the suspects together and interrogate them." That is, if they could be found.

"I'll pick up Viago," Deke said.

Brack hung up and phoned Cohen. For once, Cohen didn't argue, but agreed to meet him at his office and to pick up Dr. Waverman on the way. "I'll have my deputy find Tripp and bring him in."

"And I'll find Dr. Priestly," Brack said.

He hung up, phoned the Denver police, explained

his theories and asked them to pick up Stan Silverstein for questioning.

One of the men had to be their guy. He couldn't allow himself to consider the consequences if he was wrong.

He jumped in his SUV and phoned Priestly, but the man's answering service responded. "Tell him to call Brack Falcon as soon as possible. This is an emergency." His tires screeched as he maneuvered the corner and barreled into the police station parking lot. He jumped out and ran inside, his pulse pounding.

Cohen rubbed sweat from his neck as he escorted Dr. Waverman inside. "My deputy said that guy Tripp is not at the B and B. He's looking through town now."

"What the hell's going on?" Dr. Waverman bellowed. "You have no right to drag me out of the ER and down here—"

"This maniac has Katie, and Sonya has gone after her," Brack snapped.

"Damn." Waverman dropped into a chair beside the desk and ran a hand over his neck.

Brack folded his hands around the edge of the desk and leaned forward. "If you know anything about this killer, speak up now, Waverman."

Waverman's cheeks bulged with anger. "What makes you think I know something?"

"You wanted Sonya for yourself. You didn't hire someone to scare her into coming to you for comfort?"

Waverman balled his right hand into a fist as if he were going to punch Brack, but Brack straightened to his full height in a dare.

"That's crazy. You're wasting time even suggesting it."

Brack turned to Cohen. "Did you get anything back on the DNA or writing samples?"

"I'll call the lab now."

Brack paced the office, trying to think. If he knew the identity of the killer, he could figure out where he'd taken Sonya.

Dammit. He knew neither.

But the killer had to be someone in town, someone right under their noses. Who in the hell was he?

"KATIE?" Sonya pressed a tentative hand to her daughter's chest to make sure she was breathing. Her body ached as she waited. Katie was so still, pale, curled up and cold, but her chest slowly rose up and down. Thank God, Katie was alive!

Relief surged through her, and she gasped out the breath she'd been holding.

"Mommy?"

"Yes, baby, I'm here. Everything's going to be all right."

Behind her, the shuffle of footsteps crushed the dirt. She jerked around and stood, jamming her hand into her coat pocket. In the corner, hidden in the gray abyss of the shaft, a shadow lurched.

"Stop hiding and face me," she said through clenched teeth.

He remained still, watching her, waiting, a silent stalker taking his time just to torture her.

"Are you too much of a coward or a monster to show your face?" Her finger closed around the gun handle, and she slipped her finger into the trigger.

A long, agonizing second passed. Her breathing rattled into the cold, dank air. His followed. A wheezing sound that grated on her already spent nerves.

"You drugged my daughter, didn't you, you bastard? What did you give her?"

"Just some cough syrup to make her sleep." He moved slowly toward her, his craggy shape like a monster in the dark. He wore a long cloak—no, maybe a cape—covered in feathers. And a mask shielded his face, a birdlike beak protruding as if he were a hawk.

She shivered. He was deranged. Completely delusional. Probably psychotic or high on drugs.

She slowly pulled her hand from her pocket and aimed the gun at him, although her hand was shaking. "You're going to let us both leave here, or I'm going to shoot you."

Before she could pull the trigger, he suddenly pounced. She tried to fire off a round, and a shot pierced the mine shaft, echoing shrilly off the wall. A vile animal-like screech pierced the air, and he

knocked the gun from her hand with his sharp
talons, then threw her to the ground and kicked the
weapon into the dirt away from her.

She lunged for it, but he grabbed her arm and
jerked her to her feet. He grabbed the gun, stabbed
it against her back, then dragged her through the
darkness the opposite way from the entrance. She
screamed and beat at him, but he dug the talons into
one arm, and she gulped back a sob as he cocked
the gun and jerked her forward.

"Shut up, or I'll go back and kill the kid."

Pure panic seized Sonya. "We can't leave her
here, she'll die in the cold!"

"When we get away, I'll let you call. But only if
you stop fighting me."

Sonya went stone still. "How can I trust you?
You're a monster!"

His hot breath fanned her cheek. A drop of blood
surfaced where he'd sliced her skin. "You don't. But
fight me, and you both die."

AN HOUR LATER, Brack was frantic with worry. He
couldn't shake the terrifying images of the killer's
sadistic ways from his mind. Was Sonya hurt? Was
little Katie all right?

Were they still alive?

Denial made him stiffen his spine. He couldn't
accept the fact that he might be too late to save them.

Deke stalked in, half dragging Jameson Viago beside him.

"Who the hell do you guys think you are?" Viago barked.

"Listen to me, you little piece of scum," Brack said as Deke shoved the guy into a wooden chair. "A woman and child are missing, possibly in the hands of the sicko who is copying your MO, and we need answers. Do you know where they are?"

"No!" Viago cursed. "Like I told you, I write the Talon Terror, but I'm not him."

"The person who wrote that fan letter we confiscated is, though," Cohen cut in.

Brack jerked his head up.

"I have the results of the DNA analysis and writing sample." Cohen frowned. "It's not Viago."

"I told you," Viago snapped.

"How about Tripp?" Brack asked.

"No match. And no match with our vet."

Brack muttered a string of vile words. If not those men, then who the hell was he? And how would they find him in time to save Katie and Sonya?

Dr. Waverman looked up from the files on the desk and gestured toward the letter. "This is the letter the killer wrote?"

Brack nodded. "Why, do you recognize something about it?"

"The way it reads…this guy sounds delusional."

"Tell me something we don't know," Brack muttered.

"No, I mean delusional as in psychotic." Waverman stood, ran his hands through his hair. "He might be on medication. Or perhaps he's seen a doctor or recently been treated at a mental facility." He strode across the room as if gaining momentum in his theory. "In fact, it seems like one of the paramedics mentioned a guy applying but being turned down for the EMT program because of his medical history."

Brack slapped the desk. "Let's check it out, guys."

Waverman unpocketed his cell phone. "I'll call the hospital, see what I can find."

Cohen rubbed at his forehead, and slumped down into his chair.

"What is it, Cohen?" Brack asked.

"I was just thinking about this kid a few years back." He scratched his chin in thought. "His father turned up dead in the woods beyond that farmhouse Ms. Silverstein rented."

Brack stiffened. "Did you question the kid?"

"I tried, but he disappeared. I'd already run him in for some petty crimes. An old lady who used to live around there accused him of killing her cat. And someone else reported their chickens being poisoned."

"Psychotics often start their abhorrent behavior as children," Deke interjected.

"And their violence escalates to humans when they get older," Brack added. "What was this kid's name?"

"I can't remember. It was over ten years ago." Cohen pinched the bridge of his nose, then opened his file cabinet and began to shuffle through the contents.

The crooked wall clock ticked away precious minutes until finally Cohen removed a folder and spread it on his desk. The family's name was Elmsworth. "His father was shot in the back, and we never found the boy."

Elmsworth. The vet's assistant. Sonya had mentioned that Katie didn't like him.

A second later, Dr. Waverman turned to them. "Elmsworth. That's the man's name who applied at the hospital. I'll place a call to the psychiatrist who treated him now."

"Let me talk to her," Brack said.

"I don't know if she can help," Waverman said. "Doctor-patient confidentiality."

"Then let's go see her in person. I'll convince her she has to help us." He glanced at Cohen "I'll call you if we find something. Stay here in case Priestly calls in, and find out where Elmsworth lives, or if he has a cabin where he might take Sonya."

Cohen nodded, and Brack and Waverman rushed out the door. Five minutes later, they stormed into the psychiatrist's office.

Dr. Waverman explained the reason for their visit, and Dr. Dilliard, a middle-aged woman with curly brown hair and friendly eyes, frowned. "I can't discuss my patients' medical files."

Brack slapped the file of the Talon Terror victims on her desk and spread out the photos of the mangled women's bodies. Dr. Dilliard gasped.

Brack stabbed a finger on the picture of the teenager. "Tell me if Elmsworth is capable of this kind of violence."

Her gaze shifted to Waverman, then him. "I-It's possible."

Brack pointed to each woman by name. "He's kidnapped a woman and her four-year-old little girl who's handicapped. He's going to do the same thing to them that he did to these victims if we don't stop him."

"My God..." She removed her glasses with a trembling hand and leaned her head on her hands.

"He fits the profile," Dr. Dilliard said quietly. "You don't understand, though. He's truly psychotic, schizophrenic. He hears voices. If he's doing this, he's delusional again, which means he must have stopped his medication."

"Tell me more, anything that might help me catch him if we find him."

"He was abused terribly as a child. His father liked to play sick, twisted games with him. He would starve him and lock him in the attic in the dark for days." She inhaled, then continued. "Sometimes he took him out in the woods and left him for weeks to survive on his own. Then his father hunted him down with a gun like he was an animal. During our sessions, he even claimed that he thought he was descended from the raptors. That his father tracked him down like he was prey."

"So he turned the table and shot his father," Waverman guessed.

She nodded.

Brack's stomach clenched, but he couldn't allow compassion to enter the picture. Not when Sonya and Katie's lives hung in the balance. When Sonya moved into his old farmhouse, it might have triggered bad memories, and he'd fixated on her.

"Do you know where he lives now?" Brack asked.

She shook her head. "He was released into a group home four years ago." She consulted her files. "Our caseworkers have changed since. It says here that he hasn't reported in for over a year. I don't see a recent address."

Dammit.

Brack punched in Deke's number. "This is our guy. But we don't have a current address."

"Priestly just phoned. Elmworth was renting a house right outside town." He recited the address.

"Good. I'll meet you and Cohen there."

He hung up and raced toward the door with Waverman on his heels.

"I want to go with you," Dr. Waverman said.

Brack shook his head. "It's too dangerous." He paused at the hospital exit and shook the man's hand. "Thank you for your help."

Waverman clenched his jaw. "Just find Sonya and save her."

Brack nodded and rushed through the door, battling his emotions. Ten minutes later, he stared at the walls in Elmsworth's house in horror. Dozens of pictures of Sonya filled a black bulletin board. There were also photos of birds of prey feeding on their quarry, pictures of the dead birds he'd destroyed in his own wake of violence, and photos of the women he'd ripped apart with his talons.

Even more disturbing, they found vials of animal blood, as if he'd drained them from the birds or maybe from other animals he'd helped treat at the clinic.

"I'm getting a crime scene unit over here ASAP," Cohen said.

Deke rushed in from outside. "I searched the property. He's not here."

Brack clenched his jaw. Where in the hell had the sicko taken her?

SHE WAS so lost. So cold. So afraid for Katie.

He dragged her through a series of tunnels. Sonya tried to memorize the way, each turn, each new smell and indentation in the long labyrinth of corridors in case she escaped, so she could retrace her steps and find her daughter. She remembered Brack saying the tunnels went beneath the city, that there were openings to the ground above. Maybe if she got back to Katie…

Despair filled her. Who was she kidding? He was going to kill her. And no one would ever find Katie.

She dug her feet in, halted and forced her body rigid.

His talons ripped into her arm. "Keep moving," he ordered.

"Not until you let me call someone to rescue Katie."

He slapped her so hard that she dropped to the ground. She tasted blood where his talon had sliced her cheek, smelled his sweat on her skin, his anger.

"Either let me call help for Katie, or kill me right now," Sonya shouted.

He made a snarling sound, but tossed her a cell phone. She only prayed it worked in the tunnel. Her hands shook as she punched Brack's number. The phone rang once, then Brack's deep voice echoed over the line.

"Brack Falcon."

"Brack, it's Sonya."

"God, Sonya, where are you are? Are you all right?"

"You have to save Katie. She's in a mine shaft at Vulture's Point."

"Are you—"

Her attacker snatched the phone and ended the call before she could respond. Tears choked her throat, and she cried out as he forced her to her feet. She tried to memorize Brack's voice, sure it was the last time she'd hear it.

Chapter Nineteen

Brack disconnected his phone with a curse. Heaven help him, he couldn't lose Sonya. But the sound of her voice...she'd sounded so far away. So terrified.

But determined to save her daughter.

So like Sonya.

Love for her swelled inside him, along with fear, forcing a knot in his throat.

"Brack?"

He swallowed hard to gather his control. "That was Sonya. Katie's in a mine shaft at Vulture's Point. We have to go."

Cohen gestured toward Elmsworth's desk. "I'll search his computer for references to a cabin or house, somewhere he might have taken her."

"Good. Question Priestly, too. Maybe Elmsworth mentioned something to him."

Brack gestured to Deke, who was already at the door. "We'll find Katie, then check the mine shaft tunnels. He may be following the tunnels underground to a hiding spot."

Deke took the keys and they raced toward Vulture's Point at full speed. "Rex called," Deke said on the drive. "Hailey's gone into labor and they're at the hospital."

Brack's chest squeezed. "You can meet them if you want."

Deke shook his head. "No, not until we find Sonya and her daughter. Then we'll go together."

Brack shot his brother a look of gratitude, gritting his teeth. He just hoped to hell they found Sonya in time.

The SUV barreled over the roads, tires grinding away at the ice, snow dotting the windshield as he careened to a stop. He and Deke both hit the ground running. Dirt and snow-crusted branches snapped below his feet as Brack skidded down the embankment. He'd spotted the mine shaft before when he'd been hiking. Deke shined a flashlight into the entrance as they slipped inside.

"Katie?" Brack called. "Honey, can you hear me?"

Water trickled down the rocks in the distance. The mine shaft smelled dank, of dirt and cold and a dead animal. Brack forced unwanted images of the Talon Terror's victims from his mind and moved slowly, scanning left and right, searching the shadows in case Elmsworth had set a trap.

Then he spotted a small bundle in the corner. He

moved forward cautiously while Deke surveyed the cavelike room, covering for him. Brack stooped down to check on Katie.

"Sweetie, can you hear me?"

She was bundled in several blankets. "Mommy?"

His heart clenched. "Katie, it's Brack. Are you all right?"

She slowly opened her terror-stricken eyes. "Mommy?"

He lifted her in his arms tucking the blankets around her. "I'm going to find Mommy now." He carried her over to Deke.

"Sweetheart, this is my brother, Deke. He's going to carry you out of here." He brushed her hair back from her cheek with his thumb. "Do you know where the man took your mommy?"

She shook her head, big tears trickling down her cheek. "He gonna hurts her?"

Brack swallowed again, his throat thick. He didn't want to lie to Katie. He had to give her hope. "No, honey, I'm going to bring her back to you, I promise." He wiped away her tears. "Now, go with Deke, okay?"

Deke's gaze met his as he cradled Katie into his arms. "You're sure you want to do this alone?"

"I have to," he said. "Take her to the hospital, have her checked out. I'll...meet you later."

Deke nodded and headed toward the exit of the cave. Brack grabbed the flashlight and moved deeper into the dark cavern.

TERROR AND DESPAIR threatened to overwhelm Sonya, but she had too much to live for not to fight. Katie.

And Brack.

Her kidnapper pushed her into a clearing, a room below ground, where it appeared someone might have been staying. An old mattress lay in one corner, a table crafted out of cardboard boxes sat beside it and a metal trash can that looked charred served as a fireplace.

As her eyes adjusted to the darkness, she searched the shadows for something to use as a weapon. A stick or rock, anything. He shoved her toward the mattress, and she shuddered as she realized his intention.

She'd die before she'd give herself to him.

Using every ounce of energy she possessed, she grabbed the trash can and flung it at him. The barrel slammed into his chest, and he bellowed in rage, jerked back and stumbled. She tried to crawl upright, but he grabbed her ankle. She fell forward, and her head slammed into the wall. She saw stars, but kicked out at him, and slammed her foot into his face. The crazy mask slid sideways, and he screeched that animal sound that she'd heard in the woods the first time he'd attacked her.

He tore at her ankle with his talons and pain splintered her leg. She kicked at him with her other foot, but he slapped her so hard that her neck snapped backward and her head hit the stone wall.

The world spun, dizzying, and she closed her eyes, fading into the darkness.

A few minutes, an hour later, she wasn't sure, she blinked to clear her vision and tried to move. Panic squeezed her lungs as she realized she couldn't.

She was tied to the filthy mattress.

And she was naked.

She shivered from the cold, then nausea rose to her throat as she opened her eyes and saw the masked man peering down at her. He tore off his mask, and shock bolted through her when she realized he was the vet's assistant. Katie hadn't liked him.

Her daughter always had good instincts.

"Why are you doing this?" she whispered.

"Because you're mine," he said in a demented voice. "I knew it when you moved into my house."

"Your house?"

"Yes, the farmhouse. That's where I grew up. My old hunting ground. Where I first learned to hunt when I was little." He paused, a sick smile twisting his lips. "My old man died in the woods behind the house. But inside those walls, he used to beat me."

Sonya wiggled her hands, trying to free them from the ropes.

"Relax," he said as he raked a talon down her neck, then over her breasts. "If you don't fight me, I won't hurt you."

BRACK HEARD a scream, and his lungs nearly exploded with fear. But relief also surged through him and sent him running toward the sound.

Sonya was still alive.

His breath came in short pants as he hurried through the tunnels. Another sound, a low cry, splintered the air. Brack paused and listened, thought he heard a voice. Muffled. Then a strangled sound. Sonya.

What was the bastard doing to her?

He inched forward around a corner and spotted a clearing ahead. Moving slowly, he peered around the turn, trying to remain hidden in the shadows of the wall. He needed to know if the guy was armed. Using every ounce of restraint he possessed, he forced himself to simply watch, assess the scene.

He nearly choked when he saw Sonya naked, tied to the bed. Elmsworth was leaning over her wearing some sort of animal costume, raking his fake talons over her bare breasts.

Fury unlike anything Brack had ever experienced fired his veins. He drew his gun but held back, still searching for signs of Elmsworth's weapon. He spotted the shiny glint of metal, his gun, against the dirt beside the mattress.

"First, I'll taste your blood," Elmsworth said in a crazed tone, "then I'll mix it with mine, and we will forever be bound together."

Sonya flinched as Elmsworth traced a line down

her thigh and drew blood. Brack clenched his jaw, his body tense with anger. Shooting him would be too good. The man had to suffer.

Releasing a pent-up breath, he exploded, ran forward and pounced on Elmsworth's back. He pummeled him with his fists, threw him to the ground, then slammed his knee into the man's face and stomped him in the gut.

Elmsworth bellowed in pain and fought back, but fury roared through Brack. He hit him again and again, then gripped the man's throat and squeezed hard, choking him.

"Brack! Brack, stop it, please!"

Sonya's cry floated into his consciousness, and his hands stilled around Elmsworth's throat. The man's eyes bulged, and he jerked, coughing and sputtering. Self-loathing kicked in as Brack realized he was acting like the sick man who'd attacked her.

"Brack, please untie me."

Sonya's anguished plea tore at Brack's heart. Elmsworth was unconscious, so he dragged himself off of him and crawled toward Sonya. Wiping sweat from his face with the back of his hand, he untied her hands and her feet, then shucked off his coat and wrapped it around her. Sonya trembled all over, her face pale, blood dotting her cheek, her chest and thigh.

He felt sick inside.

She sobbed against him. "Katie? Where's Katie?"

He stroked the side of her cheek, wiping away the blood. "She's okay. Deke took her to the hospital."

She gripped his arms. "The hospital? Is she all right?"

He cupped her face in between his hands. "Yes, she's fine. I just wanted the doctors to warm her up and check her over. But she's going to be okay, Sonya."

Suddenly the hair on the back of Brack's neck bristled, and a low sound broke through the darkness. A movement to the right. Elmsworth.

The gun. He was reaching for it.

He pushed Sonya down, grabbed the pistol from his ankle holster and fired.

Elmsworth fired at the same time. Brack threw himself in front of Sonya. She screamed and fell backward, and he dodged sideways, but the bullet pierced his shoulder. His hit Elmsworth square between the eyes. The man choked, his mouth opening wide in shock. Eyes bulging, he sputtered a gurgling sound, then collapsed backward into the dirt.

Sonya reached for him, and he dragged her against him and crushed her to his chest. "It's over, Sonya, it's finally over."

THE NEXT TWO HOURS passed in a foggy blur for Sonya. She tore the sheet from the mattress and crafted a makeshift sling for Brack's arm. He phoned the police and paramedics.

She and Brack were both taken to the ER, examined and treated. While they dug the bullet from Brack's shoulder, she was finally reunited with Katie. Katie was sleepy but fine. Sonya's mother raced in, almost hysterical, and the two of them embraced. Stan also arrived, looking shaken and concerned.

He gave her an awkward look. "I was worried about you."

"I'm okay. Brack saved my life and Katie's."

A pained look crossed his face, and she remembered that he'd wanted to talk.

He touched the stitches on her cheek. "I'll be glad to take care of that for you."

She winced. Some things never changed. Stan would always see her flaws. What about Brack? She sensed he cared for her, but he hadn't mentioned love. And he still didn't know that Katie had inherited her medical problems from her.

Did she have the courage to tell him?

"Mom, will you stay with Katie?" Sonya said. "I want to check on Brack. And I need to thank his brother for rescuing Katie."

"Sure, honey." Her mother sat on the edge of the bed and stroked Katie's hair. Katie curled up against her grandmother and sighed sleepily.

Sonya found Brack standing in front of the nursery window. He grinned and tapped at the window, then waved her over. "That's my nephew," he said with a proud smile on his face. "Rex and Hailey's little boy. They're going to call him Wyatt."

Sonya's heart clenched. She loved Brack so much. But even if he did love her and wanted a relationship, she couldn't promise him a family. And from the look on his face, he would probably want a son to carry on the Falcon name.

A son she might not be able to give him.

"He's beautiful," she said, sadness welling in her chest. She had to end it now. She couldn't bear to tell him the truth and see the disappointment in his eyes.

His smile faded, questions darkening his eyes. "What's wrong?"

"I came to thank you," she said softly. "And to tell you goodbye."

"Goodbye?"

She nodded. "I'm going to take Katie home as soon as the doctor lets me." She inhaled a deep breath. "Then I'm going to sell the farmhouse and leave Tin City." Maybe they'd stay with her mother for a while.

His jaw tightened. "What about your job?"

"I can always find another one. Besides, I can't stay at the farmhouse, not with all the bad memories surrounding it." She shivered. "It turns out Elmsworth grew up there. He was abused in that house."

"I know. He shot his father in the woods behind the house." He explained about Elmsworth's psychotic break and the medication that he needed to control his delusions. "He really was a sick man, Sonya."

Sonya hugged her arms around herself to keep from reaching for him. "Thank you for everything, Brack. Especially for saving Katie."

She turned and then ran back toward Katie's room. Back to the safety of her daughter and her mother, and the fears that held her hostage.

Chapter Twenty

Dammit. Brack couldn't breathe. He didn't want Sonya's *thanks*.

And he couldn't have just found her, then almost lost her, then found her again only to have her leave.

Old insecurities, memories of his former relationship pummeled him, and he wondered where he'd gone wrong. Had he scared her with his brutality toward Elmsworth? Did she think Katie was afraid of him? Because he didn't believe that was the case.

He took one more look at Rex standing in the nursery holding his new son, and emotions racked him. Hell. He'd thought he wanted to be alone, but he'd been fooling himself.

He was in love with Sonya. He wanted her as his wife. Wanted to have babies of his own with her. And she had whispered her love in the night when he'd held her in his arms.

He'd fought all his life for his birds. Now it was time for him to fight for the woman he wanted as his wife.

He sucked in a breath, rubbed his hands over his eyes, then strode down the corridor. When he rounded the corner, he spotted Sonya talking to her ex. Anger rallied inside him. They looked cozy, tucked together on a love seat against the back wall. He leaned against the door edge, giving them space. If Sonya wanted a reconciliation with her child's father, how could he justify standing in the way?

He waited, pain riffling through him at the thought. Stan murmured something in a low voice and put his arms around Sonya, and she hugged him in return. When she pulled away, tears glittered on her cheeks. Then she looked up and spotted him, and her face paled. Regret, wariness—and something else—flickered in her eyes.

Or had he imagined the momentary second of desire because he wanted her so bad?

Desperate to regain his composure, he headed past her to the coffee machine. He had to calm down. Let Sonya make the decision. Come to him if she wanted.

But hell, she doesn't even know you love her.

Hadn't he told her when he'd rescued her? Or on the way to the hospital?

No…things had been so crazy.

With sweaty fingers, he stuffed two quarters into the coin slot, but the dispenser rumbled noisily, then locked up. No coffee. He pounded his fist against it, and a cup dropped down into the holder. But no coffee streamed down, not even hot water.

He clenched his jaw. An empty cup, just like his life would be without Sonya and Katie.

"Brack?"

He froze, dropped his fist down to his side. His left arm throbbed where the bullet had went in, but the pain was nothing compared to the dull ache in his chest.

He forced himself to face her, although he didn't think he could stand it if he saw love for Silverstein in her eyes. Not when he wanted her for himself.

He had to know. Ground the question out between gritted teeth. "You're moving back to Denver to be with him?"

"Is that what you think?"

"You said you were leaving Tin City." He removed the empty cup from the dispenser and gripped it in his hand. "It looks like you two were getting back together."

"Things aren't always what they seem," she said quietly.

No. She was nothing like she'd seemed at first.

And he was not the tough loner he wanted everyone to think. He'd been ripped apart inside when his family had been shattered as a kid. And now it was happening again—she was being torn from him, too. It wasn't fair.

"You think I should reconcile with Stan?" she asked.

He dropped his head forward. Crushed the cup in

his hand and tossed it into the wastebasket. "You should do whatever makes you happy."

"Sometimes choices aren't that simple," she said in a strained voice.

He heard the underlying meaning. She had Katie to consider. Katie's real father.

Her hand brushed his shoulder. "What about *you*, Brack? What would make you happy?"

He shook his head. "This isn't about me."

"It's not?" Her voice took on a note of anger. "All right, then I guess it really is over between us. Like you said, it was just sex."

She turned abruptly and started to walk away. Desperation made him lunge forward and grab her arm. She glanced down at his fingers, then up into his eyes.

"It wasn't just sex, Sonya." His voice wavered, thick with emotions. He didn't care. For once he had to be honest. "I love you."

There, he'd put himself on the line. If she walked away, he'd survive. He didn't know how, but he would.

She stared at him with tears in her eyes. He ached for her to say she loved him, that she couldn't live without him in her life. "Oh, Brack."

"I…" Anguish darkened her eyes. "I wanted to hear that, but…"

"But what? You love Silverstein?"

"No."

"Then are you afraid of me?" he asked. It would hurt if she said yes, but he had to know that, too.

"No. Heavens no, not of you." She wet her lips, and her face crinkled with sadness.

He slid his fingers into her hair. "Then what are you afraid of?"

Her lower lip quivered. "Of telling you the truth."

"What are you talking about?"

"My flaws...."

Anger surged through him as he remembered her comment about Stan. "I thought we covered that when we made love. Did Silverstein say something else just then?" He'd hurt the man if he had.

She shook her head. "No, it's just...I watched you at the nursery window, saw the look on your face when you looked at your nephew."

A smile slid on his face, goofy he knew. Who would have thought one little baby could do that? "Yeah. I'm happy for my brother."

"And some day you'll want a family, too. One of your own."

"I adore Katie," he said in a rush. "I'll try to be a good stepfather to her."

She sucked in a sharp breath. "And you could love Katie in spite of her handicap?"

"She's not handicapped, she's special, an angel," he said in a thick voice. "And I'd never hurt her, Sonya. Or you."

"But you'll want children of your own."

He shrugged. "Maybe. You don't want more kids?"

She bit her lip as a tear trickled down her cheek.

"I would love more children." Her voice cracked. "B-but Katie inherited the gene for her disorder from me, Brack. If I have another child, I might pass it on again—"

He curled his hands into fists. "That's the reason Silverstein divorced you and Katie?"

She nodded miserably. "He couldn't bear to look at her, at me, anymore."

"I'm not *him*." Brack cupped her face in his hands, forced her to look into his eyes, to see the truth. "Sonya, I love you and Katie, flaws and all. Hell, it's not like I'm perfect myself." He cleared his throat, determined she believe him. "And if we decide to have another child, and she or he turns out like Katie, then I'll love them, too." He traced a thumb over her cheek, brushed at her tears. "Don't you get it? Nothing matters except that we're together."

Another tear trickled down her face. "Brack—"

"Shh." He pulled her into his arms. "I love you more than life itself, Sonya. I just want you to love me back, the way you said you did last night when we made love."

"God, Brack, I do love you. I love you with all my heart. I can't stand to think about not being with you." She traced a finger over his cheek, then kissed him tenderly. "And I never wanted or intended to go back with Stan. You're the only man in my heart."

Her words soothed away any lingering doubts. "Please say you'll marry me, Sonya. Be my wife."

She nodded against him, and he wiped the tears from her eyes and melded his mouth over hers, tasting the saltiness of her tears, the sultriness of her desire and the sweet hope of the future they would have together.

A future filled with love and a happy family that he had never dared dream about before. One that would be all the sweeter because of it.

Epilogue

It was the happiest day of Brack's life.

Easter lilies decorated the patio. Spring had arrived with sunshine and warm weather. The birds were safe again. His parents had flown in.

And he and Sonya were getting married in the garden at Falcon Ridge.

His entire family—Rex, Hailey, Wyatt, Elsie, Deke, Allison and his parents—were gathered for the ceremony. His father was the best man.

Sonya's mother and Katie were there. Katie, dressed in a shimmering long pink dress, bubbled with excitement about being their flower girl.

He adjusted his duster and stepped to the French doors, but the doorbell rang, and he frowned. Everyone they'd invited was already on the patio.

Hoping there were no problems that needed the agency's attention, he hurried to the front door, determined to get rid of the unwanted guest. Sonya walked down the steps, dressed in an ivory tea-length lacy dress that hugged her curves and made him want to rip it off

As he opened the door, he spotted Stan Silverstein standing on the stoop.

He knotted his hands. No. Nothing could go wrong today. Silverstein couldn't come and make a last-ditch effort to win Sonya back. Brack wouldn't concede. Not without the fight of a lifetime.

"What are you doing here, Silverstein?"

"Stan?" Sonya said softly.

Silverstein had the good graces to look sheepish, but he stepped inside anyway. "I want to talk to Sonya."

He stiffened. "Anything you have to say you can say to both of us."

Stan glanced at Sonya, but she slid her hand into Brack's and nodded.

"All right. I…" Stan hedged, looking down at his polished shoes.

"You're not going to stop the wedding," Brack said.

Silverstein jerked his head up. "No, that's not why I'm here." He reached inside his pocket and removed an envelope. "I wanted to give you this, Sonya. Consider it my wedding present."

Brack narrowed his eyes, and Sonya frowned, but accepted the envelope and opened it. Her soft gasp followed. "Stan, I don't understand."

Brack snatched the paper and skimmed it.

"I'm not proud of what I did, Sonya, that I lied to you. Those tests…when they came back, I couldn't face the truth. Couldn't stand the fact that I was the one who carried the genetic disorder that caused our daughter's handicap." His voice wavered. "I knew before you got pregnant that I carried the gene. That's why I was upset over the pregnancy. And then…I hoped things would be normal, but when Katie was born, I couldn't bear to look at her and know that my baby was crippled because of me." He hesitated, then forged on, his voice stronger. "I know it's not much in the way of an apology, but I am sorry."

"That's the reason you switched to plastic surgery?" Sonya asked.

He nodded. "I understand other people's needs to fix their flaws." He looked humble. "Only I couldn't fix my own and was too much of a coward to admit the truth, so I blamed you."

Tears glittered in Sonya's eyes, but forgiveness softened her voice. "I can't believe this, Stan. Why are you telling me now?"

He cleared his throat. "You deserve to know the truth. And I…I'm trying to face it myself." He extended his hand toward Brack. "You're a good man, Falcon. I hope you two will be happy. And sometime, maybe if it's all right with you, I'd like to try to forge a relationship with my daughter."

Brack's throat tightened, but for Katie's sake they had to make it work. And with Sonya's love and amazing compassion and understanding, they would. He shook Silverstein's hand, then they watched him drive away.

Sonya cuddled against him, and they walked to the garden out back. "You know what this means?" she whispered.

He pressed a kiss to her lips, loving her so much it hurt. "Yes, but you know the genetics never mattered to me."

Sonya kissed him tenderly. "I know. Your acceptance made me love you all that much more. But now, one day...maybe we'll have a little Falcon boy to carry on your name."

Emotions threatened to choke Brack. What better wedding present could they have received today?

He opened the French doors, and the sound of the wedding music filled the air. He squeezed Sonya's hand and walked to the front of the garden, surrounded by his friends,

Then he turned to watch the woman he loved and her daughter walk toward him.

Katie shocked them all by propping her crutches against a metal folding chair and walking down the aisle without them. As she dropped flowers on the lawn, sniffles floated through the garden. His mother's. Sonya's. His sisters-in-law. Katie's grandmother.

And he knew without a doubt that Katie's courage was the greatest gift of all.

His bride strolled toward him, a beaming smile of joy on her face. A falcon glided above, and love soared in his heart. Today he would become Katie's stepfather.

And one day maybe a father himself.

But most of all, today he would make Sonya his wife. And together they would start a new chapter in the Falcon family's history.

* * * * *

Be sure to pick up Rita Herron's next book of gripping romantic suspense when
SAY YOU LOVE ME
comes out in June 2007,
only from HQN Books!

*Experience entertaining women's fiction for
every woman who has wondered
"what's next?" in her life.
Turn the page for a sneak preview of a
new book from* Harlequin NEXT,
*WHY IS MURDER ON THE MENU, ANYWAY?
by Stevi Mittman*

*On sale December 26,
wherever books are sold.*

make a good husband.

"Oh, you can tell that from across the room." I

Ambience is everything. Imagine eating a foie gras at a luncheonette counter or a side of coleslaw at Le Cirque. It's not a matter of food but one of atmosphere. Remember that when planning your dining room design.
—Tips from *Teddi.com*

"Now that's the kind of man you should be looking for," my mother, the self-appointed keeper of my shelf-life stamp, says. She points with her fork at a man in the corner of the Steak-Out Restaurant, a dive I've just been hired to redecorate. Making this restaurant look four-star will be hard, but not half as hard as getting through lunch without strangling the woman across the table from me. "*He* would make a good husband."

"Oh, you can tell that from across the room?" I

ask, wondering how it is she can forget that when we had trouble getting rid of my last husband, she shot him. "Besides being ten minutes away from death if he actually eats all that steak, he's twenty years too old for me and—shallow woman that I am—twenty pounds too heavy. Besides, I am *so* not looking for another husband here. I'm looking to design a new image for this place, looking for some sense of ambience, some feeling, something I can build a proposal on for them."

My mother studies the man in the corner, tilting her head, the better to gauge his age, I suppose. I think she's grimacing, but with all the Botox and Restylane injected into that face, it's hard to tell. She takes another bite of her steak, chews slowly so that I don't miss the fact that the steak is a poor cut and tougher than it should be. "You're concentrating on the wrong kind of proposal," she says finally. "Just look at this place, Teddi. It's a dive. There are hardly any other diners. What does *that* tell you about the food?"

"That they cater to a dinner crowd and it's lunch-time," I tell her.

I don't know what I was thinking bringing her here with me. I suppose I thought it would be better than eating alone. There really are days when my common sense goes on vacation. Clearly, this is one of them. I mean, really, did I not resolve less than three weeks ago that I would not let my mother get to me anymore?

What good are New Year's resolutions, anyway?

Mario approaches the man's table and my mother studies him while they converse. Eventually Mario leaves the table with a huff, after which the diner glances up and meets my mother's gaze. I think she's smiling at him. That or she's got indigestion. They size each other up.

I concentrate on making sketches in my notebook and try to ignore the fact that my mother is flirting. At nearly seventy, she's developed an unhealthy interest in members of the opposite sex to whom she isn't married.

According to my father, who has broken the TMI rule and given me Too Much Information, she has no interest in sex with him. Better, I suppose, to be clued in on what they aren't doing in the bedroom than have to hear what they might be doing.

"He's not so old," my mother says, noticing that I have barely touched the Chinese chicken salad she warned me not to get. "He's got about as many years on you as you have on your little cop friend."

She does this to make me crazy. I know it, but it works all the same. "Drew Scoones is not my little 'friend.' He's a detective with whom I—"

"Screwed around," my mother says. I must look shocked, because my mother laughs at me and asks if I think she doesn't know the "lingo."

What I thought she didn't know was that Drew and I actually tangled in the sheets. And, since it's possible she's just fishing, I sidestep the issue and tell her that Drew is just a couple of years younger than me and that I don't need reminding. I dig into my salad with renewed vigor, determined to show my mother that Chinese chicken salad in a steak place was not the stupid choice it's proving to be.

After a few more minutes of my picking at the wilted leaves on my plate, the man my mother has me nearly engaged to pays his bill and heads past us toward the back of the restaurant. I watch my mother take in his shoes, his suit and the diamond pinkie ring that seems to be cutting off the circulation in his little finger.

"Such nice hands," she says after the man is out of sight. "Manicured." She and I both stare at my hands. I have two popped acrylics that are being held on at weird angles by bandages. My cuticles are ragged and there's marker decorating my right hand from measuring carelessly when I did a drawing for a customer.

Twenty minutes later she's disappointed that he managed to leave the restaurant without our noticing. He will join the list of the ones I let get away. I will hear about him twenty years from now when—according to my mother—my children will be grown and I will still be single, living pathetically alone with several dogs and cats.

After my ex, that sounds good to me.

The waitress tells us that our meal has been taken

care of by the management and, after thanking Mario, the owner, complimenting him on the wonderful meal and assuring him that once I have redecorated his place people will be flocking here in droves (I actually use those words and ignore my mother when she rolls her eyes), my mother and I head for the restroom.

My father—unfortunately not with us today—has the patience of a saint. He got it over the years of living with my mother. She, perhaps as a result, figures he has the patience for both of them, and feels justified having none. For her, no rules apply, and a little thing like a picture of a man on the door to a public restroom is certainly no barrier to using the john. In all fairness, it does seem silly to stand and wait for the ladies' room if no one is using the men's room.

Still, it's the idea that rules don't apply to her, signs don't apply to her, conventions don't apply to her. She knocks on the door to the men's room. When no one answers she gestures to me to go in ahead. I tell her that I can certainly wait for the ladies' room to be free and she shrugs and goes in herself.

Not a minute later there is a bloodcurdling scream from behind the men's room door.

"Mom!" I yell. "Are you all right?"

Mario comes running over, the waitress on his heels. Two customers head our way while my mother continues to scream.

I try the door, but it is locked. I yell for her to open it and she fumbles with the knob. When she finally manages to unlock and open it, she is white behind her two streaks of blush, but she is on her feet and appears shaken but not stirred.

"What happened?" I ask her. So do Mario and the waitress and the few customers who have migrated to the back of the place.

She points toward the bathroom and I go in, thinking it serves her right for using the men's room. But I see nothing amiss.

She gestures toward the stall, and, like any self-respecting and suspicious woman, I poke the door open with one finger, expecting the worst.

What I find is worse than the worst.

The husband my mother picked out for me is sitting on the toilet. His pants are puddled around his ankles, his hands are hanging at his sides. Pinned to his chest is some sort of Health Department certificate.

Oh, and there is a large, round, bloodless bullet hole between his eyes.

FOUR NASSAU COUNTY police officers are securing the area, waiting for the detectives and crime scene personnel to show up. They are trying, though not very hard, to comfort my mother, who in another era would be considered to be suffering from the vapors. Less tactful in the twenty-first century, I'd say she was losing it. That is, if I didn't know her better, know she was milking it for everything it was worth.

My mother loves attention. As it begins to flag, she swoons and claims to feel faint. Despite four No Smoking signs, my mother insists it's all right for her to light up because, after all, she's in shock. Not to mention that signs, as we know, don't apply to her.

When asked not to smoke, she collapses mournfully in a chair and lets her head loll to the side, all without mussing her hair.

Eventually, the detectives show up to find the four patrolmen all circled around her, debating whether to administer CPR, smelling salts or simply call the paramedics. I, however, know just what will snap her to attention.

"Detective Scoones," I say loudly. My mother parts the sea of cops.

"We have to stop meeting like this," he says lightly to me, but I can feel him checking me over with his eyes, making sure I'm all right while pretending not to care.

"What have you got in those pants?" my mother asks him, coming to her feet and staring at his crotch accusingly. "*Baydar?* Everywhere we Bayers are, you turn up. You don't expect me to buy that this is a coincidence, I hope."

Drew tells my mother that it's nice to see her, too,

and asks if it's his fault that her daughter seems to attract disasters.

Charming to be made to feel like the bearer of a plague.

He asks how I am.

"Just peachy," I tell him. "I seem to be making a habit of finding dead bodies, my mother is driving me crazy and the catering hall I booked two freakin' years ago for Dana's bat mitzvah has just been shut down by the Board of Health!"

"Glad to see your luck's finally changing," he says, giving me a quick squeeze around the shoulders before turning his attention to the patrolmen, asking what they've got, whether they've taken any statements, moved anything, all the sort of stuff you see on TV, without any of the drama. That is, if you don't count my mother's threats to faint every few minutes when she senses no one's paying attention to her.

Mario tells his waitstaff to bring everyone espresso, which I decline because I'm wired enough. Drew pulls him aside and a minute later I'm handed a cup of coffee that smells divinely of Kahlúa.

The man knows me well. Too well.

His partner, whom I've met once or twice, says he'll interview the kitchen staff. Drew asks Mario if he minds if he takes statements from the patrons first and gets to him and the waitstaff afterward.

"No, no," Mario tells him. "Do the patrons first."

Drew raises his eyebrow at me like he wants to know if I get the double entendre. I try to look bored.

"What is it with you and murder victims?" he asks me when we sit down at a table in the corner.

I search them out so that I can see you again, I almost say, but I'm afraid it will sound desperate instead of sarcastic.

My mother, lighting up and daring him with a look to tell her not to, reminds him that *she* was the one to find the body.

Drew asks what happened *this time*. My mother tells him how the man in the john was "taken" with me, couldn't take his eyes off me and blatantly flirted with both of us. To his credit, Drew doesn't laugh, but his smirk is undeniable to the trained eye. And I've had my eye trained on him for nearly a year now.

"While he was noticing you," he asks me, "did *you* notice anything about him? Was he waiting for anyone? Watching for anything?"

I tell him that he didn't appear to be waiting or watching. That he made no phone calls, was fairly intent on eating and did, indeed, flirt with my mother. This last bit Drew takes with a grain of salt, which was the way it was intended.

"And he had a short conversation with Mario," I tell him. "I think he might have been unhappy with the food, though he didn't send it back."

Drew asks what makes me think he was dissatisfied, and I tell him that the discussion seemed acrimonious and that Mario looked distressed when he left the table. Drew makes a note and says he'll look into it and asks about anyone else in the restaurant. Did I see anyone who didn't seem to belong, anyone who was watching the victim, anyone looking suspicious?

"Besides my mother?" I ask him, and Mom huffs and blows her cigarette smoke in my direction.

I tell him that there were several deliveries, the kitchen staff going in and out the back door to grab a smoke. He stops me and asks what I was doing checking out the back door of the restaurant.

Proudly—because, while he was off forgetting me, dropping by only once in a while to say hi to Jesse, my son, or drop something by for one of my daughters that he thought they might like, I was getting on with my life—I tell him that I'm decorating the place.

He looks genuinely impressed. "Commercial customers? That's great," he says. Okay, that's what he *ought* to say. What he actually says is "Whatever pays the bills."

"Howard Rosen, the famous restaurant critic, got her the job," my mother says. "You met him—the good-looking, distinguished gentleman with the *real* job, something to be proud of. I guess you've never read his reviews in *Newsday*."

Drew, without missing a beat, tells her that Howard's reviews are on the top of his list, as soon as he learns how to read.

"I only meant—" my mother starts, but both of us assure her that we know just what she meant.

"So," Drew says. "Deliveries?"

I tell him that Mario would know better than I, but that I saw vegetables come in, maybe fish and linens.

"This is the second restaurant job Howard's got her," my mother tells Drew.

"At least she's getting *something* out of the relationship," he says.

"If he were here," my mother says, ignoring the insinuation, "he'd be comforting her instead of interrogating her. He'd be making sure we're both all right after such an ordeal."

"I'm sure he would," Drew agrees, then looks me in the eyes as if he's measuring my tolerance for shock. Quietly he adds, "But then maybe he doesn't know just what strong stuff your daughter's made of."

It's the closest thing to a tender moment I can expect from Drew Scoones. My mother breaks the spell. "She gets that from me," she says.

Both Drew and I take a minute, probably to pray that's all I inherited from her.

"I'm just trying to save you some time and effort," my mother tells him. "My money's on Howard."

Drew withers her with a look and mutters something that sounds suspiciously like "fool's gold." Then he excuses himself to go back to work.

I catch his sleeve and ask if it's all right for us to leave. He says sure, he knows where we live. I say goodbye to Mario. I assure him that I will have some sketches for him in a few days, all the while hoping that this murder doesn't cancel his redecorating plans. I need the money desperately, the alternative being borrowing from my parents and being strangled by the strings.

My mother is strangely quiet all the way to her house. She doesn't tell me what a loser Drew Scoones is—despite his good looks—and how I was obviously drooling over him. She doesn't ask me where Howard is taking me tonight or warn me not to tell my father about what happened because he will worry about us both and no doubt insist we see our respective psychiatrists.

She fidgets nervously, opening and closing her purse over and over again.

"You okay?" I ask her. After all, she's just found a dead man on the toilet, and tough as she is that's got to be upsetting.

When she doesn't answer me I pull over to the side of the road.

"Mom?" She refuses to meet my eyes. "You want me to take you to see Dr. Cohen?"

She looks out the window as if she's just realized we're on Broadway in Woodmere. "Aren't we near Marvin's Jewelers?" she asks, pulling something out of her purse.

"What have you got, Mother?" I ask, prying open her fingers to find the murdered man's ring.

"It was on the sink," she says in answer to my dropped jaw. "I was going to get his name and address and have you return it to him so that he could ask you out. I thought it was a sign that the two of you were meant to be together."

"He's dead, Mom. You understand that, right?" I ask. You never can tell when my mother is fine and when she's in la-la land.

"Well, I didn't know that," she shouts at me. "Not at the time."

I ask why she didn't give it to Drew, realize that she wouldn't give Drew the time in a clock shop and add, "…or one of the other policemen?"

"For heaven's sake," she tells me. "The man is dead, Teddi, and I took his ring. How would that look?"

Before I can tell her it looks just the way it is, she pulls out a cigarette and threatens to light it.

"I mean, really," she says, shaking her head like it's my brains that are loose. "What does he need with it now?"

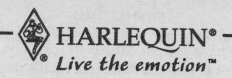

HARLEQUIN®
INTRIGUE®

BREATHTAKING ROMANTIC SUSPENSE

Shared dangers and passions lead to electrifying romance and heart-stopping suspense!

Every month, you'll meet six new heroes who are guaranteed to make your spine tingle and your pulse pound. With them you'll enter into the exciting world of Harlequin Intrigue— where your life is on the line and so is your heart!

THAT'S INTRIGUE—
ROMANTIC SUSPENSE
AT ITS BEST!

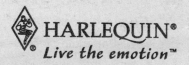

HARLEQUIN®
Live the emotion™

HARLEQUIN®
Presents

The world's bestselling romance series...
The series that brings you your favorite authors,
month after month:

Helen Bianchin...Emma Darcy
Lynne Graham...Penny Jordan
Miranda Lee...Sandra Marton
Anne Mather...Carole Mortimer
Susan Napier...Michelle Reid

and many more uniquely talented authors!

Wealthy, powerful, gorgeous men...
Women who have feelings just like your own...
The stories you love, set in exotic, glamorous locations...

HARLEQUIN®
Presents

Seduction and Passion Guaranteed!

HPDIR104

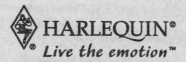